It's Wrong for Me to Love You to Love You Part 3:

Renaissance Collection

Jamie laughed a little, looking over at me. He knew I was pissed. "What's up, shawty?"

I rolled my eyes. "Kenya, Anastasia, that dark skinned dude with the limp could have played the part of Cooper. I mean, he'd already been shot before! He didn't have to act like he was in a gang because wearing all that blue, so yeah, you know he's still in one! What was wrong with him?"

Anastasia was paying me no attention. She looked Jamie over, licking her plum-colored lips. "No, he is perfect. Smile for me, Jamie."

Jamie grinned, grill gleaming. "What'cha lookin' at?"

"I wanna see your grill." Anastasia flirted.

Jamie laughed a little. "You wanna see my what?"

I was pissed. I grabbed my purse from Anastasia's desk and stormed out of the office. I had enough shit on my plate. I had to schedule an ultrasound appointment to find out how far along that I was, let alone tell my boo about the baby in the first place. My health wasn't up to par. I wanted to help pick out furniture for our new home, I wanted to build a life with my boo, and there Jamie was, crashing down on my heart again.

Anastasia caught up with me before I made it half way down the hallway. "Wait!" She grabbed my arm.

I pulled from her, pushing her off of me. "No, I'm not doing this! Flirt with Jamie on your own time! And find someone else to play the leading role of 'Katrina,' 'cause I'm not doing it! Shit, you like the muthafucka, why don't you play the part?"

Anastasia sighed. "Calm down for a minute. I mean, you're seriously gonna let your feelings for this dude interfere with your career? Grow up! This isn't about your personal life, Ne'Vaeh, it's about business. You're a grown ass woman, so you need to start acting like it."

"It's not about my personal life? No, Anastasia, it's not about *your* personal life! You drive all of us like you're a fuckin' slave driver! That's what they all call you behind your back! Most of these chicks are married with children! You're lonely, and you're fuckin' miserable, and since Darryl's never around, you could care less if we have our husbands around! You miss him, and it hurts you just as much as it hurts me to be away from Aaron! Working as hard as you do is how you channel your pain. Don't tell me that this shit isn't personal, because it is! The reason why you hate Aaron so much is because he came to save me the way that you wish Darryl would come back home to save you, huh? You brought Jamie here to break us up, didn't you? Didn't you?" I pushed Anastasia.

She just looked at me, her brown eyes searching my face. She was like a statue. The only thing moving on her were her eyes. She wanted to snap on me for putting my hands on her, but she didn't because she knew that I was right. "I don't like Aaron because he's a part-time husband, just like mine, but then he wants to come up in here like he's running shit. You keep that part-time family shit at the crib. When you're here, it's all about business. Now, Jamie Green is the perfect match for our role, like it or not. Deal with the shit. If you couldn't take the heat, you shoulda stayed your black ass out of the fuckin' kitchen, I'm just sayin'."

"How the hell am I supposed to explain this shit to Aaron?" I talked to Anastasia's back as she walked away from me, strutting down the hallway back to her office.

"Play rehearsal is at ten o'clock tomorrow morning. I expect to see you there on time, little girl," Anastasia replied, walking into her office, slamming the door behind her.

***

It's Wrong for Me to Love You Part 3:

Renaissance Collection

Krystal Armstead

www.urbanbooks.net

Urban Books, LLC
300 Farmingdale Road, NY-Route 109
Farmingdale, NY 11735

It's Wrong for Me to Love You Part 3:
Renaissance Collection
Copyright © 2018 Krystal Armstead

ISBN 13: 978-1-62286-683-0
ISBN 10: 1-62286-683-5

First Trade Paperback Printing March 2018
Printed in the United States of America

10 9 8 7 6 5 4 3 2 1

This is a work of fiction. Any references or similarities to actual events, real people, living or dead, or to real locales are intended to give the novel a sense of reality. Any similarity in other names, characters, places, and incidents is entirely coincidental.

Distributed by Kensington Publishing Corp.
Submit orders to:
Customer Service
400 Hahn Road
Westminster, MD 21157-4627
Phone: 1-800-733-3000
Fax: 1-800-659-2436

It's Wrong for Me to Love You to Love You Part 3:

by

Krystal Armstead

Acknowledgments

I am truly humbled by this journey that I had the opportunity to take this year. Words cannot really begin to express the vast amount of emotions that I am feeling, but I will try my best.

I want to start by thanking Carl Weber and Racquel Williams for taking the chance on me. Without Racquel, none of this would even be possible! She really didn't have to give me this opportunity, but she did, and I will always be indebted to her! I am so proud to be rockin' with this motivated group of individuals. I have never seen a team work so hard to uplift one another daily. I am truly blessed! Racquel gave me the opportunity to spread my wings, and damn it, I'm gonna fly!

Over these past few months, I have met some amazing people, authors, and readers alike. Carmen Doster Johnson is one of the first readers that I started "talking" to on a daily basis. She came into my life at a time that I was really going through a lot. She gave me the brilliant idea to start a reading group. So I started a group called "Krystal's Motivation" and when I tell you that my Facebook Homies on this page give me life, I mean they literally give me life! There isn't a day that goes by that I don't talk to Robin Watkins, Mishelle Neal, or Mesha Turner! They keep me motivated. They give me the strength to go on when I just feel like giving up, throwing in the towel. When my books drop, Nicki Ervin and Glenda Daniel are the first people in my inbox, telling me that my book is live! My readers know that my book is live even before *I* do! And that's love. I appreciate you all. There are too many to name, but you know I appreciate the love.

Thanks to my mother and father, Jennifer and Conrad Artis, Jr. I love them more than words can express. There isn't a day that goes by that I don't thank God for you both. Thank you for always being in my corner.

This book is for my four beautiful children: Jada, Adrian, Jordan, and Angel. A life without you four is not worth living.

And lastly, my husband, James. Thank you for taking me on this emotional roller coaster ride. Without it, my books would not be the same.

Thank you all for your support. Thank you, God, for the opportunity. All right, y'all, *let's do this again*! Whoot!

Chapter 1: The Rescue

Ne'Vaeh

"Push!" The doctors cradled my baby's head in their hands as I struggled to push her out. Two nurses braced my legs as I struggled to bear down.

I screamed out in agony, not because I was in pain, but I was crying because my baby was suffocating. As I pushed my baby out, the doctor's unwound the cord that was tightly wrapped around her neck. I could tell by the horrified looks on their faces that my baby was already gone.

I screamed out as the baby's shoulders passed through, and she slipped out into the doctor's hands.

Renée cried with me, patting my forehead with a wet towel.

Anastasia stood to my left, hand over her heart, watching the doctors as they took my child without handing her to me.

"Please tell me Sara's okay!" I cried, my heart in denial. "Let me hold my baby, please! Let me see her!"

Anastasia looked down at me, squeezing my hand in hers.

I watched as the doctors rushed my baby over to a table. She wasn't moving. She was totally purple. They tried resuscitating her, but couldn't bring her back.

I screamed out, nearly passing out, wet hair stuck to my face. My little Sara was gone. The only part of Jamie that I had left was gone.

***

I lived in Atlanta, Georgia, in a huge mansion with my cousin, Darryl Allan, and his wife, Anastasia Jones-Allan. I had been living with them for almost three months before I came clean that I was pregnant with Jamie's baby. They didn't force me to go back to Maryland, they didn't force me to go back to Jamie, and they didn't force me to slow down, but they should have. I worked too hard, I sang too hard, I didn't take care of myself. I was in and out of the hospital the entire time that I was pregnant with the baby. My blood pressure was up and down. I was dehydrated constantly, and I couldn't keep any food down. It wasn't until I was a little under seven months pregnant that I stopped feeling my baby moving. Anastasia rushed me to the hospital on June 26, 2015. I was already in labor and had no idea until my water broke in the passenger's seat of Anastasia's Maserati. By the time I made it to the hospital, I felt the urge to push.

I stayed in bed for nearly three months after my baby passed away. I could still see them lowering my baby's casket into the ground in my head. I lost my baby before I even got the chance to tell Jamie that I was pregnant. I heard through Alisha that Charlie had a healthy baby boy in May. Hearing about Charlie's blissful life made me hate my life even more than I already did. She was modeling, walking the runways, traveling the world, and probably still fuckin' Jamie. I didn't want anything to do with anyone or anything, except Darryl, Anastasia, and Renée.

Renée used all of her sick and vacation leave to stay with me in Georgia. I wouldn't eat or drink anything. I was under a nurse's care, but Renée (who was a nurse herself) did most of the work. She hooked me up to IVs. She helped the nurse bathe me. She brushed my teeth and combed my hair. She even paid an African hair braider to come and braid my hair. She didn't leave my side until I no longer needed an IV. It was August 30 when Renée was ready to head back to Maryland.

Renée sat at the edge of my bed that morning to say good-bye. "I hate to nurse and run, but—" She tried to crack a joke.

Tears slid down my face. "Thank you, Renée. You didn't have to come, but you did, and I thank you."

"Girl, what do you mean I didn't have to come? You're my boo—when you call, you know I'ma come runnin'!" Renée grinned, "I needed an excuse to get away from Maryland anyway. I got tired of chasin' behind that sorry-ass nigga. Life is boring without you, girl. Ain't shit going on there but the same old shit," Renée rolled her eyes. "Besides, I was worried about you."

I can't begin to tell you how many anti-depressants the doctors had me on. Sedation was the only way to keep me calm. There were a few failed attempts at ending my life that summer. I wanted to end all the pain. I felt like a prisoner in my own body. I needed to escape. I left Maryland to get away from pain, only to end back in the same situation in Georgia. I couldn't catch a break. All being in Georgia did was force me to confront the fact that I really needed help. That I couldn't run from myself.

"I should have never left him." I cried.

Renée shook her head. "Sweetie, it isn't your fault that Sara died. You can't keep blaming yourself. You were lucky to even *get* pregnant, Ne'Vaeh. All your life, the doctors have been telling you that you wouldn't be able to have children."

"Well, I guess they were right, because my little baby is gone! She was the only piece of him that I had left." I cried, tears stinging my cheeks. After she died, the doctors wrapped her in a towel and let me hold her. I could still feel her in my arms.

"Miss," Anastasia's maid, Beth, knocked on my room door. "You have a visitor."

I looked at Renée. "Are we expecting someone?" My heart jumped in my chest because I just *knew* it was Jamie.

She looked at me and shrugged. "Not that I know of."

The door opened, and there he was. Not Jamie, but Aaron.

I sat up in my bed. Aaron Whitehaven was the last person that I expected to see. He had moved halfway across the world to get away from me and there he was, standing in my doorway, looking like he stepped off the cover of *Source* magazine.

I lost my breath and my motor skills for a second or two.

Renée got up from the bed, just as shocked to see him as I was. "Aaron? What are you doing here?"

Aaron smiled at her a little. "What's up, Renée? I was in town for a conference, and I ran into Darryl Allan. He said I needed to check up on baby girl, so, here I am."

I couldn't believe it was Aaron. Not Jamie, whose baby that I had just lost, but Aaron.

Renée looked at me. "Ummm, I'll leave you two alone for a few minutes." She walked up to Aaron, her eyes glistening.

Aaron looked at her. "How is she?" He whispered.

Renée looked at me then back at him. "Not good." She whispered back, looking up into his face. "Do you know that you're the only one who's come to see her?"

Aaron shook his head. "Not Jamie? Not even Charlene?"

Renée scoffed. "Charlene who? Ne'Vaeh hasn't heard from her since New Year's. And Ne'Vaeh mailed Jamie an invitation to see her at the BET awards, but the mutha-fucka never showed up." Renée shook her head, looking up into Aaron's face. "She needs you."

Aaron just looked at Renée at a loss for words, probably shocked that Renée would even admit to herself that Ne'Vaeh needed him.

"Thank you for coming. She needs to know that someone still cares about her." Renée patted Aaron on the shoulder.

Aaron stepped in the room as Renée and Beth stepped out, closing the door behind them. Aaron looked around the room, eying a bassinet and tons of gifts from the baby shower that I had in May. He looked in the empty bassinet that stood beside my bed. Then he looked back at me, eyes lighting up a little. He seemed hopeful for a split second. "Shorty, you had a baby?"

I shook my head at him, and cried out loud, "She's gone!"

Aaron approached my side, sitting down in a chair that sat beside the bed. He reached for my hand. I tried to pull away, but he grabbed my trembling hand anyway. "I'm sorry, Heaven."

"She was so tiny!" I cried. "She was so beautiful. I held her lifeless body in my hands. How am I gonna get over this? Everything that I love, I lose!"

Aaron held both of my hands, pulling me up from the bed, sliding me down onto his lap. He didn't care whether or not he was making me feel uncomfortable. He knew I needed to be held. I cried like a baby on his lap, in his arms. I was so frail and weak. The only thing that had gone into my body for three months was fluid through my IVs. And even that, my body often rejected.

Aaron held me tight against his warm body. I held on to him, crying, face buried in his neck. "Baby, you'll be alright. Nothing lasts forever, even pain." Aaron whispered in my ear. I hadn't seen Aaron since his New Year's party, eight months ago. Though I was in excruciating pain, it felt so good to see that boy.

"Thank you for coming, Aaron." I cried, gripping his jacket in my hands. "Oh, my goodness, it feels *so* good to see you!"

"I told you I was comin' back for you. What, you thought I was playin'?" He rubbed my back, feeling the bones of my spine through my tank top. "Babe, you gotta eat something."

Anastasia's cook sat a bowl of chicken soup on the dining room table.

Aaron sat in a chair next to me. Anastasia and Renée stood alongside me, watching me struggle to eat.

Aaron held my hand, taking the spoon from me. I was too weak to even feed myself. I looked up at him, lips trembling.

"I got you," Aaron whispered, scooping noodles into the soup spoon.

"Well," Anastasia choked back the tears, trying her hardest not to cry. She couldn't stand to watch me sink into the depression that I was in. She tried her hardest to build me up those eight months that I'd been there. She gave me a better life. She took me places that I never thought I would go. She put my name in the spotlight. She had music producers and songwriters all over the country begging to work with me. But she knew she couldn't give me what I really needed. "Sweetie, umm, I'm gonna ride with Renée to the airport, okay? If you need me, just hit me on my cell." She kissed my cheek.

I nodded, as Aaron fed me the warm soup.

Renée hugged me around my neck. "Well, cuz, you know the number. I picked up some extra hours at the hospital. They needed someone to be on-call, so I volunteered. And I don't know if you knew, sweetie, but I've been visiting Alisha in the hospital. I mainly volunteered so that I could spend some time with her during the night."

I looked at Renée, struggling to eat the soup. Alisha had been my girl since middle school. Yeah, she gossiped more than the *Enquirer,* but she never steered me wrong. I should have listened to her in the beginning about Jamie, and maybe then I would have never gotten hurt. Alisha had a massive brain tumor, and it was a wonder she'd lived as long as she did. Twenty years old, and she was dying.

"How is she?" I whispered.

Renée shook her head. "Lucky to be alive," she said as she fought back tears.

"Yeah, the last time that I talked to Ashton, shorty couldn't even talk." Aaron wiped a drop of soup from my lips with his thumb and then licked it from his finger. He was still doing that sexy shit. I don't even think he realized what he was doing.

That was until Anastasia laughed a little. It was the first time I'd heard her laugh in months. "Oh my goodness, boy, you are too cute! Who does that? What kinda man sucks the soup off of a woman's lips? You gotta love that!" She shook her head at Aaron.

Aaron grinned a little.

Renée elbowed Anastasia, rolling her eyes. Though she was impressed that Aaron showed up when he did, she still wasn't his biggest fan. "Anyway, sweetie, Patty will be here around eleven thirty to check on you. You need to do *everything* that the nurses are asking you to do. Otherwise, your ass is gonna end up back at the hospital! You're like ninety pounds, Ne'Vaeh, and you just had a baby!" She glanced at Aaron.

Aaron looked at her.

"How long are you staying?" Renée folded her arms.

I looked at Aaron.

Aaron looked at me. "A few days, then I'm headed to Cali, then to England with my people." He looked at Renée. "Why? What's up?"

Renée shook her head at him, "I'm just making sure that my cousin has someone to keep her company for a few days. I'm sure you'll make sure she does what she's supposed to. Just make sure *you* do what you're supposed to do."

Aaron laughed a little. He knew the real Renée would show up sooner or later. "Still playing mom, huh? You still haven't gotten any business of your own, so you can stay the fuck out of other people's?"

Anastasia laughed, pulling Renée back by her arm, "Okay, kids, play nice! It was nice seeing you, Aaron. C'mon, Renée, you're gonna miss your flight."

Renée pulled from Anastasia, throwing her arms around my neck. "Take care of yourself, cuz. And keep your hands to *your*self, Aaron." Renée snuck one in before leaving us alone.

Aaron laughed a little, scooping more soup up in the spoon. "Your cousin is something else, I tell you." He said as they left the room. "She looks out for you though. That's what's up." He fed the soup to me.

I looked at him, swallowing the soup. I nodded. "She's not so bad. She just worries about me, that's all. At least *somebody* does."

Aaron looked at me. He was afraid to ask me about my baby, but he did anyway. "What happened, Heaven? What happened to your baby?"

I really didn't want to talk about my loss, but I knew Aaron wouldn't let up until I said something about her. "H–her umbilical cord was wrapped around her neck. I went into labor just a week or two shy from being seven months pregnant. By the time I got to the hospital, my water had broken, and I was already pushing her out. It was too late. My baby wasn't breathing. Her own umbilical cord killed her." The tears started to slide down my face as I saw my baby's face in my head. She was so tiny, so beautiful, so Jamie.

"Jamie should be here, Heaven." Aaron's temples twitched as he sat the spoon down on the table. "Why the fuck isn't he here with you?"

I dried my tears, shaking my head at Aaron.

Aaron looked at me, realizing by the look on my face that I hadn't even told Jamie about his child. "You didn't tell him?" Aaron shook his head. "Heaven, you didn't tell him he had a baby? You just left the dude in Maryland and didn't tell him that you were pregnant? Is *that* what happened?"

I looked at him. "He already *has* a baby, Aaron. I know you've seen the commercials!"

Pictures of Jamie with his first-born son were all over sports magazines across the country. August Carter Green was the most beautiful baby boy you could ever see. He had a father who looked like he jumped straight out of a photo shoot for *GQ* and a mother who looked like a got-damn Playboy Bunny. Jamie was making a name for himself in both the NFL and the fashion industry, and Charlie wasn't doing so bad herself. I saw her face in a few fashion magazines, and even saw her on a few catwalks on *E!* She may not have gotten to dance, but her name was still in lights. Little August would never have to want for anything. The bitch had gotten what she wanted—for her and her baby to be in Jamie's life.

Aaron shook his head. I knew he thought that I was wrong, but he left the subject alone. He yawned. "Shit. Excuse me."

I looked at him. "Tired?"

Aaron looked at me, eyes coated in tears from yawning. "Hell yeah. I've been up for like two days straight. They got me running back and forth to press conferences and shit. Miami Heat wants me now, Heaven. I'm thinking of coming back stateside. My agent is trying to talk me out of it, but I miss home."

I looked at him.

"I miss *you*," Aaron admitted.

I was so cruel to that boy. As soon as Jamie and I got back together, I dissed the *hell* out of Aaron. Made him really feel like he wasn't shit. Aaron was bold enough to approach me at Jamie's father's funeral, and I shot him down. *All* the way down. Aaron was a great guy, but I couldn't help who my heart belonged to at the time. Aaron was with Charlie, and we had no business being involved with one another. Had we both known Charlie and Jamie were sleeping together, we would have saved each other a whole lot of heartache, that's for damn sure.

Tears slid down my face. I just couldn't believe that Aaron actually came; that he didn't forget about me; that he still cared.

Aaron held my face in his hands, drying my tears. "How's singing going?" He changed the subject because he knew it wasn't the right time.

I nodded. "Okay, I guess. I didn't get a chance to promote my album. It dropped a few weeks ago, but here I am, in bed. Anastasia canceled my tour and tried to cancel the album release date, but it was too late. Anastasia worked my *ass* off, do you hear me?"

Aaron laughed a little, watching me force myself to try to smile.

I looked at him, shaking my head. "Anastasia, Darryl, their staff, their managers, their songwriters, their producers, their promoters, their fans . . . this is my family now. My life has been nothing but tour buses, studio time, photo shoots, voice lessons, and dance rehearsals—and you know I'm so not a dancer!"

Aaron grinned.

"I don't really have any friends of my own. Anastasia's life has become my life. Renée comes when she can.

Juanita writes every once in a while from prison. Autumn came to the BET Awards this past summer to see me; she tried to come when Renée told her that I lost the baby, but I didn't want her to see me like this. You already know me and Charlie don't speak. And Jamie hasn't said a word to me since I turned his proposal down at the airport," I said as I rolled my eyes.

Aaron looked at me, his eyes searching my face. "Why? Shorty, why did you turn him down? You loved dude! You dissed me for that nigga, and you turned him down? Why?"

I dried my face. "I found out I was pregnant, and it all hit me that he was having a baby with my own fuckin' sister! That our kids would be sister-cousins or brother-cousins! I wanted to forgive him, but as soon as the words 'you're four weeks pregnant' came out of that doctor's mouth, I saw my life flash before my eyes, and I didn't like what I saw."

Aaron just looked at me, not sure what to say.

"Jamie showed up to the airport that next morning and proposed to me in a terminal full of people. I didn't mean to embarrass him, but I couldn't marry him. Jamie is not the marriage type, and no matter how much he wanted to be, that just isn't him!" I exclaimed. "I'm not gonna say that I'm over him, because you never get over someone who's changed my life the way that he has, but I will say that it just wasn't meant to be. The fact that I lost his baby, and he's flaunting the baby that he has with her further proves that!"

Aaron sighed, shaking his head at me. I'm sure he didn't plan on seeing me that way when he stopped by the Allan mansion that day. He probably expected to see a shining star, who had just recorded her first album with a superstar that everyone in America wanted to record a song with. Out of hundreds of thousands of talented people who sent Anastasia demos and dance audition videos on the regular, she chose me, a real nobody, just a cousin of her husband. A cousin he didn't even know he had until just a few years ago.

"I'm sorry, Aaron. I hate that you have to see me like this." I shook my head. "But I have to say that this is my first time out of my room in over three months."

"Baby steps," Aaron smiled, not realizing what he was saying.

I burst out crying.

Aaron sighed. "Oh, shit, Heaven, baby, I'm sorry! Wrong choice of words."

I shook my head, drying my face. "No, it's okay." I struggled to stand up from the chair.

Aaron rose to his feet, catching me before I fell. "Let me help you back to bed, sweetheart."

Aaron tucked me into bed that morning. He sat at my side, looking like he couldn't believe that I was the same person that he left just months ago. "I have to catch up with my agent, shorty. He'll cuss my ass out if I miss this meeting." Aaron laughed a little.

I nodded. "Okay."

"But, I'd like to come back over if you don't mind. I mean, it's been eight months since I've seen you. You're not the same person that I saw then, but I know she's still in there. I wanna see her before I go back to France." Aaron's eyes traced my face before he got up from the bed.

I watched him as he walked out of my room.

I sighed, covering my face with my hands. Why did that boy show up when I was feeling vulnerable and unlovable? I'd been watching Jamie on TV for months. I can't tell you how many commercials had that fool in them. He signed a contract with Nike, not to mention he had his own clothing line that had just dropped. Little August was like in every fuckin' commercial. I know that

I already said that shit a few times, but the shit was really bothering me. My baby died, and everyone else's life seemed to go on as normal. I wasn't jealous of Charlie on any level, but I was tired of her getting everything she wanted when she *so* didn't deserve it. My little nephew was adorable, but my heart wouldn't let go of the fact that he was supposed to be mine.

It was about 8:00 that night when Beth knocked at my door and let Aaron in. He was dressed in a completely different outfit, like he was ready to head to the club. I was still in the same tank top and sweatpants, probably smelling like a bag of hell. The only thing on me that looked presentable were my Poetic braids, thanks to Renée.

Aaron stepped into the room, and Beth stepped out.

I sat up in the bed.

Aaron grinned, holding a bag in his hand.

"You going out on a date or something?" I looked him over. He was dressed to impress, in some urban French designer's outfit that I'd never seen before. Damn, he was fine as hell. That body of his, OMG, was perfect.

Aaron laughed a little. "Well, I was supposed to be meeting my agent and his niece at the club at ten. Yeah, it's supposed to be a date."

It was nice to see Aaron out and about, not giving a fuck about Charlie. "What's in the bag?" I asked.

"Oh," Aaron walked over to me, sitting the bag on my nightstand. "Just something I picked up from *Victoria's Secret*."

I looked at him, and then at the bag. "You got some fuckin' lingerie in that bag, Aaron?"

Aaron laughed out loud. "What, girl? Naw, some body wash! You know me better than that, Heaven. I don't see a point in lingerie. I would rather see you naked than with *any* clothes on, you know that."

He had me blushing less than a minute into our conversation. "Wh–what kind of body wash?" I stuttered.

Aaron grinned, knowing he was jump-starting my weak heart. "Vanilla."

My favorite. I looked up at him, lips trembling. "Why are you *still* so fuckin' awesome?" I shook my head.

There was a knock at my room door. Nurse Patty popped her head in, holding a towel, a wash cloth, and a change of clothes in her hands. "Hi, sweetie, you ready for your shower?"

"Yes, Patty, thank you." I pushed my covers from off of my legs.

Patty was making her way over to me when Aaron caught her by the arm. She looked up into his face when he took the towel, wash cloth, and clothes from her hands.

"I got this, Miss Patty. Let me do it." He grinned at her.

My eyes widened. I shook my head frantically at Patty. I really didn't want that boy touching any part of my body the way that he was touching my heart.

Patty laughed a little to herself, blushing, her white cheeks turning red. "Oh, my, okay, well . . . have fun, I mean." She didn't even know what to say. She just hurried her old ass out of my room.

"Aaron!" I exclaimed.

Aaron laughed, coming over to me, helping me up from the bed. "Where's your shower?"

I shook my head, looking up into his face as I stood from the bed. "Aaron, you know, you got some nerve."

"I just wanna help you. I can't stand to see you like this." Aaron's eyes traced my face. "I won't try anything, I swear. I got a date tonight, remember?"

Aaron sat on the edge of the tub. I held his shoulders, balancing myself as he helped me slide out of my clothes. Aaron was trying his damnedest not to look at me. By the time I undressed completely, his eyes were fixated on my belly button ring.

I looked down at Aaron. He'd grown his hair out a little, about an inch or two. His hair was curly and I never even knew it. I ran my fingers through his hair just a little. "You grew your hair out."

Aaron looked up at me, smiling a little.

I loved the bathroom in my bedroom. It was the first time I had lived in a house that had a shower separate from the bathtub. Aaron held my hand, leading me over to the shower. He opened the frosted door and reached in to set the water at just the right temperature.

I stepped inside, holding the body wash that he'd brought me in my hands, closing the door behind me. I sat down on the stool that sat inside of the shower.

Aaron cleared his throat. "You good, shorty?"

My heart was beating so fast. Usually, the nurses helped me bathe. It was hard to wash myself. I was so weak and in so much pain. The pain in my heart had penetrated my entire body. It was going to take everything I had in me to move on from Sara's death.

"I–I'll let you know when I need to stand up to wash," I whispered.

"A'ight." I saw Aaron going over to the vanity table in the bathroom, to sit on the stool.

We both sat there in awkward silence. I knew there was a lot that he was dying to ask me, because there was a lot that I was dying to ask him. We both started to speak, cutting each other off.

"My bad, shorty," Aaron cleared his throat. "You go first."

"Naw, boo, you go first." I started to wash off.

"So, what's wrong with you, Heaven? What are the doctors saying?" He asked.

I sighed. I really didn't feel like talking about my plethora of health issues. "Aaron, where do I start? Ummm, I have lupus and autonomic neuropathy."

Aaron hesitated. "Autonomic neuropathy? What the hell is that? Something to do with nerves, I'm guessing."

I nodded. "Yeah. It's a nerve disorder that affects your involuntary body functions like your heart and blood vessels. I'm just finding this out now, too. It would have saved my Aunt Joyce a lot of money when she was helping cover the costs of the surgeries that I had as a kid. They could never figure out what was causing the heart failure until now. And it's all thanks to Anastasia for sending me to the right people for testing."

"Is there a cure for this?" Aaron hesitated.

"No. And I'm sure my depression and anxiety aren't helping." I sighed.

Aaron was quiet. He wasn't sure what to say. What *could* he say? Instead of avoiding stress, it seems like I went looking for it.

"So," I broke the tension, "how is Paris?"

Aaron laughed a little. "Oh, it was amazing the first few weeks. Shit, I went sightseeing. I ate at some of the best restaurants and went to every club that there is. My agent and manager had me meeting all kinds of fashion designers and shit. I was in a few fashion shows, too. Shit, I can't tell you how many free clothes I got just by showing up to photo shoots. I'm talkin' about clothes by Giuseppe Zanotti, Versace, Gucci, Dolce and Gabbana—every damn body! My basketball coach is cool as a muthafucka. My parents and my aunt came out to visit me at least four times in the past eight months. My apartment sits right over the water. I swear, shorty, it feels like a paradise. Life is good. That is, until I realize I'm living that life alone."

My heart skipped a beat as the water beat down against my skin. "C'mon, Aaron, you can't tell me that you haven't met *one* girl in eight months!" I tried to play off my nervousness by flattering his ego. "A guy who looks like you should have *no* problem getting a girl!"

Aaron laughed. "I'm not saying I have a problem getting a girl—I'm just saying that the girls have a problem getting to *me*. I didn't go to Paris for that shit, Heaven. Jeremiah, my agent, seems to think I need a girl, too, which is why he's introducing me to his niece tonight."

I started to lather my body with soap, trying my best to calm myself. My heart beat rapidly in my chest. "Yeah? What does she look like?" I tried pacing my breathing.

Aaron hesitated. "Like something I'm not even trying to deal with."

I needed help washing my back, but was too nervous to tell him. Renée was right, I was skinny as hell. I had lost every ounce of fat that I had on my bones. It was going to take months to gain back the little weight that I had. Other than the ten pounds I gained while pregnant, I never weighed more than 115 pounds soaking wet. I couldn't afford to lose any weight. I felt so ashamed of looking the way that I did. I'm pretty sure the chick that Aaron was supposed to get fixed up with that night was stacked. Aaron and Jamie kept some hot bitches around them. That was the crowd they rolled with. Even Charlie. She was like Beyonce, Lauryn London, Cassie, Nicki Minaj, Jennifer Lopez, and Melissa Ford all rolled up into one. A bad bitch, I had to admit. I didn't have shit on her as far as looks were concerned. But Aaron thought different.

"My agent doesn't know that I met his niece before. She ain't nothing but a girl trying to meet some rich dude to take care of her. Yeah, she's fine, in *any* man's book. But she's too much like my last girl. You know, light-skinned, thick, seductive, you're-all-about-her-but-she's-all-about-hers type of chick." I heard Aaron's voice approaching closer to the shower. "I would never involve myself with Draya—she's gonna end up bleeding some nigga dry, but shit, it's not gonna be me. I'm just going on this double date with my agent so he can stop fuckin' talking about her, trying to sell the girl to me."

I had to say something. Aaron tried to find fault in every female that wasn't me. It took him years to tell me how he felt about me, and once he let everything all out in the open, he couldn't bring himself to keep anything else inside. In front of everyone at his wedding rehearsal dinner last December, in front of his parents who didn't like me, in front of *Jamie*, and in front of *Charlie*, he told me that whenever I wanted him, he was ready. His entire family was there to see him marry Charlie, but he couldn't have cared less. Once he found out the truth about Charlie and Jamie, he was free to be himself, and he refused to go back into that cage.

"Aaron, you are too wonderful to be single all your life." I sighed, trying to reach my back with the bath sponge, but I couldn't.

"I'm just not trying to settle anymore. I did that shit with Charlie, and I promised myself I would never do that shit again." Aaron responded after a short pause.

I sighed, irritated that I couldn't reach my back on my own. I was feeling really vulnerable, and I really didn't want to get caught up in Aaron's touch.

I saw Aaron's blurry figure turn to me, hearing my struggle. "Heaven, you straight? You need me?"

I hated to answer that. "Y—yes." I watched him not hesitate a second to remove some of his clothing. "I mean, I just need you to help me wash my back."

Aaron was silent. He opened the door to the shower. He had undressed down to his tank top and boxers, something that wouldn't have me more uncomfortable than I already was.

I looked up at him, as he held out his hands to help me up.

I reached out to him, and he helped me up by my hands, pulling me up against him. I looked up into his face, and he took the sponge from my hands. I had to tell someone how I felt, no matter how much it made that person feel uncomfortable. "I've known that boy all my life! He won't have anything to do with me anymore! I'm lost without that asshole! I ain't shit without him." I whispered.

Aaron slid the sponge across my back, firmly pressing it against my back. "I'm not gonna lie, it hurts like hell to hear you talk about dude." I felt like I was getting a deep tissue massage, his touch was so intense. "You're letting your feelings for this dude cloud your judgment, Heaven. You don't need that muthafucka. You're too *good* for that muthafucka. He knows that shit, too, which is why he hasn't showed his face. Trust me, he knows what he had." Aaron looked down into my face.

"He just . . . he made me fall back in love, he gave that girl *my* baby, and then he just cut me loose like I wasn't shit!" I cried out. "I was holding onto my secret about Sara because she was the only thing that he couldn't take back from me and now she's gone, too. I'm just a mess, Aaron. There's no way that I'm gonna recover from all of this. You should just go out on your date. You really don't need to see me like this or hear me talk about that asshole. I'm sorry."

The pressure from the water beat down on us that night in the shower. I will admit, it felt good to feel his warm body against mine. It made me think of the time we'd spent at the hotel in Alexandria, Virginia. It took weeks for my body to register that he was no longer inside of me. His touch was still intoxicating. Aaron loved me, there was no doubt about that, but why wouldn't my heart accept that? I knew Jamie loved me, but he didn't cherish me the way that Aaron did. Jamie knew he could have whoever he wanted—that was his attitude 24/7, which is why it was always hard to accept an "I love you" from him. He talked a good game; that was Jamie, all day. He was a smooth talker. He knew all the right words, all the right moves, all the right places to touch. He spoke to your heart. He got women to fall for him all of the time, and once they were hooked, he walked away. He did us all that way. The only one stupid enough to stick around for the heartbreak was Charlie.

"I don't have to go out with Jeremiah tonight. I can stay here with you. I *want* to stay here with you, Heaven." He whispered, hands gripping my waist then.

I looked up into his face, as he licked his lips. Man, he was gorgeous. I shook my head, "Aaron, you gotta stop trying to find something wrong with every female who isn't me. Look at me. I'm not the same person you saw in January. I'm sick. I'm not dying, but I'm not living either. Losing my baby took something from me that I won't be able to get back. And I don't know what happens next."

"Me—*I'm* what happens next, sweetheart," Aaron whispered.

I just looked at him, eyes tracing his lips.

"I can help you, Heaven." Aaron looked down into my face, eyes tracing my lips, too. "Come with me to Paris. Just for a little while."

I looked up into his face, my lips trembling. Lord knows I wanted to say yes, but I couldn't. Not just because I was sick and under a doctor's care, but because I wasn't ready to lose myself in another man just yet. "No, Aaron, I can't." I shook my head, looking up at him.

"Heaven, I won't hurt you. I'm not him. I swear I'm not." Aaron held my face in his hands. "C'mon, Heaven, we're friends. Let me be your friend. Let me help you. You know you can trust me. And you know you need me."

He *did* show up just when I needed him. He didn't let his pride get in the way. Even though I totally dissed him for Jamie, he still found it in in his heart to love me.

"I'm only gonna be in Paris about another two months if I sign a contract with Miami. I promised my Mom and Pop that I'd go to England with them for about two weeks. It's been a minute since my grandparents actually wanted to see me. I'll spend some time with Pop's family, and then I'll come back here to get you." Aaron dried my tears. "Please. Just think about it and give me a call."

Chapter 2: Oui

Ne'Vaeh

"Aaron wants you to do *what*?" Anastasia exclaimed the next morning, as she sat at the foot of my bed, sliding her boot socks on. She was so shapely that everything she wore fit her like a glove. Her body exuded sex. Even though she wasn't a stripper anymore, everything that girl did was seductive. She was dressed to kill as usual. She had Puma make her the tightest, sexiest, sportiest dress and matching jacket. She had on Puma sporty high-heeled boots. She had a style that no woman I knew could touch.

I sighed, watching her get cute, or should I say *stay* cute. "Go with him to Paris for a little while."

Anastasia looked at me, then grinned, shaking her head at me. "He doesn't give up, I can say that much about him."

"So should I go?" I whispered, eyes watering. "Or nah?"

Anastasia scoffed. "Shit, why not? I'm sure the boy will make sure you're medically taken care of. You're well enough to fly, boo. He'll make sure your heart, mind, body, and soul are taken care of. I saw the way that boy looked at you. He is *infatuated* with you!" Anastasia exclaimed, zipping up her boots. She stood from the bed. "It's not too often a girl meets a guy who worships the ground that she walks on. He's a keeper, girl, you *know* he is."

I just looked at her, not sure what to say.

"Sweetie, your album just dropped. We're gonna promote you the best way we know how while your body heals. So go to Paris. Relax and get back to being you, boo. When you get back, we'll start your tour. I got a few artists that are dying to tour with you and me, sweetie! So get ready to put in work when you get back!" Anastasia smiled, swinging her long hair over her shoulder.

I still wasn't so sure traveling with Aaron was the best idea. "I'm scared, Anna. Scared to let him love me. Or maybe I'm scared to love him, I don't know. All I know is that Aaron came and Jamie never showed up. That has to mean something, right?"

Anastasia shook her head, straightening out her jacket. "Well, I told you eight months ago when you left dude that once you walked away from him, there was no looking back. I know dudes like him. You shot him down. You crushed his ego. You know better than me how cocky that muthafucka is! To him, you were just like every other woman who left him! I'm just being honest with you! I'm not saying the dude doesn't love you—I'm just saying that the ship with him has sailed, and more than likely isn't coming back. Aaron, on the other hand, is here, so you might as well just jump on board. Ya feel me? Now go pack!"

So, I went to Paris with Aaron. Nurse Patty had gotten me to finally eat the two weeks and three days that I waited for Aaron to come back to get me from Anastasia's mansion. I might have gained about five pounds in two weeks. I looked a little better, I felt a little better, and I had the energy to walk on my own without help. Of course, Anastasia wouldn't let me go unless Aaron made sure he had a doctor set up for me to see in Paris. She helped me pack a few things, though Aaron told her I wouldn't need anything. I think I slept the entire flight to France. It was the best sleep I'd had in eight months.

When we arrived in Paris, a limo was waiting for us outside of the airport. It took us straight to Aaron's apartment, and he wasn't lying—his apartment looked like it sat right over the river that led to heaven. I just stood in the middle of his living room as he wheeled our luggage inside of the apartment. His apartment looked like something out of the "Lifestyles of the Rich and Famous." My jaw almost dropped to the floor when he went over to his windows and opened the curtains, revealing the river view from the balcony.

Aaron grinned, coming over to me, taking my jacket and purse from my hands.

I just looked at him, the same way that I looked at Anastasia and Darryl when they took me to their mansion in Atlanta. I was awestruck. He had truly made it. He was a star. I'm sure he wasn't as excited as I was about his fame and riches—he came from money. I guess he played basketball so that he could make a name for himself and stop living in his father's shadow.

"So, you like it?" Aaron grinned, biting his bottom lip, enjoying watching me prance around the place like a kid in a candy store.

I looked at him, eyes widened. "What? *Like* it, Aaron? This is the doorway to Heaven! Oh my God, I'm—" I couldn't even find the words to tell him how grateful I was. "You wanted to share this experience with me, and that means a lot."

Aaron's nodded. "Well, I saw how you were lookin' back in ATL. You needed a friend. You needed a heart. You needed some love. I couldn't leave you like that. How could *he* leave you like that?"

I just looked up at him, heart trembling in my chest. I exhaled deeply. "So, you must have a busy schedule. I'm pretty sure that I'll be spending most of my nights alone, huh?"

Aaron shook his head. "Nah, I'm in the process of leaving my team here. Just wanted to take a vacation before signing with Miami. I need a break. I have a few appearances to make. Maybe even a few parties to go to, but for as long as I have you here with me, I'm all yours. You just need to get some rest."

Aaron was the perfect gentlemen. He had changed so much from that Aaron who had no problems showing me how he felt eight months ago. Y'all remember that night in his weight room? And don't get me started on what happened in his bedroom on my birthday. He'd changed. He was different. He was more mature. He had me alone in the shower two weeks earlier, and he didn't touch me inappropriately. He just held me up against his body and washed me like he was washing his car.

That night, in his cozy apartment in Paris, we ordered out and ate together in bed. We were like old friends catching up on old times. I hadn't laughed so hard in months. It hadn't felt so good to be around someone in months. I wasn't exactly my old self, but I was getting there.

For dessert, Aaron made this fruit cocktail milkshake that tasted like God made it! It felt so good to be around Aaron. It felt even better when he began to massage my calves, ankles, feet, and toes.

"Oh," I moaned, leaning back against his oversized pillows. "This shake is *too* good!" I sipped from the straw. That shit was so good, it made my eyes cross.

Aaron grinned, "What about my hands?"

I looked up at him, trying not to pee on myself when his hands moved past my knees to my thighs. "Oh, they–they feel alright." I stuttered.

Aaron laughed a little.

I looked at him as he looked down at my thighs, fingers kneading and squeezing them. "You're different."

Aaron looked up at me, emerald green eyes searching my face.

"Something's different." My eyes coated themselves in tears. "I don't know what it is, but you've changed."

Aaron grinned. "Well, you've been through some rough shit this year, shorty. *I* took you through some rough shit last year. I should have never approached you when I was with someone else. As a matter of fact, I shouldn't have even *been* with someone else. I was wrong as a muthafucka. I wanted you, I *took* you, and I was wrong. I didn't show you that I wanted more than your body. I want your everything; your heart, mind, body, and spirit. You're everything I want in a woman, Heaven, and this time around, I'm hoping that you give me the chance to show you. It feels good as muthafucka being here with you. I'm doing everything that I can to be a good friend, and not rush your heart into anything. I just—I just wanna be next to you, and I'm hoping that you decide to stay here with me for the next two months. I hope what I'm saying isn't scaring you away."

The tears had already started flowing halfway through his speech. "I'm—" I choked back the tears as best as I could. "I'm not going anywhere, Aaron."

Aaron stopping massaging my legs but held on firmly to my thighs. "I didn't expect to see you like this when I showed up to the Allan Mansion. When Darryl said that you needed me, I expected to see you recording in the studio or throwing an album release party. I didn't expect to see my girl thirty pounds lighter than she was eight months ago! I didn't expect to see that my girl let some nigga break her! Losing Sara was devastating, I know it had to be, but baby, you gotta live your life! I couldn't leave you in Georgia like that, around people who are only gonna tell you what they think you wanna hear because you're gonna make them millions! You're priceless, Heaven. You're my heart, and I want you. You know I'm a better man than him. You know I'm what you need." Aaron held my legs, grabbing them behind my knees, pulling me closer to him.

I nodded. "Yeah. Yeah, you are."

"So, tell me, do I have you, Heaven? Do I have you?" Aaron's eyes traced my lips.

I looked up into his face, lips quivering, speechless.

"Heaven, I'm here to help you, not hurt you, I promise. I love you. I've loved you since the first day I met you." His eyes searched my face. "I'll move as slow as you want me to go. I won't rush you. Just give me a chance, please. Let me help fatten your ass up, a'ight?" Aaron grinned.

I burst out laughing and crying all at once. "This shake is *really* good, Aaron! Keep making these and I'll gain weight in no time! Strawberries, and bananas, and cherries—Oh, my!"

Aaron laughed, watching me laugh. "It's good to see you smiling."

I nodded, my eyes searching his. "I really needed this. Aaron, I really needed you. You came to rescue me, and I appreciate you for that."

Aaron held my face in his hands, drying my cheeks. "You know I'll do anything necessary for you, Heaven."

I looked up into his eyes, "Aaron, I came here with you because I wanted to feel whole again. I'm not gonna lie, I'm afraid to let you love me. I'm tired of getting hurt. I'm tired of broken promises. I'm tired of losing everything that I love. If you really want me like you say that you do, then you gotta give me some time."

Aaron nodded, "A'ight. I can do that."

***

Those two months that I spent with Aaron in Paris felt like I was floating on air. He made sure that I went to the doctor once a week. He made sure that I was fed. He made sure that I showered. He made sure I kept my hair done. He made sure that I had a pedicure and manicure every week. He made sure that I rocked the hottest clothes. He made sure that we went to the gym every day. He got me back into shape. He got me back to living my life. He gave me something to look forward to every day. He cooked for me every night, and we went out to eat on the weekends. I had gained about ten pounds that first month, and ten more the second month. I was happy. I was free. To prove to myself that I could get over Jamie, I turned his "J" tattoo on my neck into "Joy." I didn't forget about Sara, but I could at least go to sleep at night without seeing her face every time I closed my eyes.

The night of October 18 was our last night in Paris. I hated to leave. Facing reality was something that I wasn't ready to do. Anastasia had a tour schedule that was going to stress me the fuck out. Not to mention she had even produced a play for a local screenwriter, Kenya Love. She wanted me to try out for the leading role. I had no idea how I was going to star in a play and go on tour, but Anastasia had it all mapped out.

I wanted to stay with Aaron, at least just a little while longer. He was so sweet and so gentle. The entire time that we'd spent in Paris, the dude didn't try to touch me *once*. Not even a kiss. The closest that he had gotten to me in Paris was the night we went dancing at this restaurant that sat right on the beach. We were dancing so close I could feel the blood rushing through his veins.

"You finished packing, shorty?" Aaron tapped at my room door.

I sat on my bed in a sports bra and boy shorts, packing my last suitcase. I sighed. "Just finishing up." I looked up

at Aaron as he strolled into my room, dressed in a tank
top and baggy sweatpants.

We were staying the night in a hotel. We had spent the
day before packing up Aaron's apartment. His things had
been shipped off to his new house in Miami. I can't tell
you how much I hated the fact that Aaron was going to be
in Miami, while I lived all the way in Atlanta. I never told
Aaron how I felt about him the entire two months that I
was there. Sure, I thanked him every day that I was there,
but I never told him point blank that he made my heart
race every time he stepped into the room. Aaron was a
breath of fresh air. His very presence gave me wings. If it
weren't for him, I would have still been wasting away in
Atlanta, never leaving my room.

"Guess the honeymoon is over, huh?" Aaron laughed a
little.

"Oh my goodness, time flew by! I don't want it to end,
ugh!" I made a pouty face. "Aren't you gonna miss Paris?"
I asked, looking into his face, as he sat down on the bed,
next to me, facing me.

Aaron's eyes searched mine. "Yeah, but I'm gonna miss
you more, shorty. These past two months with you have
been the best two months of my life. I'm serious, Heaven.
You're entertainment, that's for sure! You kept a brutha
rolling on the floor laughing my muthafuckin' ass off!
You had a nigga watching *Sex and the City* and shit!"

I laughed out loud. Yeah, that was my show, and if
he wanted to cuddle with me, his ass was gonna have to
watch that shit with me.

"It feels so good to see you laughing and smiling, when
just two months ago, you looked like you were on your
death bed! You're beautiful, Heaven, and as long as I
have known you, you never knew how beautiful you are."
Aaron held my face in his warm hands, fingers grazing
against my lips.

My heartbeat sped up a little. I thought about Aaron in Miami, on a beach, laid up with some sexy, Brazilian bitch. "Talk about beautiful, those bitches in Miami are beautiful."

Aaron looked at me, grinning, taking his hands from my face. "You don't even have to worry about me dealing with anyone of them, shorty, believe that shit."

"Are—are you gonna be okay in Miami all by yourself?" I stuttered.

"Naw." Aaron shook his head, his eyes searching mine.

"I'll come visit you once my tour is over. Well, if I land this part in the play that Anastasia wants me to try out for, then I'll have to visit you after that. I can't believe she has me not only singing, but acting, too!" I rolled my eyes. "She doesn't want me to be 'one-dimensional.' She seems to think I can do it all. She's all work and no play. She and Darryl barely even see each other. I don't want a life like that, Aaron." I looked at him.

"What kind of life do you want?" Aaron asked.

"I wanna be able to come home to my man after a long day's work. I wanna talk to him, ask him about his day, and tell him about mine. I wanna cook dinner together every night, except for on the weekends when we go to either his or my favorite restaurant. I wanna take long showers or hot baths together. I wanna make love at least four or five days a week. I wanna lay up and cuddle, naked, watching movies! I want a man who will help me take my braids out!" I laughed a little. "I want a man who can see my heart, who understands me, who doesn't try to change me, who accepts me for who I am. I want a man who I don't have to tell, because he knows exactly where it hurts. I want a man who knows when I need him to just hold me and tell me everything is gonna be okay. I want a man who wants *me,* and only me." I stopped talking because I realized that the man I was describing was sitting right in front of me.

Aaron's eyes searched my face. He pulled me closer to him by the elastic in my boy shorts. "It took me like two hours to get all them damn braids out of your head, girl."

I laughed, my whole body blushing. He knew I wanted him. He knew I needed him. He knew that I was his, but he also knew that Jamie wasn't out of my system.

Aaron shook his head at me. "Jamie is gonna come looking for you eventually. What you gonna do when he comes for you?"

I couldn't help but think about *Cops* when he said that. I shook my head back at Aaron. "Aaron, I'm through with him."

"No, you're not." Aaron gripped my boy shorts in his hand.

"He hurt me, Aaron. Yeah, I was in the wrong when I slept with you while you were with Charlie, but I told him the truth! I never kept anything from him. He got that girl pregnant and to avoid telling me the truth, he just dumped me! Yes, I still feel something for him. I've known him all my life! But I can move on. I'm tired of losing." I didn't want to cry over Jamie when I was with Aaron, but I couldn't hold it in any longer. "Aaron, you came and got me when I needed to be rescued from myself. You gave me my life back. I owe you a lot. So whatever I can do to repay you, I'll do it."

Aaron shook his head. "Baby, you don't owe me anything. I just wanna see you happy, not heartbroken over some nigga who didn't deserve you in the first place. He was foolish to let you slip away. I know you're not mine, but I'll be damned if *he* ends up with you."

I hesitated. Aaron was gripping the shit out of my panties like he wanted to snatch them off. "Who says I'm not yours?"

Aaron's eyes searched my face. He was speechless.

My lips trembled. "You're gripping my panties like you wanna take them off or something."

Aaron's eyes traced my lips. "Can I?"

Truth be told, he could have taken them off two months ago had I had the strength. He had me from the moment he held me in that shower.

"You don't even have to ask." I looked into his face. "I've been ready, to tell you the truth. I was just waiting on you."

Aaron's eyes shined. He pulled me closer to him by my waist. "I finally have the chance to be with you. You have no idea what that means to me. I've wanted you since high school, Heaven. I can finally call you my girl? Is that what you're telling me?"

I nodded as Aaron gently kissed my lips. He gave me that slow, I-wanna-fuck-right-now kiss. I missed his lips, I can't even lie. He had lips that left you breathless after one stroke. His lips caressed mine until my clit throbbed. He sucked on my lips, his tongue tickling mine.

"Aaron, thank you for coming to get me," I whispered.

The time for talking was over. Aaron waited two and a half months to get to me. He snatched my panties from my body before standing up from the bed to remove his shirt and slide his pants and underwear from his body. I pulled my bra from my body before Aaron hovered over top of me.

My heart pounded in my chest as Aaron kissed from my lips to my neck, all the way down to my nipples, and then to my stomach. He nibbled on my belly button ring as he slipped his fingers inside of me. My legs shook as he dug his fingers into me. I hadn't been touched in ten months, so you know I was dripping wet. I nearly bit my own lip off as Aaron kissed from my belly button to the insides of my thighs. My nerves were jumping, heart was racing, and hormones raging. Aaron gripped my thighs in his hand, as he kissed the insides of my thighs, before planting his lips on my clit. My legs immediately locked around Aaron's neck.

"Oh!" I moaned, running my hands through his curls.

"Mmmm," he moaned, too, as he slipped his fingers in and out of my pussy, sucking on my clit like he was sucking from a bottle. He more than ate my pussy, he devoured that bitch. He sucked my pussy until I squirted all over his lips. As soon as I came, he licked from my clit to the crack of my ass, then back to my clit again. I covered my face with the pillow to keep from screaming out. My legs were shaking, one of them damn near going numb. My pussy squeezed tight around his index and middle finger before releasing again. Aaron sucked and nibbled on my clit until I came all over again. By then both legs were numb. I couldn't take anymore.

I squealed, gripping his curly hair in my hands. "Aaron, please stop!"

Aaron laughed a little as he loosened his lips from my clit, but began to gently kiss my pussy lips like he was kissing the lips on my face. "Your pussy tastes good as a muthafucka," he said between kisses. "Fuckin' delicious."

My body jumped each time his lips touched me.

Aaron finally came up for air, hovering over my body, his dick sliding up my leg. He gently kissed my lips, as he slid his way inside. He kissed my face, my cheeks, my shoulders, my hands. I held onto him, damn near digging holes in his back with my fingernails. He dug into my soul that night. He worked my pussy like he was never gonna get the pussy again. When he came, he was still going at it, dick hard as a rock. I just held on and enjoyed the ride. He moaned, biting down on my neck, one hand on my waist, the other around my neck.

"I missed this pussy, Heaven." Aaron moaned in my ear. "I love this pussy, yo."

I moaned, gripping his ass in my hands as he dug deeper. My pussy pulsated, squeezing the dick as Aaron let out a sigh, cumming inside of me again. I cried out loud as Aaron's weight rested on my body.

Aaron buried his face in my neck to hide the tears in his eyes from me. His heart beat steadily against my chest. "Damn, I hate to leave this," he whispered. "Shit."

The next morning, I woke up to the smell of cinnamon and brown sugar. I opened my eyes, facing the clock on the nightstand. It was 6:00 and our flight was leaving at 8:00. I hopped up from the bed, grabbing Aaron's tank top and throwing it on. Aaron was always up before I was, cooking something.

Aaron smiled when he saw me entering the kitchen, hair looking wild as hell. "Good morning, gorgeous."

I grinned, going over to him, hugging him from behind, and surrounding him in my arms. There was nothing sexier than watching that man cooking over the stove. "Good morning. Mmmm, it smells so good in here! You always cookin' up something!"

Aaron looked over his shoulder at me, "Baby, can you reach in that drawer and get the spatula for me?"

I nodded, letting go of him. I went over to the drawer that he was referring to and opened it, about to grab the plastic spatula from it when I saw a tiny ring-sized gray box sitting in the drawer. My heart nearly shot out of my chest.

Aaron looked at me, removing the frying pan from the heat before turning to face me. He saw the horrified look on my face. "I know you're scared, Heaven, but just listen."

I backed up a little as Aaron reached inside the drawer to get the box. He flipped it open, showing me the ring.

It wasn't his grandmother's ring, the one he'd given to Charlie the year before. It was a beautiful pink oval diamond in a platinum setting. I'd never seen a ring so beautiful in all my life. It was so Aaron to know exactly what my heart needed. I looked up into his face, as he took the ring out of the box and sat the box on the countertop.

Aaron looked at me, pulling me closer to him by my left hand. "Heaven, I love you, you know that. I found the woman that my soul loves. We have fun together, we laugh together, we cry together, we make each other feel good, and we *belong* together. I know our lives are hectic as shit, but I don't care. If you want me to give it all up to be with you, I'll do it. I'll do whatever it is I have to do to get you and keep you."

I shook my head, placing my hand over my heart, looking down at the ring in his trembling hand. "No, Aaron, don't quit basketball for me. You're so good at it! This is your dream! You love basketball!" I looked back up into his face.

Aaron nodding hating to admit that I was right. "Yeah, I do love it, but I love you more."

"How are we gonna do this though? You're gonna be in Miami, and I'm gonna be in Atlanta." I shook my head to myself.

Aaron's eyes searched mine.

"I'll quit," I replied.

Aaron shook his head. "Hell naw! Are you crazy? Your voice is phenomenal! You have a gift that shouldn't be thrown away for anyone, shorty. Don't give that up. You deserve this; nobody deserves a better life more than you do, Heaven, and that's real."

"Aaron, your parents—they don't wanna see you with me." I sighed.

"Man, I could care less about what my parents have to say about it," Aaron said with pride. "I'm tired of trying to live up to their standards. It's exhausting."

"How are we gonna do this when we live so far apart?" I shook my head.

Aaron's eyes searched my face. "We'll figure it out. Basketball season started already. I gotta jump straight into the swing of things when I get to Miami. But the season is over in April. I don't mind staying with you in ATL for a few months, taking a break from training for a little while. Long distance works for me. I'll take what I can get from you, Heaven. I've waited too long for this. I'm not about to be picky, for real. Baby, I wanna be with you; I *need* to be with you."

My lips trembled. Aaron made me happy. Aaron hated to see me in pain. Aaron never wanted to see me cry. He kept a smile on my face. He was drawn to me. Just being in my presence was good enough for him. I never met anyone who cherished my heart the way that he did. I'd lost Jamie. I'd lost Sara. And God brought Aaron back to me. I would have been stupid to just let him go, right?

"Aaron, I love you so much." I bit my lip to keep from crying out loud. "You came to rescue me. . . . You didn't forget about me, and that means so much."

Aaron held my left hand in his, sliding the ring on my finger. "I promise to love you forever, Heaven. I'll never hurt you. Marry me, Heaven, please."

How could I say no to a face like his? To a heart like his? To a smile like his? There was no doubt in my mind that I was in love with him. I trusted Aaron. He made me feel complete, and I didn't feel the need to hold back the way that I felt with Jamie. I never knew that someone could love me so much. I didn't know what true love was until I met Aaron.

I nodded, tears rolling down my face. "Yes, Aaron. Yes, I'll marry you."

Aaron pulled me closer, surrounding me in his arms. "Baby, we'll figure this out."

I held onto him, then held my hand up looking at my ring. *No turning back now, Ne'Vaeh. Don't hurt this boy.*

Chapter 3: Love 'em All

Charlene

I woke up bright and early to the sound of little August crying from his nursery. My baby had the softest, most gentle cry, almost as if he were singing. I loved waking up to the sound of his voice. My baby was destined to break hearts, just like his got-damn daddy.

I peeled my body from my satin sheets, rubbing my eyes, looking over at the clock. It was 6:48 a.m., and I was supposed to be out the door by 8:00. I still had to find something suitable to wear and do my hair. Man, I shouldn't have had that fifth drink the night before.

"Lilia!" I called out, reaching for my tank top, pulling it over my head quickly before the nanny bust through my door, catching a glimpse of my 36Ds.

In seconds, my nanny Lilia slowly peeped her head in. She had learned about busting up in my bedroom. The last time she burst through my door unannounced, she caught me on my knees, mouth full of dick.

Lilia was a cute, young Spaniard woman with long black hair and a face full of freckles. She could sing her ass off and had no business working as a nanny. She helped me through some very stressful nights for the past year of my son's life. Little August had colic up until he was about four and a half months old. Her voice seemed to be the only thing that soothed him.

I grinned at her.

"You want me to get Agosto up and ready, señorita?" She grinned back.

"Please, and thank you." I sighed as she shut the door. I had a long day ahead of me.

I looked over my shoulder at the man lying on his stomach beside me. His name was Tyler Anderson. He was a tall, brown-skinned, muscular, sexy muthafucka. The way he touched me, held me, grabbed me, licked me, kissed me made my pussy *drip drop*. I met Tyler freshman year at Morgan State. I was dating Aaron at the time and didn't pay him much of any attention. I happened to bump into him on March 1, 2016, at a party in DC. I was out celebrating the contract I had just signed with Diva Game, a huge modeling agency in DC. Tyler was out celebrating being traded from the Cowboys. I'd been around pretty black men before and wasn't impressed by his perfectly white teeth . . . that was until I found out that he was being traded to the Baltimore Ravens. You know I'd do anything to get Jamie's attention, including fuck his teammate.

I nudged Tyler's shoulder. "Babe, you gotta get up. I gotta go to my girl's funeral."

"Hmmm?" Tyler mumbled, putting the pillow over his head.

I pushed him a little in his side. "C'mon, Tyler, I'm serious. I'm already running late. I need to straighten my hair. Do you see all of these curls on my head? Yeah, it's gonna take my stylist hours to do this shit. Get up!"

Alisha died in her sleep on May 15, 2016, my son's first birthday. The girl who hated me with every inch of her soul since we were in elementary school had become my best friend over the past year. I watched her shrivel away for 365 days. The night she died, her boyfriend Ashton and I sat with her. She knew that she was fading on us, and didn't want anyone else but me and Ashton in her bedroom that night. Ashton held her in his arms and didn't get a wink of sleep that night. He shook with every breath Alisha took, afraid it would be her last breath. She died in his arms at 3:35 a.m.

Ashton and I weren't exactly on speaking terms. He hadn't said a word to me ever since the night he told me that he loved me, at Jamie's NFL party over a year and a half ago. But that night that Alisha died, I held him in my arms and let him cry until he couldn't cry anymore. He nearly lost it when the paramedics carried her away on a stretcher. Ashton had lost his homie, his lover, his best friend. There was no replacing Alisha. I sure as hell wasn't ready for her funeral, but I really wasn't ready for Tyler to think that he was going to lay up with me all day. We had a fuck-me-nigga-then-leave kind of situation going on, and I planned on keeping it that way.

Tyler was Tuesday's treat, if you know what I mean. I had to do something to get my mind off of Alisha. Sunday night, I called Lee. He was Japanese. He knew how to make love to my mind. On Monday, I called Montego over. He was Caribbean. The brutha could cook and fuck like a champ. And I ran into Tyler at the gym the evening before Alisha's funeral. A quickie in the locker room turned into an all-nighter at my place. He had me in tears from the time we left the gym at 8:30 that night until about 4:00 the next morning. As you can see, after Aaron left me and Jamie dissed me, my heart beat for no one.

Tyler sat up in the bed, pulling me closer to him, kissing my shoulders. His lips were so gentle and soft, capable of making me do just about anything he wanted me to do. He was phenomenal in bed, and that was all I allowed myself to know about him. Knowing anything else was too dangerous.

"You need me to roll wit'cha, sweetheart?" He squeezed my waist with his strong hands.

I looked up at him, shaking my head. "Naw, I'm good. And why would you wanna go to a funeral for a girl you didn't even know?"

"Because *you* know her. Because she was your friend. And because if you needed me to be there with you, I would." Tyler's eyes traced from my eyes to my lips. "You shouldn't have to go to a funeral alone."

I shook my head, fighting back the tears. "I—I'm not gonna be alone, Tyler. I promised Ashton's mother that I'd sit with him today at the funeral. You know, my girl has everything planned out for today. She even planned a huge party after her funeral!" I laughed off my pain, "She said she didn't want folks depressed about her death, but that she wanted us to be happy for her because she wasn't suffering anymore." I wiped the tear away that broke through.

Tyler reached for my face, but I quickly turned away, getting up from the bed.

"I think you should go. Jamie will be here to get his son in a little while." I stood before him.

Tyler laughed to himself, grabbing his boxers then getting up from the bed.

The only chance I got to see Jamie was when he came by to visit his son. He wasn't my biggest fan. He blamed me for chasing away Ne'Vaeh. She hadn't stepped foot in Maryland since she left with Anastasia Jones for Atlanta, Georgia last January. When she left Maryland, she took Jamie's heart with her.

Tyler looked at me, standing before me, "That heart of yours doesn't feel a thing, does it? That's how you can live the way you do, huh?"

"Tyler, I don't need you judging me, okay?" I watched Tyler pick up his pants from the floor. "Men break hearts all the time and walk away. Why can't I? Why can't I have a different snack every night? Don't y'all do that shit?"

Tyler laughed to himself, sitting down on my bed to put on his socks and shoes. "You don't have to convince me that what you're doing is right, sweetheart. If you think you need another man to get over the other one, that's on you. You got a son in there who needs a woman to look up to. Now, if you think what you're doing is something that your son will accept, go 'head, ma. Do you."

I shook my head. "Don't bring my son into this, Tyler. You know what, I don't need this. Get your shit and get out." I picked up his shirt and jacket, shoving it into his chest. "Leave."

Tyler stood up looking down into my face, shaking his head at me. We fought almost every week. He was always saying some shit about my lifestyle that pissed me off. I shouldn't have gotten mad at him, because he was right. Ever since my six-week checkup, my pussy was on the hunt. My heart shut down, and my pussy just took completely over me. That hole that was in my soul had to be filled with something, so I filled it with dick. As many as I could find it seems.

I no longer lived in that tiny apartment in Baltimore City. I was living it up in a decent-sized mansion in Washington, D.C. I inherited the home along with her maids, nannies, and cooks from my great-aunt on my mother's side. She left the house to me when she died the previous summer. She had no children of her own, and I was her favorite niece. I loved the fact that I was a little closer to Jamie. It made it that much easier to get to him when I needed him, though he made it a habit to make sure that he was always occupied. He replaced Ne'Vaeh with photo shoots, commercials, weight-training, football, and groupies.

I stood in the mirror that morning, smoothing out my tight, long-sleeved black dress. It hugged my curves and cupped my breasts. It had a split that came up to my thigh on the right side of my dress. My hairstylist, Holly, straightened my hair in no time. I sat my black pillow-box hat with netted veil and feather on top of my head, just when the doorbell rang. I knew it was Jamie coming to pick up August. His aunt wasn't going to Alisha's funeral and agreed to watch our son while we went to the funeral.

I held my long dress up a little so that I could hurry out of my room, and to the top of the steps so that I could make an entrance when the maids opened the door for Jamie. I stood at the top of the stairway and slowly made my way down the steps when Carlita opened the front door. There he stood, in a crisp blue buttoned-down shirt, brown dress pants, and polished brown Italian leather dress shoes. A brown hat hung over his eyes a little. When he greeted Carlita, I could see his ice grill gleaming. He couldn't give up Memphis, Tennessee for nothing. That Southern sex appeal still drove me wild. I had the hardest time keeping my distance from him. Co-parenting with a man as fine as him was tough, I mean *tough*. Going over his place, seeing bitches laid up in his house, drove me fuckin' crazy. He did respect me enough to put the hoes out when our son stayed with him.

Jamie's eyes traced up my legs as I strolled down the steps and over to him. He grinned a little, tilting his hat up a little to get a better view. "Sup, shawty?"

"Hi, Jamie," I played it cool.

His eyes traced my red lips as Carlita stepped aside, letting Jamie into the house.

"Carlita, can you please go tell Lilia to bring little August?" I smiled at Carlita. "Thank you," I said as she hurried off to get her. I looked at Jamie. It had been a little over a month since we'd seen each other face to face. For the past month, he'd been picking up August from my mother's house every Friday and dropping him back off at my mother's on Mondays.

Before Aaron and I broke up, he had hooked me up with Jamari William Davis, one of the top modeling managers on the East Coast. His wife, Golden was friends with the owner of Diva Game, and that's how I landed that contract. When Jamari wasn't flirting with me, he had me modeling for all sorts of fashion designers for the past five months. He took me all over the world. For about six months, all I was known as was Jamie Green's baby's mama. Once Jamari showcased my talent to the top glamour magazine editors, that was a wrap. I started with the fashion shoots for the top fashion magazines. From there, I had at least ten or twelve designers asking for me to walk on their runway. And the rest is history. I had to make a name other than "slut" for myself. I still danced from time to time, but once Alisha was too weak to dance, I quit the dance team. She'd travel with me when she wasn't too sick. But for the most part, she'd show her support from home. I stayed as busy as I could to avoid watching Alisha die, Ashton suffering, and Jamie fuckin' other women.

"If you didn't have that hat on, I'd think you were goin' to a club or somethin', shawty." Jamie grinned, teeth glistening.

"Is that supposed to be a compliment?" I smoothed out my dress a little.

"I don't have to tell you how good you look, as if you didn't know." Jamie tilted my hat a little.

I looked at him, so glad that the veil covered my face just enough so he couldn't see my eyes watering. Jamie was so fuckin' hot. I loved looking at that muthafucka. You know the feeling you get in a restaurant when your plate is coming, and the waiter sets it right down in front of you? Yeah, that's the way I felt whenever Jamie Green walked into a room. Jamie appealed to all five senses, and he knew that shit, too.

"So, which one of your hoes are you bringing with you to my girl's funeral?" I played off my attraction.

Jamie laughed a little. "Man, nobody. I'm about to drop my son off, and then I'm headed to the church. I ain't goin' with anybody, shawty."

I looked at him. He was hoping Ne'Vaeh showed up. I hadn't seen or heard from her since New Year's 2015. And from what I knew, Jamie hadn't seen or heard from her since she turned down his wedding proposal at the airport. The shit was all over YouTube. Ne'Vaeh went straight to Atlanta and didn't look back. I'd seen her in a few videos with Anastasia Jones. Anastasia even brought her up on stage with her after winning her fourth BET Music Award in 2015. When I ran into Renée at the mall last fall, she said that her cousin wasn't doing well. I had no idea what to think. I wanted to go see her, but I knew she wouldn't want to see me. And even though Renée assured me that Ne'Vaeh really needed my support, I still didn't budge.

"You think she'll show up today?" I hesitated to ask Jamie. "It would be nice to see Ne'Vaeh, wouldn't it?"

Jamie just looked at me, as Lilia walked down the steps with little August. The look on Jamie's face was priceless. He loved our little boy. From the moment little August came into this world, Jamie was right there. I remember the night that my water broke. I was lying in bed, watching Lifetime, when I felt a pop between my legs. It felt like a reflex to pick up the phone and call Jamie. Luckily he was already in the area and got to me in no time. He got me to the hospital and stayed with me, holding my hand through it all. I just knew the man would bail on me, but he didn't. The first sight that my baby saw when he opened his eyes was his daddy. And they've been inseparable ever since.

My baby boy nearly jumped out of Lilia's arms that morning, happy as hell to see Jamie. "Daddy, daddy!" He squealed, as Jamie took him from Lilia.

Lilia smiled, taking the diaper bag off of her shoulder, handing it to Jamie. "He's been asking about you all morning, Señor Green." She grinned at Jamie.

I looked at Lilia. That bitch. You should have seen the look on her got-damn face, watching Jamie playing with our son. Either they were smashing, or she was crushing. Either way, I was going to put an end to that shit.

I cleared my throat, snapping her out of her thirsty-ass trance. "We're good, Lilia. You can get back to work."

Lilia smiled at me nervously, then scurried off to finish her work.

Jamie looked at me, holding August in his arms.

I folded my arms, looking at him. "Nigga, are you fuckin' her?"

Jamie grinned, shaking his head to himself. "Are you fuckin' my teammate?"

I shut my mouth real quick.

Jamie nodded, "Yeah, shawty, so don't question me about what the fuck I do, *especially* when you got niggas braggin' about your head game in the locker room. But naw, I ain't fuckin' with shawty. I could; trust me, I could, but I'm not. Is everything I need for little man in the bag, Charlene?"

"Y—yeah," I stuttered. "Everything should be there."

"A'ight. Good. Our son is all we need to be talkin' about. All that other shit is irrelevant, shawty." Jamie's eyes searched my face.

I shook my head at him, then kissed my baby on his rosy cheeks. "See you later, baby. Be good for your auntie, okay? Mommy loves you!"

Jamie turned around and left.

***

Like I said earlier, I was not prepared for that funeral. People I hadn't seen in years showed up to the Newman's house that day. Alisha's entire family on her mother's side was there. Of course, the entire dance squad from Morgan was there. Not to mention our old teammates from high school and middle school were there to support Alisha. Some of our old teachers were there. The entire basketball team and football team from both high school and college were there. Renée showed up like she did everywhere else—with about ten of her friends. Jamie showed up alone as promised. My mother, sister, and brother showed up. Of course, Ashton's entire family was there.

Alisha's father, who was nowhere to be seen in the girl's life while she was alive, showed up. Ms. Danielle Newman was feeling some type of way about that, but she kept her cool. I helped Ms. Newman give out the obituaries. I could barely look at Alisha's face when I went to the wake the day before, let alone look at her face on the obituary. Alisha was beautiful even when she was on her deathbed. She looked tired, but she was still so pretty. Tyra held my hand that day we viewed her body in her casket. Alisha didn't even look like she was dead, but looked like she was peacefully sleeping.

Ashton didn't say a word to anyone. His mother, Ashley Chester-Brookes, made me promise that I wouldn't leave his side during the service that day. I was supposed to ride in a limo that carried Alisha's body. Why they wanted me up close and personal with her dead body, I don't know. Why they embraced me the way that they did when they knew our previous history, I don't know. But Ms. Newman treated me like family. Alisha was her only child, and I couldn't even imagine the pain that she was experiencing at that time. Alisha was talented. She had several chances to leave

Maryland, and go to any art institute that she chose, but her mother clung to her with all her might. We had no idea that Alisha was sick until Ashton told me that night at Jamie's Ravens party back in 2014.

Ashton sat alone in the corner of the room. He sat in a chair, struggling to fix his tie. Frustrated, he threw the tie down on the coffee table. I excused myself from the crowd of people that I was mingling with, and went over to try to comfort him.

"You need some help, Ashton?" I stood before him.

Ashton looked up at me, eyebrows knitted together. He sighed, grabbed the tie, and then stood up from the couch. "I can't get this shit right," he mumbled, handing me the tie.

I took it from him, then wrapped it around his neck, tucking the tie underneath his crisp collar. He looked so handsome. I couldn't look up into his eyes. I didn't want to cry, but my makeup was perfect. "Boo, you look so handsome." I had to tell him.

He looked down at me, looking my body over a little. "You look nice, too."

I tried not to grin. "Thanks, sweetie."

Ashton cleared his throat a little. "Alisha's mother really appreciates what you did for her."

I opened up a dance studio named Alisha's Dream for Alisha in the heart of Baltimore City. She often talked about opening a dance studio for little girls who couldn't afford the dance lessons. A few of the Morgan Girls agreed to volunteer once a week to teach classes. I was rockin' with some of the best dancers on the East Coast, so these little girls were going to make Alisha's dreams of helping little girls achieve their goals come true.

"It was no problem, Ashton. It's the least that I could do for her." I tied a knot in his tie.

"And she really appreciates you helping us pay for that statue, too." Ashton's voice shook. We had a marble statue sculpted of a girl dancing to place next to her grave. The figure was looking up, arms reaching upward, as if she were dancing toward heaven.

My lips trembled, but I refused to cry. One of us had to be strong that day. Ashton was so angry with me that he had a hard time showing me that he really appreciated me being there for Alisha despite our differences.

"Your girl was a bitch, Ashton, but she always told the truth. I could have saved myself a lot of heartache if I'd only listened to her. The past year that I spent with her was awesome. She was a great friend, and I wish that I would have gotten to know her like that growing up. At least we can all rest assured that she's not suffering anymore, Ashton." I whispered, straightening out his tie.

"That picture on her obituary is perfect, too. Thank you." He finally thanked me.

I tried to help out with the funeral arrangements as much as I could. Ms. Newman wasn't in her right frame of mind, and her family couldn't afford to spend the time away from work helping her prepare for the funeral. My mother's God-parents owned a funeral home and covered the entire expenses of the funeral. Ms. Newman couldn't thank us enough. We just wanted to make sure that she sat on the life insurance money, instead of having to spend it all on funeral costs.

"Ashton, really, it's no big deal. Please don't make me cry right now, okay?" I tried to smile, finally looking him in the face.

Ashton's light eyes searched my face.

I smoothed out his shirt a little.

Ashton grabbed my hands in his. His hands were so warm, so smooth, and so gentle.

I looked up at him. "Ashton, sweetie, you're gonna make it. I'm here for you. I've *always* been here for you." I slipped my hands from his. I wasn't going to let him make me cry. "So, is everything set for Alisha's party?"

Aston nodded. "Umm, yeah, everything's set. Ms. Newman isn't coming. Matter fact, I don't think any of the older crowd is comin'. Just the Nineties crew will be up in the spot. I hope Aaron's flight makes it in time for the funeral. He called me about three o'clock this morning, and I haven't heard from him since."

I looked at him. I hadn't seen Aaron in person since the New Year's party last year. I watched a few of his games overseas, even seen a few video clips of fashion shows of him in them. He was a really big deal overseas. Not only was he awesome at playing basketball, but he was beautiful to look at. I admit I missed him a little. I didn't appreciate him when I had him. I didn't realize what I had in him until I was all alone. I had been with him so long that I had forgotten how the single life was. I missed spending the night at his apartment and falling asleep in his arms. True, he loved Ne'Vaeh, but it took him nearly three years to approach her. It was my own fault for trying to get to him first when I already knew that he was feeling her.

"How is he?" I sighed.

Ashton grinned. "Fine, I'm sure."

It was the first time I'd seen Ashton attempt to smile in a long time. "What's that grin for?" I questioned.

Ashton tried to wipe the smirk from his face. "My man is finally happy, that's all. He's in Miami, in case you didn't know. Plays for Miami Heat."

I shook my head. "No, I didn't know." I had a feeling deep down in my soul, telling me that it was best that I didn't know anything about his life without me in it. Apparently, whatever he had going on put a smile on Ashton's face that I hadn't seen in over a year.

***

I had to compose myself as I stepped inside of the hearse that carried Alisha to the church. I sat in the limo next to Ashton and Ms. Newman. I had to count to ten about a hundred times to keep from hyperventilating. Ashton put his arm around me to try and comfort me, and I lay my head on his chest to try and comfort him. The ride to the church was the longest ride that I'd ever taken. My mother's God-parents did a fantastic job setting up the flower arrangements at the church. I felt like we were more at a wedding than at a funeral. The Phillips made the event seem more like a celebration than a catastrophe, something Alisha would have wanted.

Alisha's and Ashton's family filled about 80 percent of the church. There was not enough space for everyone; people were lined up and down the aisles, and along the walls. I sat in the first row, alongside Ashton. I sat and watched as more people flooded their way into the church. Jamie sat down right next to Renée. He just knew Ne'Vaeh was coming. He acted as if he was over that girl, but I was no fool. He was angry with her for leaving him, but his heart just wouldn't let go. I'm not going to lie and say that shit didn't hurt like a muthafucka, but I've known that boy was in love with her since elementary school. I don't think there was anything that girl could do to make Jamie stop loving her.

No sooner than Jamie sat down next to Renée, did Aaron stroll into the church. He was dressed in a royal blue dress shirt, dark brown-striped tie, and dark brown dress pants. He looked amazing. And he'd grown his curly hair out. He sat down next to a few of his old teammates. Maybe ten seconds later, Ne'Vaeh strolled into the church. The petite little thing had on this brown, tight-fitted designer dress that had a short train. She looked like a million dollars. Her sleek hair fell just below her shouldcrs. Renée caught sight of her and waved for her to come over. You should have seen the look on Jamie's face when Ne'Vach grinned at her cousin and then went to sit with Aaron. Jamie turned around and looked at me. "Look at this shit" was written all over his face. I turned back around, heart pounding in my chest, and I looked at Ashton, who had that same stupid grin on his face that he had back at Alisha's mother's house.

I looked back at Renée, who was looking at Jamie like she expected him to go over and put an end to whatever the fuck was going on. Jamie just sat there, slouched back in the pew. He was pissed, but he was still a fool in love. He sat there, cool, calm, and collected. Renée's dramatic ass got up from her seat, shoving passed people until she made it over to her cousin.

I should have known that Ne'Vaeh would show up with her got-damn entourage. Anastasia Jones and Darryl Allan burst through the church doors with about eight other people, strolling down the aisle like they were on the got-damn red carpet at the Grammy's. It was supposed to be Alisha's funeral, yet everyone was looking at Anastasia. I hadn't seen Ne'Vaeh's ass in almost a year and a half, and there she was, in Aaron's arms, surrounding herself with a crowd of celebrities, making it damn near impossible to approach her that day. Yeah, Ne'Vaeh was there to try and stunt on my ass with Aaron at her side. My Aaron.

Alisha's home going was one of the most depressing days of my life. I didn't cry. I didn't shed one tear that morning. Ashton tried his best to be strong for Miss Danielle, who nearly lost her mind at the grave site. Her brother had to carry her away, kicking and screaming, before Alisha's body was lowered into the ground. I watched everyone weeping and wailing over Alisha. I watched half of the dance squad hyperventilate, some even passing out. I watched Ne'Vaeh burry her face in Aaron's chest, unable to look at Alisha's dead body. I think seeing Aaron with Ne'Vaeh kept my mind off of the despair that I felt from the past few months that I watched Alisha fade away. Watching the way Aaron cherished that girl, despite what anyone thought, only made me miss him even more. I needed love from someone, no matter how hard I tried to fight that need.

The crowd began to dissipate, leaving only Ashton and me standing there. We stood there, watching as Alisha's ivory casket was lowered into the ground.

"My baby sure could dance, couldn't she?" Ashton's voice shook, eying her marble statue.

Our hands intertwined.

I lay my head on his chest, his heart beating in my ear. "Yeah, boo, she could," I whispered.

Alisha's Farewell party was supposed to be uplifting, but I sat there alone at the bar, depressed as hell. I must have been on my forth Mango Tequila Sunrise. I watched as Aaron mingled with his old teammates and Ne'Vaeh purposely talking to everyone but me. Jamie left as soon as the church service was over. Seeing Ne'Vaeh after not seeing her for over a year was overwhelming enough, let alone seeing her with another man. Jamie was devastated. I'm pretty sure Ne'Vaeh got a thrill out of hurting him. Otherwise, she wouldn't have been so visually blunt about her relationship with Aaron.

"Cute couple, huh?" I heard the irritating sound of Kelissa's voice over my shoulder.

I didn't even bother to turn around to see her face. I rolled my eyes as she sat down on the stool next to mine, looking like a damn African beauty queen. She must have gained about fifteen pounds this past year and a half. She and her husband had a baby, born on Christmas Day. Kelissa never looked so beautiful. She'd finally gotten some hips, probably went from a size 5 to a size 9, but it looked great on her. She always did look good in all of her clothes, slim or thick. She wore a skin-tight, long-sleeved black lace dress that met her ankles. Her Senegalese twists were swept up into a bun. She'd cried so much that her foundation had begun to run, but still, her face was flawless. She looked like a got-damn black Barbie Doll. That bitch.

I hadn't heard her voice since she put her two cents in at my wedding rehearsal dinner back in 2014. Whenever she came to visit Alisha, I made sure I wasn't anywhere in sight. I hadn't forgotten the events that had taken place at my baby shower. It didn't have to go the way it did, but that bitch wouldn't shut her mouth.

"OMG, just when I was starting to enjoy the sound of not hearing your voice, you just had to say something, to me at that." I sipped from my drink.

Kelissa laughed a little. "Oh, are you still salty about the way your own mama set you up, talking you into having your baby shower at your best friend's—Ooops. No, your sister's boyfriend's house, who just happened to be your baby's father? Someone should have smacked some sense into your mama, too, shit. No, it didn't have to go down like that, but I couldn't stand by and watch Ne'Vaeh be so blind. She always looks for the good in the wrong muthafuckas."

I looked at her. I mean, really looked at her. Her eyes were puffy as hell. She'd been crying since she stepped foot inside the church. Kelissa and Alisha had been best friends since they were in elementary school together. They had met in ballet class, and they had been inseparable ever since. They didn't always get along, trust me, they fought like alley cats on many occasions. But let someone fuck with either one of them, oh, they were fuckin' that person up on sight. I kind of felt sorry for

Kelissa. I don't know what she was going to do without Alisha. She admired Alisha, looked up to Alisha, and worshipped Alisha.

I looked at her, watching the concealer running down her face as she began to cry over her friend again. I signaled the bartender to make me two more drinks. Then I handed a Kleenex to Kelissa.

She looked at me, hesitating before taking the tissue from me. She dried her face, then blew her nose. "Thank you." She looked at me, as she balled up the tissue. "It's nice to see that your bitchery only lasts part time."

The bartender slid me the two colorful drinks, and I slid one to Kelissa.

"To Alisha, one of the most talented dancers I've ever met." I held up my glass.

"Naw, bitch, *the* most talented dancer." Kelissa held her glass up to me.

I grinned at her, watching her take a sip of her drink. Her eyes grew bigger as she sipped from her drink.

I laughed out loud. "Good shit, huh?"

"Hell yeah!" Kelissa laughed a little, whipping her lips. "Girl, how many of these have you had?"

"This makes my fifth one. Wait, it might be my sixth." I sipped from my drink.

Kelissa shook her head at me. "Girl, that shit is gonna sneak up on you. I sure as hell won't be drinking anymore after this one, no ma'am!"

I watched as she drank damn near half the glass. "So, how are you holding up?"

She looked at me, setting her drink down. "I've known Alisha a long time, you know? She was so strong and so beautiful. Even when she found out she was dying, she didn't let that stop her. She danced until she couldn't dance anymore. I miss her already, Charlie."

I nodded, going through my purse for my cigarettes.

I hadn't cried all day, and I wasn't about to start now. "Yeah, me too, 'Lissa."

Kelissa watched as I started to light the cigarette. "What the fu—Charlie, when the fuck did you start smoking cigarettes? You don't even look right doin' that shit."

I damn near choked off that bitch. I didn't know how muthafuckas smoked that nasty, strong-ass shit. "Girl," I coughed, "I found this shit in little August's diaper bag. I forgot to give it back to Jamie when I saw his ass today."

Kelissa sipped from her drink, "Well," She swallowed, "since you and I are on speaking terms again, and while we're on the subject of Jamie's ass, you need to check him, because he's about to lose his fuckin' job. You know the dude has been fuckin' the coach's eighteen-year-old daughter? I mean, the bitch *just* turned eighteen on May first. The bitch got pictures *all* over Instagram and Facebook! You ain't see that shit?"

I looked at her. I was pretty used to Jamie fuckin' nothing but the hottest, richest chicks. Ne'Vaeh was the only mediocre chick he dealt with. Well, yeah, she's cute, but compared to the thick chicks he fucks with, she was considered mediocre. "Girl, I have never been Facebook friends with Jamie for that very reason. He's fuckin' with Coach Frost's daughter?"

"Yes, li'l Brittany Frost got her a taste of that chocolate! And you know how the sayin' goes: once you fuck with Jamie . . ." Kelissa bust out laughing, nudging me in my shoulder.

I rolled my eyes. "Girl, bye."

"Girl, shut up. I'm tellin' you, Jamie must have that golden Donkey Kong magic dick, because you bitches be sprung over that nigga, for real! That nigga's dick put a spell on y'all ass!" Kelissa shook her head at me. "The dude is even fuckin' Kent Sanderson's wife! You know he married that pretty Hawaiian chick last year."

My eyes widened. Oh, he was looking for trouble. "The team owner? Oh, Jamie, why? Dude, why?" I attempted to take another hit of my cigarette, but that smell was giving me a fucking headache, so I put it out.

Jamie's behavior was similar to mine—self-destructive. He wasn't satisfied with his life unless he had some type of chaos going on. Jamie had everything anyone could ever ask for, yet he still wasn't satisfied. The fame, the looks, the talent, the money, the cars, the house, the clothes, the fans . . . He was a part of something amazing, and he was about to fuck that up.

"Losing that girl fucked that nigga's head all the way up." Kelissa drank the rest of her drink. "Li'l Ne'Vaeh was messed up for a while, too, according to Alisha."

I looked at her. "What do you mean?"

Kelissa shook her head at me. "You don't even keep up with your own sister. That's crazy. Typical Charlene— always thinkin' more about herself than anyone else. I know Renée told your ass to go and visit her. It didn't dawn on your selfish ass that Renée might have told you to go see her for a reason?"

I rolled my eyes. "Bitch, don't start."

"She was in the hospital, almost died and shit. Aaron had to go and damn near save the girl's life. That's how they hooked back up. The girl was sick as shit. Would have died if it hadn't been for him." Kelissa watched my nostrils flare. "Renée was Alisha's nurse. When she came back from staying with Ne'Vaeh in Atlanta for a few months, she told Alisha the deal."

I was pissed. Yeah, I know you're thinking that I have no right to be mad, and maybe I don't. But she always gets what she wants, and it's always at my heart's expense.

"Charlie, you mad, or nah?" Kelissa smirked, looking over her shoulder as Anastasia Jones and her girls hit the dance floor. It was time for the dance tribute to Alisha.

"Hell yes, I'm mad. What the fuck kind of question is that?" I exclaimed.

Kelissa looked back at me, laughing to herself. "Well, you shouldn't be. Look what you took from her! She loved Jamie, always has, probably always will. You had a baby with the nigga, and you have the audacity to be mad at her relationship with Aaron? Bitch, you can't have your cake and eat it, too."

"Well, ain't that what you're supposed to do with cake? Eat it?" I rolled my eyes.

Kelissa laughed at my jealousy, as the room went completely black before white lights flashed around the room. Anastasia and her girls could work their bodies like nothing I'd ever seen. I'm not a lesbian (okay, maybe just a little), but that girl was sexier than a muthafucka. Those hips, those thighs, that ass—she worked every part of her body in a way that had the entire room of people dazed. Fuck the other dancers around her—they didn't exist as long as she was on the floor. Darryl had to be one strong man to be able to have a wife as sexy as she was. I'm sure it made him want her even more when he saw her dance. He stood alongside the dance floor, watching her dance. He probably was thinking of all the shit he wanted to do to her as soon as he got her back to the hotel. It was a hot little tribute they did for Alisha. Anastasia had studied all of Alisha's videos of our performances, and she did a dance melody so to speak. It was fantastic. Anastasia deserved an award for bringing Alisha back to life. I'm sure Alisha was in heaven smiling down at her.

Kelissa wasn't lying—that alcohol started to hit me as soon as my ass stepped foot in my Bentley. I didn't bother to stay all night. After we ate dinner that night, I left. It had to be around 9:00 when I got tired of looking at Aaron and Ne'Vaeh hugged up. After Ashton left, it was safe for me to leave, too. It was still early enough to catch Kendrick. He was this record producer out of D.C. who also deejayed at DC Live. He wouldn't go into work until around 12:00, so if I could just make it home around 10:00, I could catch him just in time for a quickie. A dose of that long, chocolate dick would put me right to sleep.

I had so much on my mind. I had to do something to clear my mind of Alisha, Jamie, Aaron, and Ne'Vaeh. I cared about Jamie. I didn't want the idiot to lose his job because of his weakness for new pussy. I had to do something to convince his coach and owner not to end his contract. Jamie had the opportunity of a lifetime, and he was blowing it. After I helped Ashton clean out Alisha's apartment, I would pay Coach Thomas Frost a little visit. Oh, we had our history. I might have teased the dick a time or two back in high school. Both Coach Frost and Kent Sanderson were just as bad as the players they coached. Age was nothing but a number to any of them back then. I'm sure they hadn't changed much. Their wives had no idea what type of lifestyle they lived. Coach Frost had no business being mad at Jamie for messing with little Brittany. Coach Frost was just sixteen when he had his first child. He was a young, sexy white man, who had a secret love for black women, as a lot of them do. I was not going to have a problem getting to him, nor to Kent Sanderson, who had been trying to get me in bed again since senior year in high school.

I was so deep in thought that I didn't even realize that I was speeding, *and* over the solid yellow line at that. I made it half way home before red and blue lights flashed behind me.

"*Shit!*" I cursed out loud, pulling onto the shoulder of the highway. I hate fuckin' cops. Cocky, arrogant, uneducated muthafuckas who are bitter because most of them make less than thirty thousand dollars a year. They get a thrill off of having so much control, and they often misuse it and take advantage of those who don't know the law.

I rolled down the window, then placed my hands on the steering wheel as I heard the officer's footsteps approaching.

He aimed a flashlight straight at my face. "Driver's license and registration, ma'am."

I laughed a little, reaching for my purse, grabbing my wallet. "Aren't you gonna tell me what you're pulling me over for, Mr. Officer?" I shoved my license and registration into his hands.

"Ma'am, you were driving left of center." He huffed. "And you were going eighteen miles over the speed limit." I didn't look at him, but from the corner of my eye, I saw him aiming the flashlight at my license. He hesitated for a second. "Charlene Campbell?" He flashed the light in my face again.

I covered my face. He was blinding me with the light. "Dude, damn!"

He laughed a little, removing the beam from my face, bending over, getting a better look at me. "I apologize. Damn, it's been a long time. I almost didn't recognize you."

I looked up into his brown eyes. It was Jayson Taylor. We went to school together. He was kicked off the basketball team when he got into a fight with one of the referees. The boy had skills, his temper was just off the chain. Did we have sex? Of course. He was the first man to give me multiple orgasms in one round. Until this day, it's still hard to say that man's name without getting wet. Ummm, Kendrick was gonna have to see me another night.

I smiled up at Jayson, "Officer Taylor? Wow, it's been a few years. How have you been?"

He grinned. "You've been drinking, Charlie?" He handed my license and registration back to me.

"What you gonna do? Handcuff me?" I grinned.

"Yeah, if that's how you like it." Jayson smiled, biting his juicy lips.

I laughed a little.

"My shift is almost over. I worked a little overtime tonight." He looked back at the police car, parked behind mine. "Wait here."

I sighed as he walked back to his car. I put my license and registration away, then I checked my face in the mirror.

In about five minutes, I saw the police car cut off its lights then drive off. Just when I started to say, damn, where is Jayson's ass going, he was standing outside my window. "Get out of the car." He took off his campaign hat.

I made a face, looking up at him. "What?"

"Charlene, you're drunk. I don't know why any of your friends even let you out of their sight, as drunk as you are." He opened my door. "Let me drive."

I sighed, unbuckling my seatbelt, stumbling out of the car, making my way over to the passenger's side. I got in, looking at him as he put the car in drive and sped off down the highway.

"Make yourself at home." I kicked off my shoes as we entered into my bedroom that night.

Jayson grinned, removing his jacket, watching me as I bent over to pick up my shoes off the floor. "You have a nice place. The modeling industry must be treating you well. You're doin' the damn thing like I always knew you would."

I approached him, turning around so he could unzip my dress for me. I pulled my hair to the side as he unzipped my dress, sliding the sleeves over my shoulders. I grinned as he grabbed me by the waist, gripping my dress in his hands. "So you've seen me on the runway?"

"My wife is a press rep. She goes to lots of fashion shows. She really admires you." He gently kissed my neck.

I quickly turned around to face him. Oh, I was so tired of those thirsty, horny, depraved men who used me to take care of whatever needs their wives or girlfriends neglected. All too often, I was fuckin' or suckin' some guy who only wanted me when his wife or girlfriend didn't want him.

I looked up at him, "Isn't your wife expecting you home?"

Jayson shook his head, pulling my body up against his. "No, she's at a business conference in New York. The kids are staying over her mothers."

I shook my head at him, laughing to myself. "Kids, Jayson? Okay, umm, I'm drunk, but I'm not that drunk. Why did you come here tonight other than to get some ass?"

"Why did you bring me here?" Jayson's brown eyes searched my face.

"Well, you didn't much give me a chance, now did you?" I looked up at him. He was tall, brown skinned, built. He was so handsome and wasn't at all cocky like most men who looked like him.

"Couldn't let you drive home drunk, Charlene. Where were you coming from anyway?" Jayson let go of my dress.

I sighed, sliding my dress down, standing there in front of him dressed in a lace nude camisole, lace boy shorts, garter belt, and stockings. I unhooked my garter belt and sat on the bed to slide off my stockings. I looked up at him. "Alisha's funeral."

Jayson's eyes widened. "Alisha as in Alisha Newsome?"

I nodded. I wasn't ready to come to terms with my feelings about her death. I had just gotten to know Alisha on a personal level that past year and a half. She was so fuckin' funny and passionate about the things she loved the most. She always kept it real. She never sugarcoated anything. She was honest even when you wanted her to lie to you. I should have gotten to know her back in middle school. Instead of chasing dick, I should have put more heart into dancing the way that she did. She could have made it very far in life. She had agencies and celebrities all over the country asking about her. Anastasia Jones even wanted her. I wasted so much time hating that girl.

"Wait, when did y'all become friends?" Jayson sat down on the bed next to me. "The last I remember, y'all hated each other. Some shit about you sleeping with Ashton."

I shook my head at him. "First of all, I didn't sleep with Ashton. We moved passed all the rumors and shit last year. I found out that she had cancer. I wasted so much time hating that girl when I should have gotten to know her. Twenty years old, Jayson. The girl was twenty fuckin' years old!" I couldn't fight the tears any longer.

Jayson tried to hold my face, drying my tears,

I pushed his hand away. I wasn't gonna let another man suck me in the way Jamie once had. "I'm good, Jayson." I laughed away the tears, drying my face. "I just wish we could have spent the last seven years being friends, instead of enemies. She taught me a lot about life. It's too short to waste." I looked at Jayson. "I'm sick of just fuckin', Jayson. Do you know how much dick I've sucked? How many dicks I've rode this year? I do this shit every night!"

Jayson laughed to himself. "I think you're being too hard on yourself, sweetheart."

I shook my head at him. "I have a son, Jayson. He looks up to me, he worships me. I love him. I don't want him to look at me and think that every woman is like this. I want to make my baby proud. If he knew I was a thot, he wouldn't love or respect me. He'd treat me like all the other men in my life."

Jayson put his arm around me. "You're single, Charlene—you can do what the fuck you want."

I looked up into his face. "Yeah, I'm single, but you're not. You're not even supposed to be here, honey. I don't know what's lacking in your relationship, but you're not gonna find it here tonight."

Jayson laughed to himself. "It was pretty bold of me just jumpin' in your ride like you didn't have other plans, huh?"

I smiled a little. "Yeah, just a little."

"Well, my partner isn't gonna come all the way here from the other side of town, Charlie. He's working until at least two o'clock. I could call him, but he won't get here until around three. So can I at least get some sleep? Maybe even a beer or something to drink?" Jayson's brown eyes searched my face. He wasn't even mad at me, and I really appreciated that. Another nigga probably would've been disrespectful or forceful. But I should have known Jayson would be cool. I've known dude since middle school.

I smiled. "Yeah, I'll get you something to drink. No problem. Lilia!" I yelled.

Chapter 4: Smash-n-Dash

Charlene

I awoke to Lilia frantically shaking my shoulder. I pushed my hair from my face, sitting up in my bed. I had the worst fuckin' headache of my life, right in the middle of my face. Jayson and I had been up drinking until at least 1:30. We just sat up talking, laughing, and tripping about high school. I was only dressed in a bra and panties, and we just talked, though I know it didn't appear that way.

Lilia was standing over me, with her arms folded, and big ass pink rollers in her head.

I looked up at her, "What?" I was frustrated as hell, being that there were no sun rays coming through the drapes in my room. It was the middle of the night. And I probably had only been asleep for an hour or so.

"Señor Jamie Green is downstairs waiting for you, señorita." Lilia shook her head at me, looking over at Jayson who was lying next to me, asleep in all of his clothes except his jacket and Kevlar vest. "*Necesitas poner algo de ropa, puta.*" She muttered before leaving my side, walking toward the door.

The bitch didn't know I knew she was telling my bitch-ass to put some fuckin' clothes on. I did listen in Spanish III. "Oh, Jamie has seen me in much less, honey," I shouted at her back as she reached the door.

Lilia stopped in her tracks, clenching her fists before leaving the room.

"Jamie, it's—" I looked at the grandfather clock that stood in the corridor, "Two forty-eight in the morning." I tied my robe around my waist, meeting Jamie at the bottom of the stairs.

Jamie stood there in a crisp white t-shirt, ankle length gray shorts, and brightly colored K.D.'s. He held a matching brightly colored cap in his hands. He always dressed like he was ready to hit the club; he always looked his best no matter how bad he felt on the inside. He had to be feeling pretty shitty to come over my place at damn near 3:00 in the morning.

Jamie looked down at me as I looked up at him.

"You okay?" I looked up in his face.

His eyes seemed to connect the freckles on my cheeks. "I need to talk to you, shawty."

I shook my head. "Jamie, this really isn't a good time. I have company."

Jamie made a face, pulling me to him by my hand a little. "And? Tell the nigga to leave, yo."

I laughed a little. "What? I'm not telling him to leave! Would you put your bitches out for me?"

Jamie didn't hesitate. "Yeah, you know I would."

I looked at him, my heart skipping a few beats. "Well, Jayson's asleep, so . . ."

Jamie looked at me. "Jayson? Jayson who?"

Just when I opened my mouth to speak, Jayson spoke for himself. "Taylor—Jayson Taylor." Jayson came down the steps, putting on his jacket. "What's up, Jamie Green? It's been a long time, man!" He was actually excited to see Jamie. They weren't the closest friends in school, but they'd pretty much hung with the same crowd.

Jamie wasn't really in the mood for a high school reunion at the moment. He had some shit he wanted to get off of his chest, and Jayson was stepping on his toes. Jamie looked at me, grinning a little before looking back at Jayson, "What's up, homie?"

Jayson approached Jamie, giving him a little brotherly, ain't-seen-you-in-a-minute love. "How have you been, man? I mean, I know the game is treatin' you nice, but outside of that, what you been up to?"

Jamie just looked at Jayson. I knew Jamie well enough to know he wasn't about to talk to Jayson like they were old friends at 3:00 in the morning. Jamie and I were nowhere near being together, but he couldn't tell me it didn't bother him to see other dudes in my house. "Dude, I ain't tryin' to be rude or nothin', but you gotta get the fuck up outta here."

My mouth dropped open a little. He had some fuckin' nerve.

Jayson laughed a little. "What?"

"You heard me, nigga, I said you need to get the fuck up outta here," Jamie repeated himself.

"What, are y'all seeing each other or something?" Jayson grinned.

"What the fuck does it matter to you? Aren't you married, bruh? Got a wife and three kids, my nigga? You ain't even supposed to be here, yo." Jamie snarled.

"Jamie, no, you can't do this." I faced Jayson. "Jayson, sweetie, you don't have to go anywhere."

Jayson smiled down at me. "No, Charlene, it's all good. My ride just called and said he was outside waiting on me anyway. It was nice talkin' to you. I'll be sending your tickets in the mail, sweetheart." He walked past us and headed toward the door.

I shook my head at Jamie before rushing to the door to catch up with Jayson before he left out the door. "Jayson, wait! I'm sorry. It's been a long day. Forgive Jamie—anything that comes out of his mouth right now should not even be taken seriously! We just buried our friend yesterday!"

Jayson smiled at me, "No need for the apology. Your baby daddy pops up at this time in the morning to talk to you, maybe you should see what he wants."

I watched Jayson walk over to the police car parked in my circular drive way, right behind another one of Jamie's pimped-out rides. Jamie's car was black, lime green, and chrome. It looked like someone pimped the Batmobile.

"Jamie, what kind of car is that?" I shook my head at the candy-painted car before closing the door.

"A Chevy Creeper." Jamie sat on the third step from the bottom of the stairway. "It's not on the market yet, shawty."

I went back over and sat next to him. "Jamie." I sighed, eyes tracing his profile, "What was that about?" I knew what it was about. He was already having a fucked-up day. First he sees his ex-girlfriend with the man he swore he wouldn't let her end up with. And then he sees me, the woman he wished he never had a baby with, still sleeping around with every nigga in town.

Jamie couldn't even look at me. "I needed someone to talk to."

I laughed a little. "Since when do we ever talk, Jamie? The last real talk we had was back on that beach in Miami, a year and nine months ago."

"They're married, Charlene." Jamie looked at me.

"Who's married?" I looked into Jamie's face. He didn't even have to say who. The flaring nostrils and the twitching temples pretty much gave it away. "Who told you this?"

"Nobody had to. I saw the rings on their fingers today at the funeral, shawty." Jamie shook his head to himself. "I went out of my way to change for shawty, Charlene. Yeah, I fucked up, but I changed who I was for her!"

I shook my head. "Jamie, we weren't honest with Ne'Vaeh, and you know it. And the shit that went down at the baby shower only made the situation worse. Aaron is a great guy. You know he'll take care of her."

Jamie looked at me like I was fuckin' crazy, and then looked away from me to really contemplate about what I had just said. "So, I'm just supposed to let him have her?" he asked after being silent for a few seconds.

I shrugged. "He already does, sweetie; like it or not, she's gone."

"This hurts like hell, Charlene. I'm barely breathing. My chest hurts. I couldn't sleep. I felt like I was having a heart attack or something, shawty. I ain't never felt like this before. What is this feeling?" Jamie buried his head between his knees.

I knew that feeling all too well. "Heartbreak," I whispered.

"How long does it last?" Jamie whispered back.

I shook my head, trying not to cry. "I'll let you know when I start to heal from mine."

Jamie lifted his head looking at me. His eyes were glistening, but he refused to let himself cry in front of me. "Shawty, I didn't mean to bail on Alisha's funeral, but I couldn't stay and watch those two muthafuckas together, all hugged up and shit. Was Ashton okay?"

I shook my head at him. "No, he wasn't. I'm not sure when he'll ever be okay, to be honest."

"Are you okay?" Jamie put his hand on my bare thigh. That damn touch of his, oh my fuckin' goodness, always sent a jolt straight to my damn g-spot.

I lost all my senses for a few seconds. He hadn't touched me in so long. He hadn't so much as accidentally bumped into me or grazed his shoulder up against mine. I missed his touch so much. Yeah, I had been with a lot of men over the past year, but no one could compare to Jamie. I felt connected to him. Not just because we had a son together, but because I could still feel that boy inside of me. Since I knew that we would never be together, I guess I was just searching for something that even came a little close to that feeling that he gave me. He'd entered my soul, and my soul had a hard time letting go.

"J—just wish I hadn't wasted so much time, ya know?" I regained my ability to speak. "Alisha was awesome. I spent so much time hating her instead of listening to her."

"Well, I know she appreciates what you did for her family. She's probably gonna be dancing in heaven along with you and those little girls in that dance studio that you started!" Jamie laughed a little. "That was real decent of you, shawty. Them little girls are gonna be thankful, ya know? A lot of them come from rough neighborhoods and broken homes. You're giving them a place to feel safe. You're giving them a reason to believe in themselves. I wish they would have had something like that for me when I was a kid, something to keep us little niggas out of trouble. I'm proud of you for doing this, shawty, real talk."

I blushed a little. "Oh my goodness, am I in the twilight zone? Is Jamie Green actually saying something nice about me? Whoa, I must be dreaming!"

Jamie laughed a little. "Naw, shawty, I'm trying to be serious. Y'all were at each other's throats since we were kids, yo, and you know it. The fact that y'all could move past all that and get to know one another is beautiful, that's all I'm saying."

I looked at Jamie. We hadn't really sat down and talked in a long time. I hated how it all went down, but

I didn't regret having a baby with him. "Little August is the best thing that's ever happened to me, Jamie." I finally admitted out loud to him. "I'm sorry about you and Ne'Vaeh, but I'm not sorry that I kept my baby. He's awesome."

Jamie agreed. "Yeah, he is. Little Man is the only thing keeping my heart beating right now. That laugh of his, boy, it gives me life."

I looked at Jamie. I had to talk to him about what Kelissa had told me while I had the damn nerve. "Jamie, what are you doin' fuckin' with your coach's daughter and the damn owner's wife? You're fuckin' crazy! Those two can end your NFL career! And you know that shit!"

Jamie looked at me like he could care less about what I was saying.

I shook my head at him. "You worked too hard for this, boo, to just throw it all away over her. You have a son to think about! You have yourself to think about, Jamie. I'm gonna have to pull some serious strings to keep your career afloat."

Jamie shook his head. "Naw, I'm good, shawty."

"No, you're not! Now, the season doesn't start back until September. You have at least three and a half months to do something else with your time. You need to occupy your time with weight training and extracurricular activities other than fuckin' bitches and partying! You're so talented, Jamie. I've been hearing that you can sing, like really sing. They're calling you the next Tyrese! Do something with that shit, Jamie! You gotta show that you're an asset to the entertainment industry, that you're more than just football and fashion. Market your talents everywhere. You've made your mark in the athletic industry. You've made your mark in the sports apparel industry. You need to start showing your skills in the music industry, too. Kent doesn't play about his wife, honey, I'm trying to tell you."

"Oh, y'all are on a first-name status, huh?" Jamie shook his head at me.

I rolled my eyes, "Jamie, please, okay? You know my past, don't even front."

"Your past?" Jamie laughed out loud. "Was that your muthafuckin' past that just walked the fuck up outta here? Looks like your history likes to repeat itself to me, shawty."

I shook my head at Jamie's emotions. He was really on some other shit early this morning. "Wow, you were really in your feelings today, Jamie, and I really don't have time for it. I'm just trying to help your ol' horny, arrogant, conceited ass, but no. You're trying to point the finger at me. You need to get the fuck over that bitch and concentrate on your career, the same shit you were doing before you even got back with that girl. Suck the shit up and move the fuck on. And don't come back to my fuckin' house crying over her, because evidently, the bitch isn't crying over you!"

I'm sorry. Jamie needed that shit. He was starting to get on my last fuckin' nerve. We hadn't sat down and talked in over a year, and he had the nerve to come up in my house and act like he was running shit. He had me fucked up, all the way up.

Jamie just laughed to himself.

I wasn't in the mood for laughing; I was irritated as hell. "What the hell is so got-damn funny? I'm trying to help you, and you're over here judging me! I don't tell you how to fuck your bitches, do I? No, I stay in my lane. But you have the nerve to come up in here, and throw my company out so you can sit here and talk to me about another girl? Bruh, I'm really not in the mood for this shit."

Then Jamie grabbed my hand.

I looked up at him, my emotions immediately changing from anger to sympathy. He was really hurt. He really needed me. He really needed a friend, and it was obvious he didn't have any, or else he wouldn't have come to me.

"Can we go somewhere and get a drink or something?" Jamie asked.

I didn't even hesitate or stop to think. "Yeah." I nodded. "Let me go change my clothes."

There it was, 5:00 in the morning, and we were sitting at a booth in Tipsy's, a bar in the middle of Baltimore City. I was dressed in a pair of dark denim skinny jeans, a black spaghetti strapped shirt, and a pair of black Red Bottoms. I was on my third Corona, and Jamie was barely through his first bottle. He just stared at me, as I licked the beer from my lips.

We had been sitting there for damn near an hour and a half, and we had barely said five words to each other. It was getting late, and I was working on barely an hour of sleep. I had to be at Alisha's apartment at 9:00 that morning to help Ashton clean up and pack her things. There was no way that I'd be able to go all the way back to DC to my house, and then have the strength to drive all the way back to Baltimore. I was going to have to check myself into a hotel in the city.

"I appreciate you coming to chill with me, shawty." Jamie finally said, his brown eyes searching my face. "I didn't mean to kick your company out."

I shook my head, sitting the bottle of beer on the table. "It's all good. He was about to leave anyway. We weren't having sex, Jamie. I mean, it started out that way, but when I found out he was married with children,

I changed my mind. I'm tired of fuckin', Jamie. When am I gonna get to make love again? I don't wanna be someone's jump off, someone's side chick, someone's smash-n-dash. I don't wanna be a main chick, I wanna be an *only* chick. Is that too much to ask?"

Jamie just sipped from his bottle. Apparently, it was.

I sighed, crossing my legs, shaking my foot anxiously. I really loved that boy, but his mind was far from me. He was just trying to fill the void in his heart that Ne'Vaeh left. The groupies couldn't fill it. I guess he went for the next best thing, his desperate baby's mama. "Look, Jamie, it's getting late. I'm about to check into a hotel. I gotta meet Ashton in a few hours to help him clean out Alisha's crib. We've been sitting here over an hour, and you've barely said a few words to me. What you tryin' to do this morning, Jamie? Talk, or what? I don't have time for this!"

Jamie looked at me, setting his bottle down on the table. "You're right about me, Charlie. I am fuckin' up my career. Nothing in my life outside of football is going right. My mama, who never fuckin' picks up the phone to call me, decided to call me last night, asking for money to pay her mortgage because she was four months behind. She only calls a nigga when she wants some shit."

I shook my head at him. I knew him well enough to know that he gave that woman what she'd ask for. "How much money did you give her?"

Jamie looked at me. "She asked me for six thousand dollars; I gave her fifteen thousand."

I shook my head at him. "Dude, you're better than me. I wouldn't have given her ass a got-damn thing! The way she treated you all those years! She used to beat the shit out of you, Jamie! Hammers, extension cords, irons; do you remember that shit? Your own sister told us all about how your mama treated y'all! Do you remember sleeping on the floor in the back of Walgreens? Do you remember begging your neighbors for food? Do you remember how you were dressed when you came here to live with your sister? That bitch doesn't deserve shit but an ass whoopin'!"

Jamie shook his head, disgusted with himself for falling weak to that woman. "She's my mama, man. I've wanted her love all of my life. I guess her calling me for money is the only time I get to hear her voice."

I held his hand in mine. "You can't make your mama be your mama, Jamie. You're a great son that any mother would be proud to have. Her own insecurities and emotional issues kept her from loving you. It wasn't anything that you did. You need to stop beating yourself up over this woman and move on. I know it's easier said than done, but you deserve to be happy. And holding on to pain and hurt isn't going to get you to that point. You need to just tell the woman how you feel, whether she wants to hear the shit or not. You deserve love in your life, Jamie. I don't know why you find it easier to accept hate. You run from love, which is how you lost Ne'Vaeh."

Jamie just looked at me.

"You know she would have stayed if you'd only told her the truth. Better yet, when your father came to get you that summer before tenth grade, you should have woke Ne'Vaeh up and taken her with you! That girl would have done anything for you! You lost her, so get over it, dude!" I exclaimed. As bad as I wanted Jamie, I knew where his heart was. Ne'Vaeh only went to Aaron for love because that boy cherished her the way that Jamie never did.

I stood from the table, grabbing my purse.

"Where ya goin', shawty?" Jamie looked up at me.

"To a hotel, to get some fuckin' sleep. I can't with you right now," I fought back the tears, scooting out of the booth.

Jamie got up, too, catching my arm before I went dashing out of the bar.

I pulled from him. "What, Jamie? I love you, and you know that shit! I use niggas left and right to try to mask this feeling that I'm feeling inside for you! I even started fuckin' with your teammate, Tyler, just to make you fuckin' jealous!"

"Yeah, I noticed." Jamie's eyes searched mine.

"I've had sex from the moment the doctor gave me the okay, just so I could get over the fact that you're never gonna love me the way that I love you! It hurts to sit here and reminisce with you like we're old friends catching up! I know you need a shoulder to cry on, but so do I got-damn it! I refuse to let you into my heart again! I've wanted you for so long, and you've always wanted her! I don't mind you coming to get your son and spending time with him, but I will never let you back inside my head again, do you hear me?" I pushed him in his chest.

Jamie grabbed my waist, pulling me to him, his lips instantly pressed against mine. My knees went weak, and Jamie caught me in his arms, holding my body up against his. I held his face in my hands, my lips stroking his. It felt so good in his arms. I hadn't felt his lips in almost two fuckin' years. Yeah, I was stupid for letting him kiss me when I knew he was just vulnerable and needed to feel love from someone at that moment. He knew that I loved him. He knew where he could get love when he needed it.

Jamie sucked on my bottom lips just a little before letting go. "Let's go to the Four Seasons, shawty."

Before I could even say no, Jamie was already holding my hand, pulling me along with him out of the bar.

The minimum stay at that hotel was for three days, but they let Jamie rent a suite for just a few hours. Spending damn near three hundred dollars for just a few hours; yeah, Jamie was that kind of spender. The valet, the front desk manager, the concierge; everyone there that morning already knew Jamie by face. Not just because he was an athlete, but because he had been there several times before. The housekeepers even giggled as we walked down the hallway to our room. I turned to him as soon as we got into the room.

"Jamie, how many times have you—" I could barely get the words out when Jamie pulled my body up against his, kissing my lips and unbuttoning my jeans at the same time. "Wait," I pulled my lips from his, "Is this just gonna be a smash-n-dash? If so, I'll pass."

"Kinda." Jamie's eyes searched mine, "I mean, I gotta get our son at eight o'clock from my aunt's crib. She has to be at work at eight thirty."

My eyes searched his beautiful face. Oh, I wanted to fuck that nigga's dick off, but I wasn't about to let him try to play me. "Jamie, you're not gonna just fuck me and dismiss me this time. You wanna fuck with no strings attached, that's cool. But you're not gonna just fuck me and act like I don't exist in your world. I wanna at least spend some time with you every now and then, Jamie. I wanna mean something to you, boo. I really do. You know I do."

Jamie kissed my lips, sliding my pants over my hips a little. "You're the mother of my child. You'll always mean something to me. I'm not trying to use you, Charlie. I could've gone to any chick at damn near three o'clock in the morning, but I went to you because I needed you. I'll come around more. I promise, shawty."

I was speechless. I had never heard him say that he needed me, not once. Those words were like honey. They were the sweetest words that I'd ever heard. No, he didn't say that he loved me, but the fact that he needed me meant everything.

He swooped my shirt over my head, tossing it to the floor. I pulled his shirt over his head, damn near ripping off his wife beater underneath. He had Ne'Vaeh's name tattooed over his heart. I ignored it, but I knew it was there. I sighed as he slid my jeans over my hips. I stepped out of them as I unbuckled his belt, pulling it from his jeans. I slid off his boxers as he snatched off my panties. I gasped as he lifted me up, and I wrapped my legs around his waist. He held me up with one arm, unsnapping my bra with his free hand. We kissed and moaned in each other's mouths as he carried me into the back room. I knew the dude wanted to fuck me, but I wanted him to make love to me. I didn't want him to bust quick and then fall asleep; I wanted him to stroke me to sleep.

"Ride this dick," he moaned in my ear as he sat down on the bed, one hand gripping my waist, the other on my thigh.

I sighed as Jamie began to suck on my neck, running his fingers up and through my hair. I loved it when he massaged my scalp with his fingertips. I loved it when I was close enough to him to feel his heart beating, and the air circulating in his lungs. Jamie was so sexy, so charming, and so sensual.

I lifted my ass a little as Jamie held his dick and eased it inside of me. My legs jerked a little as he eased his way through. That monster bumped my cervix just enough to make my whole body lift up. Jamie pressed my ass down on it, stopping me from running.

"Ride it, shawty, c'mon." He whispered, gripping my ass.

I sighed, locking my knees, beginning to grind on him. He moved with me; oh, I could feel him in my stomach. He gave my body all types of sensations that I hadn't felt since that night on the beach in Miami. I was already drunk as fuck, so you know I was floating on air. I rode him until my knees started to burn from rubbing against the silk bedspread.

Jamie gripped my hips in his warm hands, backing up until he reached the middle of the bed. He held me tight against his body as he quickly rolled over. He was on top of me, his body temperature rising, his heart beating against my breast. My legs trembled with every stroke he delivered. He had me speechless, breathless even.

"It's been a long time, Charlene." Jamie kissed my lips. "I needed this. Nothing feels like this, shawty."

Jamie got me every way that he wanted that morning. I'd had my share of dick that year, but Jamie's dick talked to my soul. I missed his dick in my mouth. His nut was so smooth and sweet. When he slid it in my ass without a heads-up, shit, I didn't even put up a fight. I hadn't had a taste of that boy in almost two years. I needed that dick. I'd been craving that muthafucka. But more than sex, I was craving Jamie's touch. It felt amazing being on top of him, underneath him, next to him. The way he held my hips, the way he kissed my lips, the way he ran his fingers through my hair, the way he grabbed my thighs, the way he smacked my ass—oh, there are no words to express that feeling.

I awoke the next morning to the sound of my cell phone going off. I rolled over to see that Jamie's ass wasn't lying next to me. I sat up in the bed, looking for any sign of him. He was gone. I picked up the phone, muttering "This muthafucka," to myself. I didn't even look at the time or the caller ID.

"What?" I snapped.

"Well, hello to you, too, bitch." Kelissa's voice huffed through the phone. "Ashton said he'd been trying to call your ass all morning. Weren't you supposed to be meeting him at nine o'clock?"

I rubbed my eyes. "Shit, what time is it?"

"Girl, eleven thirty! Where are you? Do you know your mama's over here helping that boy clean out that apartment!" Kelissa exclaimed.

I jumped up from the bed as soon 11:30 came out of her mouth. Why the fuck didn't Jamie wake me? Smash-n-dash, I fuckin' knew it. Didn't even wake me up to ask me if I needed a ride to Alisha's crib. The nigga just left me, naked, in the bed, ass, titties, and pussy sore as a muthafucka!

I jumped out of bed. "Kelissa, where are you?"

"At Alisha's crib. Bitch, I just told you that your mama is over here. Where the fuck you at?" Kelissa asked me again.

"I'll be there in like thirty minutes, okay? Tell Ashton I'm sorry and I'm on my way." I hung up the phone, rushing over to my clothes.

I tried to get as decent as I could that morning. Luckily, I had a brush, comb, hair band, a clean pair of panties, and Dove Powder Fresh deodorant in my purse. Not to mention Lancôme concealer, Lancôme dual finished pressed powder, and Maybelline Blackest Black Illegal Lengths mascara. I covered my eyes with Bvlgari Flora Sunglasses to hide the tired look on my face that the makeup couldn't cover. I smelled just like Jamie, and I didn't mind at all. Hopefully, no one else noticed.

I called a cab on my way out of the hotel, and just when I stepped through the revolving door, I saw Jamie's driver standing alongside Jamie's stretch Navigator, right in front of the hotel. Kalvin, the driver, tipped his hat to me, "Miss Campbell." He opened the door for me.

I sighed, getting in. "Thank you, Kalvin."

Chapter 5: Feeling Some Kinda Way

Charlene

You could imagine the look on my mother's face when I pulled up in front of Alisha's apartment building, getting out of Jamie's car. She was helping Tyra and Danita place boxes in the back of a U-Haul truck. They were are dressed in loungewear, ready to work, and there I stood in two-thousand-dollar stilettos and sixty-thousand-dollar glasses.

They all looked at me as I approached them. I removed my glasses from my face, "Good morning, mama."

My mother scoffed, then looked at her clock. "It's twelve thirty, Charlene. We have all been here since nine o'clock, helping that boy, and you're just now showing up to help? And is that Jamie's Navigator that you just stepped out of?" Mama exclaimed, watching Jamie's driver speed out of the parking lot.

I sighed. I really wasn't in the mood for any of her shit. She always had something to say in Ne'Vaeh's defense, and it got on my last muthafuckin' nerve. I was in no mood to go back and forth with anyone. I felt like I'd gotten hit by a bus. I had drunk way too much the night before, and my asshole felt like it was on fire. Not sure if y'all have ever let a man enter your back door, but the next morning (if not right afterward), you have to shit, and it stings like a muthafucka when it comes out.

"Mama, don't start. Damn!" I rolled my eyes.

"Charlie," Kelissa hopped out of the U-Haul, dressed in sweat capris, a tank top, and a pair of Reeboks, "You haven't changed a bit. It's like you just wake up in the morning like, hmmm, I think I'll be a ho today."

I laughed a little. "This bitch," I muttered to myself.

"Don't get mad at your mama. She's been here like the rest of us since nine o'clock this morning helping Ashton clean and pack shit up! The boy is an emotional wreck, Charlie! You're his best friend; you're supposed to be here, not laid up somewhere with Jamie's muthafuckin' ass!" Kelissa was pissed.

I rolled my eyes, so not in the mood for her shit either. "Look, Kelissa, you can save that shit, too. The last time I checked, I was grown. If I wanna fuck every 'Jamie' there is, I'll do that. Mind your fuckin' business, all of you." I looked right at my mother. She and I hadn't been on good terms since my baby shower.

"You are so disrespectful, Charlie." My mother shook her head at me. "Your friends are here to help your ungrateful ass, and all you can do is flaunt your promiscuous lifestyle, screwing men like it's a sport? This shit is going to catch up to you, I promise you! And when it does, these same ladies that you're turning against you are going to be the very ladies that you're going to need. Don't believe me? Just watch."

Kelissa approached me, dusting her hands on her sweats. Her eyes searched mine. She shook her head at me. "Well, isn't this situation convenient though?" She grinned. "Your sister's here, inside helping the fellas."

I rolled my eyes. "Of course Heather's here; she asked if she could borrow some damn money to pay off all of those credit cards that I told her ass to cut up months ago. Mom, you spoiled that girl and gave her everything, now she thinks she can just spend money and not have to pay the shit back!"

Mama laughed a little. "Charlene, she's not talking about Heather. She's talking about Ne'Vaeh, Aaron's little piece of Heaven."

I looked at my mother. She was enjoying my pain a little bit too much. "The fuck is she doing here?"

Tyra shook her head at me. "Aaron's in there helping his boy pack. You didn't think he'd bring his wife with him? You need to take off them Christian Louboutin's and put on these Reeboks, and get your ass in there to help straighten up."

I looked at her as I stepped out of my heels, then bent over picking them up. All of them bitches were gloating in my face. They loved the fact that Ne'Vaeh was there with Aaron.

Tyra shook her head at me as she kicked off her Reeboks. "Really, Charlie? You really fuckin' with that asshole again?" She handed me her shoes, taking mine from my hands.

I snatched the shoes from her hands. "Save the lectures, okay? This is really not the time. Why the fuck didn't either of you call or text me to tell me that Ne'Vaeh was here?"

"Because you wouldn't have come and that boy in there needs you." Mama's voice shook. "You need to put this petty shit aside because that girl in there—your sister—needs you, too."

Alisha's front door was propped open when I walked inside of the apartment. I walked right in on Ashton and Aaron placing a 46-inch LG television back in its box. I hadn't seen Aaron up close since the night of our rehearsal dinner. At the New Year's Eve party in 2014, he'd ignored me. Didn't even look my way. Aaron looked amazing. Even in a plain white t-shirt, a pair of baggy sweats, and a fresh pair of white and gray Jordan's, the nigga was still one of the most beautiful men I'd ever seen. Ashton looked up at me as I entered the room. Aaron looked in the direction of Ashton's gaze.

Ashton looked at his watch. "So, you can't tell time, Charlie?"

I sighed, placing my purse and glasses on top of a box. My feet were throbbing. Tyra's feet were at least an inch smaller than mine. Tyra put my red bottoms in the backseat of her car, knowing I wasn't going to leave without them. "Ashton, I had like ten times too much to drink last night. I just overslept."

Ashton looked at me, shaking his head to himself. "You mind helping shorty in the kitchen clean out the 'fridge, the dishwasher, and the countertops? I mean, if that's not too much to ask. I know you've had a long night. Fuckin' and suckin' every night has got to be exhausting. Which nigga was it last night? Or should I saw how many niggas was it last night?" Ashton threw a roll of tape across the room, damn near creating a dent on the wall.

"Yo." Aaron grabbed Ashton's arm. "Chill, dude."

Ashton pulled from him. "I need some air, yo. Can you handle this last box? I'm about to go smoke a cigarette." Ashton left the room to keep from creating a dent upside my head.

Aaron watched his friend leave, then looked back at me. "What's good wit'cha, Charlene? Long time no see."

I looked at him, eyeing the platinum and diamond wedding band on his left ring finger. Yeah, his ass was married alright. "Nothing much. How are things going with you? I can't help but notice the bling on your finger."

And Aaron couldn't help but grin, dimples piercing his cheeks. "Oh, this?" He looked down at it, then back up at me. "Looks good on a nigga, huh?"

I had to admit, he was glowing. I'd never seen that boy look so happy, so complete, like he'd achieved everything that he ever wanted in life. He was twenty years old and married to the girl of his wet dreams. How lovely. "What do your parents have to say about it? As a matter of fact, have you even told them about it?" I grinned, just knowing that he would be unresponsive to the question. Aaron's mother—as ignorant as that bitch was—was his heart. "I know Miss Ella is just lovin' this shit."

Aaron looked me in the face and said with so much heart and soul, "Fuck my mama and her got-damn opinion."

I damn near swallowed my tongue. "Okay, Aaron, damn. You sure grew some balls since you've been with ol' girl. 'Fuck your mama'? Wow, nice!"

"You know what I mean, Charlene." Aaron sighed, shaking his head. "If I let them run my life forever, I'm never gonna be happy. I'm doing me, with her, ya feel me?"

As bad as it hurt to know he was married to that girl, it was really nice to know he finally stood up to Ella's color-struck, stuck-up ass. "When was the big day? And why wasn't I invited?"

"We got married in Paris, last October, on shorty's birthday. We didn't invite anyone, not even my parents. We didn't tell anyone. I just let muthafuckas figure it out on their own when they saw the ring on her finger, and her signature when she signed her name. I mean, I wanted to tell the world, you know that. But Heaven didn't want her folks trippin' on her. You know, she's got Anastasia Jones riding' her ass, always trying to change her image, and then you have Renée always playing got-damn mama." Aaron looked at me for a few seconds before going over to pick up the tape that Ashton threw across the room. "Aston is pissed than a muthafucka at you, Charlie. The fuck you do to him?" Aaron walked back over to the box of trophies they had started packing but hadn't finished.

I laughed a little. "Do to him'? I didn't do anything to him."

"You sure? The shit you do affects more than just you, shorty. You never did realize that." Aaron looked at me, as he sat down on a stool. "Alisha was Ashton's heart, Charlene; we all know how much he cared about that girl. But you—"

I looked at Aaron.

"Everyone knows that you are everything to that dude." Aaron leaned forward, resting his forearms on his thighs, looking up at me. "How the fuck do you think he feels watching you pull up in Jamie's ride? You don't think he knows where you've been all night?"

I rolled my eyes. Everybody and their fuckin' mama had something to say about what I chose to do with my time.

"Why does anything that I do concern you? Aaron, I'm not your concern anymore, probably never was, so can you mind yours and I'll mind mine, thank you?" I rolled my neck at Aaron, folding my arms.

Aaron smirked a little. "Really, Charlie? You think Jamie is yours?"

Oh, Aaron always knew how to press my got-damn buttons. "Why are you worried about what the fuck I'm doin'? You have who you want so don't worry about me. You've always wanted her, now you got her. Just don't fuck it up, okay?"

Aaron grinned. "I got this."

I nodded, fighting back the tears. "I bet you do." I was genuinely happy for them, surprisingly. I was trying to be angry with them, but my heart wouldn't let me.

I heard Ne'Vaeh clearing her throat over my shoulder, behind me. I turned around to see Ne'Vaeh standing in the hallway, dressed in a tight gray tiny t-shirt and skinny jeans. Her hair was pulled up into a messy bun. She looked adorable as usual. She tossed me a pair of vinyl dish gloves.

Aaron stood from the stool, going over to slide his arm around her waist. He gently kissed her forehead. Oh, it was so adorable. "I'm gonna go check on Ashton. Make sure he's alright," he whispered to his wife.

Ne'Vaeh looked up at him. As jealous as I was of her, I couldn't help but feel overjoyed watching the way they looked at one another. Aaron always wanted that girl, and I knew his heart was rejoicing at the thought of that girl being his wife. I tried to hate her, I really did, but even I couldn't help but grin at the way he grabbed and kissed her. It wasn't a show for me; he genuinely lived and breathed Ne'Vaeh. I could tell by the way that he kissed her that he couldn't live without her.

"Aaron, baby, please don't smoke, okay?" Ne'Vaeh pleaded with him as he walked toward the door.

"I'm good, shorty. No cigarettes, I promise." Aaron winked at her before leaving the apartment.

Ne'Vaeh looked at me.

I couldn't wipe the grin off my face as I approached her.

Ne'Vaeh gave me this IDFWY face. "What are you grinning about?"

"You. This." I pointed to her ring. I held her tiny hand in mine, looking at that beautiful ring. I wanted to hate her, you know how hard I tried. But I couldn't. I looked into her face as she slipped her hand from mine. "You look like . . . like you can finally breathe."

Ne'Vaeh sighed, seeming relieved at my response, like she'd expected me to pop off on her for having the audacity to flaunt her relationship with Aaron in my face. "Yes, I can. He is a breath of fresh air. He loves me and only me, and that feels amazing. Aaron is where I'm supposed to be. Being with him feels like home."

My eyes grew misty listening to her talking about the way Aaron made her heart feel. I desperately wanted to feel that way. I slid the gloves on, fighting back the tears. "Okay, what are we cleaning?"

Ne'Vaeh walked back into the kitchen. OMG, her waist was so tiny, and though she was a petite little thing, her bodily dimensions were phenomenal. Obviously, Anastasia had that girl working out; she was finally starting to get thighs and hips. "Well, I cleaned just about everything. We just need to clean the dishwasher, the countertops, and pack the rest of Alisha's dishes."

I stood and watched as Ne'Vaeh emptied the dishwasher. We hadn't seen nor spoken to each other for almost a year and a half. There was so much that I wanted to say to that girl; so much I wanted to tell her. At one point we were best friends. She was the only girl friend that I had that accepted me with all of my flaws, and I blew it. I should have just backed away and let her have Aaron. She didn't deserve to get her heart broken by both me and Jamie.

"So, how's Jamie?" She hesitated, looking up at me as she sat the dishes on the countertop.

I wasn't sure what to tell her. That late night action I'd gotten from Jamie was the longest I spent with that boy since that night after Ne'Vaeh's birthday party, a year and seven months earlier.

"Are y'all dating or something?" Ne'Vaeh had the nerve to ask.

I didn't mean to laugh out loud, but her question seemed hilarious. "Jamie? Dating? Me at that? Girl, bye!"

"Right," Ne'Vaeh nodded, picking up a bottle of 409 from the countertop. "Y'all just fuckin' as normal, right? No labels, no strings, huh?" She shook her head to herself, as she stooped down to spray the dishwasher down. It still hurt that girl to know that Jamie hadn't changed. He hadn't gone to see that girl since she moved to Atlanta. It appeared to be easy for him to up and leave her or to just let her go. I know that had Ne'Vaeh wondering whether or not Jamie ever loved her at all.

I sighed, sweeping my hair over to one side, stooping down beside her. "Jamie loves you, Ne'Vaeh."

Ne'Vaeh couldn't even look at me. She damn near scrubbed the stainless steel off of the Whirlpool dishwasher, she was scrubbing so got-damn hard. "Yeah, says the girl who's fuckin' him."

I grabbed her hand, taking the sponge from her. "Aaron is the better man for you, and you know it! I had no business being with him in the first place. He was made for you and you were made for him. He is a good man, and you deserve him!"

Ne'Vaeh looked at me, her big brown eyes sparkling. "Yeah, he is a good man. I was losing myself to depression last summer. All I did could think about was Jamie. My soul needed that muthafucka, but he never called or even asked Renée about me when she saw him at a party in DC! I sent him an invitation to come to the BET awards to see me, but he ignored it! I couldn't eat, sleep, drink, think, anything without Jamie! When I turned his proposal down, Jamie lost interest in me altogether. I wouldn't marry him, so I wasn't shit, and that really hurt. After all you both had done to hurt me, he actually thought I'd accept that ring! Charlie, when I left here, I was pregnant."

I was stunned to silence. All I could do was start scrubbing down the dishwasher. But then I stopped to think, and looked at her. "So, where's the baby? Let me see a picture of him or her!"

Ne'Vaeh shook her head, hand over her heart. "There is no baby, Charlie."

"You got an abortion, Ne'Vaeh? You turned the nigga's proposal down knowing that you were pregnant, then you went and got an abortion?" I shook my head to myself, scrubbing the dishwasher. I was too quick to judge.

"When I pushed her out, she was already dead, Charlie. Her umbilical cord was wrapped tightly around her neck." Ne'Vaeh damn near killed me with the response.

I looked at her, speechless. She had to go through that alone. Jamie should have been there. Shit, I should have been there. "Ne'Vaeh, sweetie, I'm sorry."

Ne'Vaeh stood from the floor. "I held Sara's lifeless body in my arms! She was so beautiful, so precious, and so tiny. She looked like she was only sleeping. I thought I was going to have a heart attack when the doctors took her from my arms and covered her face with her little white blanket. I got home to a room of baby clothes, toys, and furniture, and no little baby girl. And I went straight crazy. Do you know how many times I tried to kill myself? Do you know how many times I had to stay in the psychiatric ward? I needed you both, and neither of you showed up!"

I stood up with her, trying to hold her trembling hand in mine, but she wouldn't let me. Her eyes searched my face for the key print that she left on my face the day of my baby shower, in December of 2014. It took about three laser surgeries to remove that scar from my face. The area was still slightly darker than the rest, but nowhere near as bad as she left it.

She looked back into my eyes. "Sara was the only piece of Jamie that I had left, and God took her from me . . . but he brought me Aaron. I went to the darkest place in life there is to get to the light. Aaron is the best thing that ever happened to me. He came to me when he knew I needed him, and I didn't have to ask. Aaron accepts me for who I am—he loves me, he cherishes me, he completes me, and he protects me. So you can have Jamie, Charlie. . . . Aaron is where I'm supposed to be. All the heartbreaks, the lies, the rumors, the groupies, you can have that shit! And bitch, I hope you choke on it!" Ne'Vaeh tossed her gloves on the countertop and left the kitchen. And then left the apartment altogether.

Jamie had no idea of what he'd done. And apparently neither did I.

Man, you should have seen how many people showed up to the yard sale that Alisha's mother decided to have to get rid of the things that she didn't want. Ashton was nearly in tears watching the Morgan girls go through her clothes. Ms. Newman sent Alisha's furniture and electronics in the U-Haul to her storage unit. She also kept Alisha's jewelry, cheerleading outfits, and her prom dress. The Morgan girls took just about all of her outfits and kitchenware. Ms. Newman tried giving Ne'Vaeh Alisha's brand new China set, but Ne'Vaeh was crying too much to accept it. Ashton kept all of her trophies. All I wanted were a few of her photo albums. I wanted pictures of moments that we shared and moments that I had missed. It was really hard accepting the fact that she was gone, but we had no choice.

Ashton didn't say anything to me that entire morning. Aaron and Ne'Vaeh were headed back to Atlanta that afternoon, when Aaron thought it was a good idea to take us all out to lunch. He invited Kelissa, Heather, Tyra, and my mother to go along with the four of us (me, Ne'Vaeh, Ashton, and himself). Ne'Vaeh sat quietly at the restaurant next to Aaron, barely eating a thing from her plate. Every five or ten minutes, she was excusing herself to go to the bathroom.

My mother carried on and on with Aaron about his basketball career. He didn't want to boast on and on about himself. He was more into letting us all know about Ne'Vaeh. She was back on the music scene and had gone back on tour. I saw a few of her videos on MTV2 and VH1 the year before. She was hot as hell in those videos. Anastasia transformed her into a stripper in training. I knew Ne'Vaeh hated every minute of it, she didn't have to tell me. The whole reason why she quit the cheerleading squad in high school was that the skirts were too short. The fact that Ne'Vaeh agreed to start performing in stage plays didn't surprise me. She was shy, but when it was time to act and sing, she was a totally different person. I was really proud of her, but she was too angry with me to notice the smile on my face from the moment her name came out of Aaron's mouth.

After lunch, everyone parted ways. I caught up with Ashton as he was walking to his car. I always loved the way he walked. It was cool, calm, and collected, just like his personality, except when it came to me. Man, he was really feeling some kinda way about me dealing with Jamie in any type of way.

"Ashton, hold up!" I called out, scurrying up the sidewalk in my stilettos.

Ashton just kept on walking and got in the car like he didn't hear me calling his got-damn name.

"Ashton!" I yelled as I got to his car, just as he started the engine. I tapped on his tinted windows.

Ashton rolled down his window. "What?" He looked straight ahead, temples twitching.

I bent over, peeping inside of the car, eying the gym back in the passenger's seat. "Headed to the gym, boo?"

"I'm going to work. I'll probably work out at the gym on my lunch break." Ashton finally looked at me, gazing at my cleavage for a second or two. Ashton was going to college full time, unlike myself who dropped out of college as soon as I signed my name on that phat-ass modeling contract. Even Ne'Vaeh and Aaron were taking classes online. I don't know how everyone maintained a full-time career and went to school full time as well. I could barely handle my career and motherhood, let alone going to school. Fuck all that.

Ashton was working as a paid intern at the University of Maryland Medical Center. He turned down several offers to join the NBA. Once Alisha's health started to deteriorate, so did Ashton's interest in playing basketball. He kept his head in the books and off of anything that reminded him of Alisha.

"Can I get a ride home?" I asked. "Please. My mama and the girls already left me."

Ashton looked up at me. "So, you want me to take you all the way to DC, and then drive all the way back to Baltimore to go to work? Is that what you're asking me to do?"

I wasn't even thinking. I bit my lip. "Please."

Ashton just looked up into my face before letting out a long sigh. "How about I drop you over your mama's crib? Don't cha gotta pick up your son anyway in a little while?"

I scurried over to the passenger's side.

Ashton tossed his gym bag in the backseat as I got in. His Audi was so clean and smelled so good. He kept his car neat at all times. You almost never caught him with a car full of people.

After driving about fifteen minutes down the highway to my mother's, Jamie finally decided to grace me with a text.

What's good, sleeping beauty? he texted.

I rolled my eyes, texting, RME.

Lol, Jamie texted back.

What the fuck is it that you want, Jamie? I texted back.

My assistant, Karlie, is about to drop August off at your mama's crib in about twenty minutes. She just called your mama to make sure that she was home, Jamie texted.

Okay. Whatever, I texted back. I rolled my eyes. He knew I hated that funky bitch.

Yo . . . I can still feel your lips on it, shawty, Jamie had the nerve to text. Jamie was straight wildin' out, for real. Without Ne'Vaeh he really didn't give a fuck.

I burst out laughing, texting, Boy, bye!

Ashton glanced at me "Who's that?"

I jumped at the sound of his voice, forgetting dude was even there. I powered off the home screen to my iPhone. "Oh, just Jamie texting me, saying his slut bucket sex-u-tary will be dropping our son off at mama's in a little while." I looked at Ashton.

His temples started to twitch again as he clenched the steering wheel with one hand. "I never liked that muthafucka."

I sighed, rolling my eyes. "What the hell has he ever done to you, Ashton? Jamie has never given you any problems whatsoever."

"It's not about me; it's about what he's done to you." Ashton glanced at me.

"Man, y'all are really killing me today! He hasn't done anything to me that I didn't let him do, Ashton!" I shook my head, really frustrated with everyone's outtake on my life.

Ashton changed the subject because he knew there was nothing he could say to me to make me think that Jamie was doing me any harm. "I buried Alisha in the ring that I gave her in eighth grade. Man, I saved up three hundred fifty dollars of my allowance to buy her that ring." Ashton laughed a little at the memory of Alisha. "She loved that ring. She showed that ring off like it was a fuckin' engagement ring!"

I smiled. "That girl really loved her some Ashton."

Ashton looked at me. "But I've always loved you, and she always knew it." Ashton pulled up in my mother's driveway and cut the car off. "And I always felt bad about it, but I can't help the way that I feel."

I looked at Ashton, already feeling where the conversation was headed. "Ashton, we already talked about this. You know how I feel about you. You are the perfect guy. You deserve way better than me, and you know it."

"Why are you fuckin' with this nigga again?" Ashton shook his head at me. "Do you really love him?"

I shrunk back in my seat, not looking Ashton in the face, but looking out the window. Of course I loved Jamie. My heart beat for that fool. I could still feel his hands on me and his lips sucking on my nipples. I couldn't shake the feeling of him, and I didn't want to, either.

"I know, I'm all in your mix, but I don't want to see you get hurt. He's gonna hurt you." Ashton assured me.

I looked at him, shaking my head. "I won't let him."

"I've been here for you, Charlene, and you've always overlooked me." Ashton exhaled deeply, frustrated as hell with me.

I shook my head at him, "Oh, Ashton, I never overlooked you. It's just I don't see any use in trying to fix something that isn't broken. I like where we are in our relationship. You're my friend—my best friend, and I would like to keep it that way."

"The only decent dude you've ever been with was my nigga, Aaron. That's why I never had a problem with y'all being together. He was a good influence on you. He had you getting better grades, he had you studying, he kept you out of the streets, and he kept the niggas out of you." Ashton's eyes searched my face.

I scoffed. "What?"

Ashton nodded, "Shorty, you know I ain't lyin'. And as soon as you got the chance, you went right back to your regularly scheduled program of getting dicked down by random niggas daily. Why you continue to live on the edge, I don't know. All I know is I need you, Charlene. I need you to change because I know you're better than this. You're too fine to be living like this. Just let me love you." Ashton grabbed my hand.

I sighed, interlocking my fingers with his. His hands were so warm and soft and comfortable. I'll admit that I felt so at ease with him. But he deserved better than me. I couldn't give him damaged goods. "I appreciate everything that you've done for me, babe, but I am what I am. And you don't deserve this. You deserve—"

Before I could stop him, Ashton was leaning in to kiss me. The first kiss was the softest touch I'd ever felt. Then he kissed me again, that time holding my face, fingers slipping up the nape of my neck into my hair. I swear I was lost in the stroke of his lips for a little while. The stroke of his warm, wet lips felt amazing, felt so strong, felt so . . . familiar. My mind instantly took me back to another moment in time where we'd kissed. A memory I didn't know existed. I'm telling you, it was déjà vu.

I pulled my lips from his, getting out of the car as fast as I could without as much as a good-bye. And just when I got out of the car, that slut bucket bitch pulled up in a hot red Ferrari with my baby boy in the backseat of her ride.

Chapter 6: Do You Remember the Time

Charlene

I couldn't shake Ashton's intense kiss for anything. Why his lips felt so familiar, I had no idea. We'd never kissed, so why did my mind take me back to a time that we did the moment his lips touched mine? I could even remember the cologne he was wearing. I remember the outfit I was wearing. I remember feeling his hands on my bare waist. The memories were too vivid to be my imagination. I thought I was going crazy.

Meanwhile, I had other business to attend to. I walked up the steps of Kent Sanderson' office building located in Silver Springs. Jamie was going to lose that phat-ass contract that he had by sticking his dick where it didn't belong. Kent Sanderson was expecting me. I'd called him the morning of May 30, around 8:30. I made sure to wear something tight, sexy, and silky. Kent liked anything tight, sexy, silky, and with a thigh-high split.

"How can I help you, Miss Campbell?" Kent smiled, sitting back in his big leather chair. He was a sexy ass white man with an olive skin tone, hazel eyes, and dark hair. He was a real lady killer. He reminded me of the late actor Paul Walker with darker hair. The fact that he'd gotten married shocked the hell out of everyone. The fact that she wasn't white had the media talking.

Y'all already know the deal with white man's fascination with black women, dating all the way back to slavery. The muthafuckas can't keep their hands and eyes off us, though they'd never admit it.

Kent held his hand out, gesturing me to have a seat. "Have a seat, gorgeous." His eyes traced my silhouette and ran their gaze up my thighs as I crossed my newly waxed legs.

"I'm here to talk about Jamie Green." I watched Kent's eyes trace from my thighs, past my waist, around each breast before looking back into my eyes.

Kent grinned. "Jamie Green? My star quarterback?"

"I heard that you were thinking of trading him or ending his contract altogether." I swept my bangs from my face.

"Yes, Coach and I were discussing the possibility of trading him to Dallas or just ending his football career period. He's arrogant, cocky, and won't take any advice. He doesn't get along with any of his teammates. He's causing too many problems out there on the field." Kent scoffed.

I rolled my eyes. "Oh, please. What field? The football field or your field? The bedroom getting pretty cold since she got a taste of Jamie, huh?"

Kent got up from his chair, then walked around his huge cherry pine desk, sitting on the edge of it, facing me. "What difference does it make to you?"

"Jamie is good, you know he's good! He's not just football, he's fashion, and the muthafucka can sing! Some other team is gonna snatch him up, that's for sure. He's already made his mark in history. Some other team is gonna be making all that money that you could be making. He's worth so much more than y'all are paying him, and you know it. Sure, you have connections, and you could put an end to his football career out here on the

East Coast if you wanted to, but he's got talent. One of the coaches out there on the West Coast who hate you would be glad to snatch him up. He doesn't need you to get far. You're really gonna let your ego get in the way of your money? Jamie might have put a dent in your wife's cervix a few times, so what? Shit, that's nothing compared to the things that you, me, and a few more chicks used to do when I was back in high school, and way under aged if I might add. When was it we started having sex again? You know, the statute of limitations isn't up on those several instances." I grinned.

Kent looked at me, the air growing tense. He exhaled deeply. "What is it that you want, Charlene?"

"A renegotiated contract of twenty-two million." I stood from my chair.

Kent scoffed. "Twenty-two—"

"The Forty-niners have been trying to get to Jamie since the first day he stepped foot on your field. Not to mention the Giants, Packers, and Patriots! And every last coach on those teams hates your ass." I cut him off. "Jamie's about to sign to an undisclosed record label. Not to mention his sports apparel sales are skyrocketing by the second. Jamie's the best player this team has ever had. I can get him to leave your wife alone. I can even get him to chill out on the smokin', partying, and whatever else he does. But we need him here. And I'm willing to do whatever and whoever to keep him here and to keep his career intact. I have so much dirt on the coaches and owners of so many teams, all of who you socialize with. I have enough dirt to put you all behind bars for years, or at least come out of millions to settle lawsuits." I looked up at Kent as he stood from his desk, six feet two inches from the ground.

"I know every judge there is to know in every court in Maryland, D.C, and Virginia. No judge will ever convict me off of the word of a few dancers and a slutty runway model." Kent looked me up and down. "You gotta come harder than that, Miss Campbell, to threaten me, sweetheart."

I sighed, looking up into his face. "Look, Jamie is my son's father. My son loves him. He won't even sleep without hearing his father's voice! I'll do whatever it is I have to do to keep Jamie around."

Kent looked at me as he pressed a silver button at the edge of his desk.

"What, are you calling security on me, Kent? Really?" I folded my arms.

"Of course not." Kent grinned, pulling me closer to him, unfolding my arms.

In seconds, a copper-skinned bombshell entered the room. She was about five feet eight inches without her heels. She had very long, thick dark hair that fell right below her perfect ass. She had breast, hips, legs, and ass for miles. She stood there, dressed in a tight orange halter mini-dress and matching gold Giuseppe Zanotti stilettos, holding a clipboard in her hands.

"Charlene, meet my wife, Ailani." Kent held out his hand for his wife to come to him.

She was breathtakingly beautiful. The sight of her made my pussy twitch. Yeah, Jamie hit that.

She grinned at me, holding out her hand to shake mine. "Aloha." She pulled me closer to her by her gentle hands. "Wow, you're beautiful. She looks like Cassie, Diddy's Cassie. Honey, doesn't she look like a lighter version of Cassie?"

"Yes, she does. I told you she was sexy." Kent licked his lips.

"Yes, honey, very sexy." Ailani looked me over.

I was speechless. I looked up at Kent.

He smiled at me, kissing his wife's bare shoulder. "Now, what was it you said about doing anyone to make sure Jamie stayed in the game?"

Before I could even attempt to back out of the situation, Kent was undressing Ailani, and Ailani was undressing me. She pulled me closer to her, hands surrounding my waist, lips stroking mine.

Yes, I felt like a slut when I got into my limo that afternoon after having sex with Kent, his wife, and his damn secretary Kimberly for hours. I was so over that life years ago. I got dick on a daily basis, but pussy? Nah, it's been years. I'll admit, having sex with those women was a hell of a lot better than taking pipe from two or three men at a time. I left Kent's office with a new contract for Jamie to sign and the taste of pussy in my mouth. I felt nasty, but I felt good knowing Jamie was in Maryland to stay.

I was about to hit the road with my modeling agency for a few weeks. I had a show and a few photo shoots down in New Orleans and some in San Diego. I had to do whatever I had to do so I could get Ashton's kiss out of my mind. Not to mention the things I had done with those women and Kent's perverted ass to get Jamie a $22-million contract. It was obvious that I'd do anything for that fool. He hadn't stepped foot near me in about a week. I knew he was feeling some sort of way about Ne'Vaeh. Having sex with me wasn't going to make him not miss her. Even though I hated to admit it, Ne'Vaeh needed Aaron. Jamie had no idea that she had his baby and then lost it. He needed to know, but I wasn't so sure that I should have been the one to tell him. He needed to face her and hear what she had to say. I just wasn't so sure how I was going to get him to go to Atlanta to see her.

I went home and jumped straight in the shower that afternoon. I damn near scrubbed my skin off. I washed my face, teeth, tongue, lips, everything. I must have brushed my teeth and tongue for a good twenty minutes. No matter what I did, I could still smell and taste Ailani's and Kimberly's pussies. Maybe it was the guilt that had my minds playing tricks on me. It wasn't even 4:30 and I was already fiending for a drink.

I had my cook, Tahiri, make me a nice strawberry daiquiri topped with whipped cream and red sprinkles. I sat at the bar in my kitchen, reading over Jamie's contract when I heard the doorbell chime. Hoping it was Jamie, I hopped off the stool, pulling my tiny Victoria's Secret pink shorts over my ass a little more. Come to think of it, he likes ass, so I pulled my shorts up higher over my belly button. I snatched the contract from the countertop, holding it behind my back.

"Miss, Campbell, Señor Ashton is here to see you," Lilia announced, standing at the entrance to the kitchen.

I sighed, tossing the contract back on the countertop, pulling my shorts down over my ass. I sat back down as Ashton appeared in the doorway, and Lilia stepped out. Ashton was dressed semi-casual, in a gray Gucci shirt, dark gray Gucci slacks, and non-scuff leather Gucci shoes. He must have been on his way to the hospital, or just getting off. He looked so good. My heart was racing, and my pussy was throbbing. I really needed to give my pussy a rest. There was no way I was gonna give her to Ashton, even though she really wanted him.

I ran my fingers through my hair, sweeping it all over to one shoulder. "Hey, boo."

"What's up wit'cha?" Ashton walked into the kitchen.

I sipped on my drink as I waved at him, eying the photo album he held in his hands. I swallowed a huge gulp of my delicious daiquiri. "What's that you got there?"

Ashton grinned, walking over to me. He eyed my thighs in my little shorts a little bit before sitting down on the stool next to me. "Oh, this photo album from y'all's dance competition, junior year in high school." He opened the album, laying it out in front of me.

I smiled, looking at the pictures. Alisha was so photogenic. I took one of the photos out of the plastic to look at it up close. "Oh my goodness, I remember this! We thought we were so sexy in these outfits! I hate to admit it, but Alisha looked the best in her outfit with all that ass she had!"

I eyed a picture of Alisha posing in our sexy purple lace outfits for our spring competition in Dallas. I couldn't remember the exact date of that competition, so I flipped the picture over, hoping she'd written the date on the back. Instead, I found my old telephone number written on the back in Ashton's handwriting. I looked at Ashton. "Really, dude?"

Ashton grinned, "Hey, I didn't have any paper. I had to write it somewhere."

I shook my head, putting the picture back in the album. "Putting another girl's number on the back of your girlfriend's photo? That's pretty damn bold, Ashton. And not just any girl, but the very same girl that your girl used to wish murder on! You made that girl hate me, Ashton, ugh! Y'all niggas kill me!"

Ashton laughed a little, "Naw, you did a pretty good job of that yourself. Y'all red bones singled out the dark-skinned chicks those days, yo. Look at this bullshit. Look at the pyramids. Y'all even had the light chicks on top and the dark-skinned chicks at the bottom. I felt like I was an extra in 'School Days' whenever y'all were around!" Ashton flipped through the pictures. "Alisha was beautiful, oh my God, but she never thought she was. Every time I saw her face, I'd tell her how sexy, how beautiful, how pretty she was. My opinion didn't matter all that much though. She let y'all girls control her view of what she thought beauty was." Ashton shook his head to himself. "Y'all did a number on my baby, for real. It wasn't cool how y'all did her. Ripped her self-esteem to pieces."

I sighed. He was right. We were pretty mean back then. We used every advantage we could in those days to get ahead. And yes, our complexions did get us a lot of perks. "Yeah, we were the definition of *bitch* back then, seriously," I admitted. "I must have apologized to Alisha a gazillion times this year about all the trouble that I caused her." I looked at him, eyes tracing his profile. "So, where are you off to today, lookin' and smellin' all good? Work? Lookin' like this? Oh, I know them damn horny-ass chickens at the hospital be squawkin'."

Ashton looked at me, then grinned a little. "Naw, I worked overnight. A few of the fellas and I are going to a bar in a few hours. You can roll if you want to."

I looked up into his face. I'd already had plans that night. I was going out with my manager's wife and some friends to dinner. "I already have plans, but thanks for the invite. My manager's wife, Golden, is taken me out to dinner to celebrate this deal we just got with this new makeup line that just dropped in Italy. They want me to be their spokesperson! I'm about to hit the road for about three weeks. I have a few shows in New Orleans and San Diego to go to. I wish you could come; I hate hanging around those models who only talk about dieting and how much money their nigga is spending on them. I really don't fit in with them at all, but hey, it's a job." I noticed Ashton's attention was over my left shoulder. "Hey, are you even listening to me, Ashton?"

"Yeah, shorty, I'm listening." Apparently, he was eying the contract sitting on the countertop. He reached across me and grabbed it before I could stop him. "What's this?"

I gasped, trying to snatch it from him, but he blocked me, trying to quickly read it before I managed to get the contract back from him.

Ashton laughed out loud, reading the $22-million section out loud. "What is this? Whose is this?" He didn't get a chance to finish reading it when I got a hold of it, snatching it from him. He looked at the letterhead. "That looks like Kent Sanderson's logo. You workin' for dude, too? What is that?"

"Don't worry about all that, Super Duper Snooper. It's not yours." I rolled my eyes, smoothing out the paper. "Gosh, you're nosy!"

Ashton looked at me, "What the fuck did you do to get someone to write you a contract for that much, Charlie? Or should I say who did you do?"

"It's not for me, Ashton." I blurted out without thinking. *Shit, you talk too damn much, Charlie!*

Ashton's stare was so intense that he probably could see straight through me.

I looked away from him, feeling as ugly as the look on his face. "It's Jamie's contract. And before you say anything, I'm fine."

Ashton's temples twitched. "Naw," he shook his head. "You're not fine. What's up with you, Charlie? You fucked that dude and whoever the fuck else he had you fuckin' and suckin' on just to get Jamie, a nigga who doesn't give a fuck about you, a contract that can have him set for life?"

"No, I fucked Kent, his wife, and his secretary so I can get Jamie a contract that will have my *son* set for life!" I exclaimed. "I will do anything I can to protect my son, and keep his father around him! My son lives and breathes Jamie!"

Ashton shook his head at me, "And so do you."

I sighed. "I'm just doing what's best for my son."

"Well, what about what's best for you? You running around every night, fuckin' whoever and whatever, and you never once stop to think about what you're doing. You need to get your life, shorty, and stop fuckin' around. Didn't Alisha's death teach you anything? Stop fuckin' around and get your life together before it's too late!" Ashton exclaimed, watching me shake my foot anxiously.

I just sat there, heart racing in my chest. I'll admit I was tired of living the fast life. I wanted a man to call my own, not a man who called me when he needed his dick sucked. "I want him to love me, Ashton, and he doesn't." I finally admitted.

Ashton shook his head. "Well then move on. Next, shit."

"That's what I've been doin', Ashton!" I replied.

"Naw, you've just been fuckin' niggas, and you back to fuckin' bitches, too, apparently. That ain't love and you know it. You want somebody to fuck you? Shit, I could have done that. I got a dick, too, shit." Ashton looked at me.

I looked at him, trying not to grin. "Naw, baby, you can't handle this pussy. I'm tellin' you, she'll make you fall in love with the quickness."

"I'm already in love, Charlie, you know that. And that's what you're running from. It's cool, though." Ashton closed the photo album, exhaling deeply. "Don't mind me. I've been in my feelings since my baby left me."

I looked at him. I had to know about the kiss. "Ashton? Have we ever kissed?"

He looked at me.

"I mean before the other day, have we ever kissed?" I asked.

Ashton hesitated. "Naw, not that I can remember."

I sighed, running my fingers through my hair anxiously. "Well, lately, I've been having these flashbacks of memories that I never even knew existed. Are you sure we've never kissed before?"

Ashton shook his head, then made a face like he was a little puzzled himself. "It's funny that you ask that question though, because for a little over a year and a half, I have been having this dream that you and I were at this party out in Severn, at that little white girl's house who used to be on y'all's dance team before she got sick. You remember Misty Daniels, right?"

I looked at Ashton. Misty used to be my home girl. She could dance her little ass off. She got real sick one year in high school and had to be homeschooled. That didn't stop us from going to see her. She threw the hottest parties, and if you wanted to get high, she had the party favors that could get you higher than a got-damn kite. "Yeah, I remember The Supplier, the leader of the 'Mile High' crew. She used to be my rider, for real! We haven't hung with her in a minute."

"Well, in this dream I had, we were at one of her parties, and you and I slept together." Ashton eyed my thighs for a few seconds.

I looked at him. "Slept together? So you're having fantasies about me, Ashton?"

Ashton looked back into my face. "This wasn't just any ol' fantasy, shorty. I mean, it felt so real, and it was so vivid. I can smell you, taste you, and feel you. I remember the dress you wore, the color of your nail polish, the perfume that you had on. I mean, yo, it's the exact same dream over and over." Ashton's eyes searched my face. "I mean, we did go to a few of her parties the year before last, right?"

"I vaguely remember those parties, Ashton." My heart pounded in my chest. Something wasn't right. Something happened. Something must have happened. "When you kissed me, Ashton, I started having all of these flashbacks. This can't be a coincidence, Ashton." I laughed a little.

"You don't do drugs, and I stopped doing drugs years ago—well, except for a little weed every and then—so, what is going on?"

Ashton grinned a little. "Maybe we slept together in a past life." Ashton joked.

"Come on, this isn't a joking matter. Seriously, Ashton, when could this have happened?" My pussy started to throb just thinking about Ashton's warm lips all over me.

"It didn't." Ashton shrugged.

"But why are you dreaming about it? And why is it that from the moment you kissed my lips, my mind went straight back to another time that we kissed? Yes, it felt real. And no, this can't be a coincidence. Why did you kiss me in the car the other day anyway, Ashton? You caught me off guard, didn't even give me the chance to say no." I shook my head at him, putting Jamie's contract away in the kitchen drawer.

Ashton just looked at me, not having too much to say.

I shook my head, "Ashton, baby, you don't need to be with me. You're just confused. I never did nothing good to or for you, other than sucking your dick back when you were fourteen. My head game wasn't that tight, Ashton, for you to still be sprung after all these years. You want your dick sucked? Is that what you want? Come on then; pull it out."

Ashton laughed out loud. "Naw, Charlie! I mean, yeah, but—"

I punched him as hard as I could in his shoulder. "Asshole!"

Ashton was dying laughing. I hadn't seen him laugh that way in over a year. He was too cute. He was my buddy. I loved him like he was a part of me, and I didn't want to lose him as my friend. He had been there for me for as long as I could remember. I would only end up hurting him if he got involved with me.

And just when I started to ask him for another kiss, ya know, for possibly old-time's sake, I heard my son crying over the baby monitor. I looked at the television monitor that sat on my island countertop. He was tossing in his crib.

I sighed. "I'll be right back, Ashton." I hurried out of the kitchen and rushed as fast as I could up the steps. My son had been fussy for the past few days. His nose was running, and he was feeling warm. I wanted to take him to the hospital, but my mother said he was fine and it was probably just a cold, so I just moved his crib into my room so that I could keep an eye on him. When I got to my room, my li'l bright boy was standing in his crib, rubbing his eyes.

I smiled as I picked him up, and he lay his head on my shoulder, curly hair brushing against my cheek. "Hey, li'l bright boy. You okay? Did you have a good nap?" I bounced him on my shoulder, soothing him, running my fingers through his hair. I turned to see Ashton standing in the doorway, watching me with little August. I grinned as Lilia came up behind Ashton, moving him out of the way a little.

"Señorita, I'm sorry, I was helping the housekeeper fold the linens. Do you need me to take Agosto to get a snack?" Lilia approached me, holding out her hands to take August from my arms.

I sighed as he reached for her, then laid his head on her shoulder. I felt bad that August was so close to every-one in the house. He loved me, but I was always occu-pied with modeling and my social life to spend as much time with him as I should have. He spent more time with Jamie and my mother than he did with me. Jamie had a very hectic life, but he always made time for little August. I don't think there was a time that I asked Jamie to keep our son that Jamie didn't say yes to. I felt like a bad mother, seriously.

Lilia looked at Ashton as she left the room. The bitch had the nerve to roll her eyes at him.

Ashton grinned, looking at me. "Whoa, what the fuck I do to piss the nanny off?"

I rolled my eyes, "That bitch has been lookin' at me sideways for the past few months. I don't know, but if the bitch keeps it up, I'm lettin' her ass go. Adios."

Ashton laughed a little walking into my bedroom. He looked around. "It's nice in here, shorty. So this is where you bring the niggas?" He joked, approaching me.

I pushed past him. "Boy, bye." I walked over to my dresser to pick out whichever bra and panties would go with my outfit. I planned on wearing a strapless romper and heels to meet my manager and her crew. If Ashton was gonna stand there and watch me try on clothes when I had already told his ass to wait for me downstairs, shit, it was alright with me. I had to meet my crew in just an hour and a half for dinner, and I wasn't halfway near being ready. My hair took the longest since I wanted to wear it straight those days. I changed right in front of him, pulling my tank top up and over my head. I tossed my shirt to him, standing there in nothing but booty shorts.

You should have seen the awestruck look on his face. The nigga was speechless, but he looked like he wanted to take his shirt off, too. His eyes danced from one 34D to the next.

"So, which bar are y'all going to?" I slipped out of my shorts and tossed those to him, too, then walked over to one of my walk-in (more like live-in) closets.

Ashton cleared his throat. "Ummm." I could feel his eyes on my ass cheeks. "The Power Trip, that new bar out in Columbia." He muttered, standing in the closet doorway, watching me bend over to get a shoe box that contained the new burgundy Burberry heels that I had just ordered.

I squatted down on the floor to remove the heels from the box, then slowly stood back up as I tried the shoes on to see how they looked. I stood there topless, in a burgundy thong and burgundy heels. I tossed my hair over my shoulders, looking at the full-length mirror in my closet. *Yup, these look good*, I thought as I kicked the shoes back off. I started going through my clothes to find my blue jean romper.

"Well, we're supposed to be going to Simons, that restaurant near the Harbor. They're really excited about this makeup line. We leave out tomorrow afternoon for New Orleans. We're going out to eat first, then maybe hit the club. The way my manager's wife and her friends party, shit, we'll probably be out all night. I'd ask you to come with me, but you already have plans." I looked up at Ashton. He wasn't paying my voice any attention. His eyes traced my entire body. I grinned as I went back to searching for my romper. "Do you like what you see, Ashton?"

Ashton scoffed. "Do I like what I see? Shit, I want what I see. Why you playin'?"

I grinned a little, as I found the outfit and removed it from the hanger. I threw it over my shoulder, then walked toward Ashton on my way out of the closet. He just stood there, standing in my way, looking down at me. "Ashton, are we done here? I really have to get ready to meet Golden, Serena, and them."

"Charlene, why won't you let me love you?" Ashton's light eyes looked my body over. "I can do it a hell of a lot better than these niggas you let up in you. These niggas ain't shit compared to me. They just wanna fuck you; I wanna take care of you."

I really wasn't in the mood to hear about some nigga telling me how much he'd love me and how much he could do for me. I'd heard enough from Jamie and the rest of the niggas. Jamie was a certified sweet-talker. He could get any woman to drop her panties with the quickness. I'd met my match when I met Jamie. He was driving me crazy. I was beginning to lose myself, and I hated it.

I rolled my eyes at Ashton, folding my arms, looking up into his face. "Don't you have somewhere to be, Ashton?"

Ashton unfolded my arms, pulling me closer to him by my hands. "I am where I'm supposed to be." He gently kissed my lips.

My body jumped. I tried pulling from him, but my heart pulled me in. Ashton surrounded me in his arms, lips sucking the life out of mine. "Ashton," I whispered in between kisses, "we're friends, best friends. We can't do—we can't do this."

"We're already doing it, Charlene." Ashton peeled his lips from mine.

"I don't wanna lose you. I don't wanna hurt you. I care about you too much." I whispered, looking up into his face, watching him lick my kiss from his lips. "You're all I got right now, and I can't lose you. I'm not the type of girl you need."

"You're everything I need. Your smile, your eyes, your thighs, your style, the way you talk, the way you walk, your personality—I want it all." Ashton kissed my forehead, my cheeks, my nose, my lips, my chin. Oh, he was so adorable.

"I can't lose you as my friend. I don't want this to change our status. Please don't let this change what we are." I begged him.

He ignored me. "You wanted to know if we've done this before, right? Let's see if it all comes back." He gripped my waist in his hands. Those hands, I remembered that touch. I remembered how his lips felt against mine. As he slid his hands around my ass, sliding his hands into my panties, I started to unbuckle his belt. We didn't have much time; we both had somewhere to be. He backed me up against the wall of the closet, sliding down my panties, lips sucking on my neck.

I wanted to see it; I had to see his dick as he lowered his pants, revealing his dark blue boxers. I slid his boxers down as his erection revealed itself to me. Ashton had the biggest got-damn dick I'd ever seen. Whoa, it sure had changed a lot in the last six years. It had gone from a polo sausage to a fuckin' Airwick air freshener can. Yeah, I damn sure had to be drunk or high or some shit to attempt to let him put that shit anywhere near me let alone up in me. My eyes widened as he lifted my body up, bracing me against the wall of the closet.

Ashton looked up into my face as I wrapped my legs around his waist. He watched the way my lips trembled and my eyes searching his face. "Nigga, are you serious?" was written all over my face. I braced myself.

"Charlene Campbell is finally scared of the dick, huh?" He grinned, biting his lip, looking up into my face. "You can take it. Don't be scared."

I gasped as Ashton eased his way in, one hand gripping my thigh, the other hand gripping my ass, digits in the crack of my ass. I screamed out as he shoved it as far as it would go. I grabbed onto him with all of my might, damn near passing out. My knees shook. I tightened my thighs. And the whole time he's stroking me, he's looking me in the face. And slowly but surely, whatever memory I had of whatever happened was coming back.

"Why can't I be the only one you give this to you, Charlene?" Ashton moaned, slipping a finger into my ass.

I remembered the smell of his cologne that night. I remember he was wearing a black baseball cap, a black and white long-sleeved Nike shirt, black baggy jeans, and black and white Nikes. Why did I remember all that if it hadn't happened? Why was it so vivid in my mind all of a sudden?

I gripped the back of his neck, screaming out, Ashton thrusting in and out of me. He backed me away from the wall a few inches until my shoulders were leaning against it. I wound my hips in slow circles, causing him to slow down a little so I could handle the dick. That nigga was hitting all the right spots. His dick knew exactly where my G-spot was; he didn't need any help.

My mind flashed to me giggling because Ashton was sucking on my nipples, giggling himself. I remember smelling the alcohol on his breath. I remember holding a plastic cup of red punch in my hands. I remember popping Drunk Gummy Bears.

"Charlene, I love you. Do you feel me?" He braced me back up against the way. "I said do you fuckin' feel me?" He thrust harder and a little faster.

"Yes!" I screamed out.

My mind flashed to Ashton playing in my pussy, rubbing my clit, kissing my inner pussy lips. I remember him smacking my ass, hitting it from the back. I remember being on my stomach, biting the pillow, begging him to stop.

My legs went limp around Ashton's waist, but he held my thighs, holding me up. I wrapped my arms around his shoulders as Ashton dug into me as fast as he could. It was the most intense quickie that I'd ever had. His dick caused temporary paralysis. The stimulation to my clitoris was amazing. I don't know how many times I came, but the orgasms came in multiples of three. Though it was meant as a moment of instant gratification, he made love to me. He held me, he stroked me, he looked at me, he saw me, and he loved me. Oh my goodness, he was confusing me, and y'all know I'm confused enough as it is.

I gripped his ass as he dug into me, dick tapping against my cervix, damn near bursting through it. Ashton buried his face in my neck as his dick grew thicker and harder. I knew it had been a while since he'd had sex from the amount of pressure I felt from his cum, as it spit out against my cervix at thirty miles per hour. His entire body shook up against mine. Though he'd come, his dick was still pretty firm, and I'm pretty sure he could have used a round two, but I couldn't take it.

He looked up into my face, and I looked down into his. He lowered my body a little, my breasts pressed against his shirt, my heart pounding against his chest. He wanted to do it again. I knew he wanted to call his boys and tell them to fuck that bar; he was fuckin' me that night.

He lowered me to the floor. My legs were wobbly. I braced my back up against the wall, panting, watching him pull up his boxers, then pull up his pants.

My pussy was calling his name. He was the fourth person that I'd had sex with that day, and it was the first time that I was ashamed of myself. I felt like such a slut, such a ho, such a freak. I had a different nigga every day of the week, and all he wanted was me. Our body chemistry fit like a hand in a glove. Our encounter was brief, but the way he held me, I wanted more. I wanted him. I needed my best friend.

"Ashton, baby, we did this before. I don't know when, but it happened." I whispered, watching him zip his pants then buckle his belt.

"I can't imagine when, Charlie." Ashton looked at me, "but you're right. It had to have happened. We went to so many parties. Maybe someone put some shit in our drink. Who knows? Let's just let it go and move on. It's happening now, and that's all I'm worried about."

My lips trembled. Boy, my heart was pounding. Things were going to change between us, I could just feel it.

Feelings were going to intertwine. He was going to get hurt if he thought I was going to all of a sudden be his girlfriend. "Ashton, just because this happened doesn't mean we're exclusive. You know that right? You know this doesn't mean that I'm your girlfriend, right?"

Ashton grinned, pulling me to him by my hips, "I'm gonna make you love me one way or another, Charlene, but I'm not stupid enough to think that this one moment means that you're my girl. It's gonna take more than this to get to you, and I know that. I'm not dumb."

I picked up my romper from the floor and covered myself with it. Suddenly, I was ashamed of myself. "Ashton," I looked up at him. "Can you come back over after you leave the bar?"

Ashton shook his head. "Naw, why don't you just cancel your plans and come to the bar tonight with me?" He held my hand, pulling my body up against his. "You're gonna be gone for a few weeks, and I wanna spend some time with you before you leave me."

I couldn't resist. I nodded, "Okay."

I woke up the next morning, lying next to Ashton. He lay sound asleep in his Polo Boxers. He had the prettiest feet I'd ever seen on a man. Do you know how many niggas I fucked who got completely naked but kept their socks on? Ashton and I made it back from the bar the night before. We started ripping each other's clothes off from the moment that we'd gotten in the door. He worked the shit out of my pussy, had me speaking in languages that I never knew that I even knew. His dick was something to get used to, I can say that much. His stroke was on point; he had to brace himself just to make sure he didn't rupture anything inside of me. Missionary and doggy style hurt like a muthafucka, but I loved it. Each ring inside of my vagina pulsated as that man entered me.

He fucked my pussy dry that night, and I sure as hell felt it that morning.

I couldn't shake the mystery of our past from my mind. I kept trying to remember a time in the past where we could have had sex. I had been to several of Misty's parties back in 2014 when Aaron and I were dating. The last party that I'd gone to was the night before we went to Miami for our dance retreat. I damn sure didn't remember taking any drugs that night. Come to think of it, I don't remember anything that happened at that party. All I remember was waking up the next morning at Dana's apartment, all packed and ready to go on our trip. Ashton told me to let it go, but I couldn't.

I looked over at Ashton. He looked so beautiful and so peaceful laying there asleep. I peeled myself from the sheets and got up from the bed. I grabbed his wife-beater, threw it on, then tip-toed out of the room. The help wasn't at work yet, and I was dead sure that Lilia was in her room asleep. I wanted a nice cup of coffee before jumping in the shower. And just when I strolled into the kitchen, there Jamie was, sitting on a stool at the island in the center of my kitchen. Dude was sitting there with a cup of got-damn juice and a plate of fruit, and the radio was playing next to him like he was at home or some shit.

I nearly jumped out of my skin. I was basically naked, no panties, no bra, just Ashton's tank top. I knew Jamie could see everything through my shirt.

He grinned, sitting there in a white T shirt and blue sweat shorts. He looked like he was on his way to the gym. "What's good, shawty? I see your nigga's car out there in the driveway."

I was still in shock, holding my hand over my heart. "How the fuck did you get in here?" I exclaimed.

"Oh, Lilia let me in a few minutes ago." Jamie smiled, grill gleaming. "She fixed me this plate of fruit, told me to make myself at home."

I rolled my eyes. "That bitch is about to get fired, I swear. What do you want, Jamie? I haven't seen you in a week, and you just decided to show the hell up out of the blue like I don't have a fuckin' life?"

"Oh, I can see you have a *fuckin'* life. You standing here naked and shit, and your dude's car is in the driveway." Jamie looked at me as I walked over and sat across from him at the Island. "Shawty, why you playin' with that boy like this?"

I rolled my eyes, really not feeling like hearing Jamie's worthless change. "What are you talking about, Jamie?"

"It's not a good idea to sleep with this dude. He's in love with you, and you're not in love with him." Jamie's eyes searched my face.

I looked at him. He wasn't talking to me like a jealous baby's daddy. He was talking to me like a friend. I sighed. "I know, Jamie. I tried to resist. I really did. But my heart . . . he needs me. He just lost Alisha. I'm trying to comfort him."

Jamie shook his head at me. "Well, you're going about it the wrong way, shawty. I'm sure he'd rather have your heart than your pussy, I'm just sayin'. But it's none of my business. So, I'll stay out of it."

"Yeah, bruh, you're right. It really is none of your business. But this is." I reached inside of the drawer and pulled out the contract that I fucked Kent into signing the day before, and I handed it to Jamie.

Jamie looked at me. Then started looking over the contract. You should have seen his eyes when he saw all those damn zeros. He put his fist to his mouth. "Damn, shawty!" He looked up at me.

"Before you get all excited, it's not final until Coach signs it, too." I watched Jamie read over it. "Not to mention I told Kent that you were signing with a record label this week. He thinks you're a money cow and that's the reason he's not letting you go. You need to sign with some record label. You have connections, fool, use 'em."

Jamie's eyes searched my face. I knew he wanted to ask me what I did to get Kent to agree to renegotiate his contract for that much. "The nigga was pissed at me a few days ago. Wanted to kill my ass. And now all of a sudden after he 'speaks' with you, he not only wants to keep me, but he wants to pay me almost ten times more than what he was paying me at first? The fuck did you do to the nigga, Charlie, to get him to agree to this?"

I shook my head. "Don't worry about all that. You just need to stay the fuck away from his wife and away from Coach's daughter. And like I said, you need to find a label to sign to."

Jamie shook his head at me, eyes searching my face. "Shawty, you didn't have to do this for me."

"Yes, I did, boo. You worked too hard to lose this opportunity." I crossed my legs, almost forgetting that I wasn't wearing any panties.

"*Good morning, everyone, rise and grind!*" Deejay Spinner chimed over the radio station that morning. "*Word has it that Kenya Love and the Dutchess of Crunk music, Anastasia P. Jones, are hosting auditions for the new play* Thug in Love! *They're looking for the male lead role! Stay tuned, because after the commercial break, we're gonna announce the address of the first auditions! Bruthas, you don't wanna miss this one! The lead female role is gonna be played by Baltimore's own Ne'Vaeh Washington-Whitehaven! That's right, li'l Ne'Vaeh just announced to the world that she was secretly married to Miami Heat's Aaron Whitehaven last year! More after the break!*"

Jamie looked at me, temples twitching. He was pissed, but I was thrilled.

My eyes widened. "Hell yeah!"

Jamie made a 'bitch, you crazy as fuck' face at me. "What? Hell *naw*! I ain't doin' that shit!" He got up from the stool.

I grabbed his arm, but he pulled from me. I sighed. "Jamie, I got you this phat-ass contract! You owe me this! I told this dude that you were a big money investment and that you were gonna bring him in a lot of revenue! Do you know what I had to do to get you this muthafuckin' contract? You have to do this!"

"Man, fuck this contract and whatever it is you did to get the nigga to write this shit! I ain't gonna do this!" Jamie was furious.

And I was starting to get heated. He was about to let his pride get in the way of his career. "Jamie, fuck your feelings right now, okay? This is the opportunity of a lifetime for you! Anastasia is all about the money, trust me. Please, baby, do this for your son. Do it for me. I did it for you!"

Jamie looked at me, his anger subsiding a little. "She– she won't wanna see me."

I looked at him. His heart wasn't prepared to see Ne'Vaeh, but he had to go. I wasn't going to tell him why, but he needed to go. "Baby, you need to go. This isn't about your feelings for her. This isn't about her feelings about you. This is about you saving your career. This is about you providing for yourself and your son."

Jamie was still reluctant to say he'd go. "I don't know, shawty. I don't know about rehearsals and shit. And having to read shit in front of muthafuckas. You know a nigga ain't good at that shit."

I looked at Jamie. And I knew what else was bothering him. Jamie wasn't a reader. Had to work mad over time to keep up with the rest of us in school. "Boo, you'll do fine.

You're not that much of a reader, but your memory has always been better than anyone's that I've ever known. I know one of the groupies who works for Anastasia will be glad to help you memorize those lines. Just go to the audition. What could it hurt? What harm could be done that hasn't already been done?"

Chapter 7: She Knows

Ne'Vaeh

"Mmmmm . . ." I sucked on Aaron's bottom lip that morning, running my fingers through his curls. I held onto him for a few seconds before he slid out of me. "I'm supposed to be working out this morning, Aaron."

"That was a workout." Aaron laughed, easing his way out of me. "Shit, you know I want another dose. But we gotta get goin', love." He got up, pulling me up along with him as I quickly grabbed my panties. There we were, making love on the floor, on my yoga mat.

Words can't even begin to describe how wonderful it felt being married to that man. But it wasn't easy. I didn't want to tell anyone, but Aaron, you know he wanted to tell everybody and their mama about us. I refused to have a wedding. I was okay with wearing a nice dress before a magistrate, but I just wanted Aaron. All that other superficial shit didn't matter. I'd seen tons of beautiful marriages that ended ugly. Aaron was all that mattered to me.

After he proposed to me, he went to Miami, and I went back to Atlanta ready to get back to work. After a few weeks of missing Aaron, I flew to Miami the day before my birthday, and he flew me back to Paris, where we were married. You should have seen his face the day that we were married. Watching him crying had me crying. Of course, every girl dreams of getting married in a beautiful white dress, in front of her family and friends. I would have loved to do that, but I wasn't about the drama. Aaron was everything I needed. And besides, the cheaper the wedding, shit, the more we had to spend on the honeymoon. We started our honeymoon in Paris. Then we flew to Jamaica. And then to Hawaii. I was floating on air, literally.

Months had gone by before we told Aaron's parents about us. It was my choice, not Aaron's. His mother was the first person he wanted to call. I didn't want to come between the two. I begged him not to tell her, but he told her anyway. You already know that his mother had the biggest issue with us being married. Before she could even get a word in, Aaron cursed her ass out. It was months before Aaron's father got her to speak to him. Though Aaron's father didn't approve of me at first, I think he was proud that his son finally stood up to his mother about the woman that he loved. Aaron loved me, and he didn't care who else didn't.

The next person I was forced to tell was the slave driver, Anastasia. When I tell you she was pissed . . . oh, yeah, she was pissed. You know she loved Aaron for coming to save me after my baby passed away, but her feelings for him soon changed when she realized that Aaron was all I was interested in those days. She just knew Aaron would get in the way of her making money. She knew that I'd spend every waking moment that I could with Aaron. And she was right. After sneaking off to Europe to get married, and after escaping to our honeymoon, I stayed in Miami with Aaron for about three weeks. I went to every basketball game, every sport's event, and every autograph signing with him. When those three weeks were over, I was reluctant to go back to Atlanta to face Anastasia. When I got home, Anastasia worked the shit out of me. From the moment that I got back from Florida, she had me in the studio. From the moment that I got home from the studio, she had her driver waiting to take me to play rehearsal. I'd gotten the part in the play before I even auditioned. They had me on the panel, helping them choose the other actor's in the play. So far, we had everyone we needed except for the leading male role.

And when I wasn't at play rehearsal, we were at photo shoots, shooting for my new videos, or making club appearances. But worst of all, I hated dance rehearsals. Dance rehearsals with Anastasia were the fuckin' worst. Why? Because she loved having her dance rehearsals at Crunk Shakers, the strip club she used to work at years ago. She thought I could learn a "thang" or two from those skanks. Man, I knew what the fat girls in the gym felt like watching all the skinny chicks work out. I was barely a size 3, wearing barely a 34B, maybe a C on a good day. These muthafuckin' strippers were from size 7 to size 14, with 34Ds or Fs, with asses and thighs out of this world. They had the perfect Coke-bottle figure. It was like I was in a got-damn world full of Charlene Campbells, and I hated it. I looked like a little boy compared to them, and they made sure they made me feel like it every time that I even attempted to twerk.

"Babe, we gotta shower. Don't you have to get to dance rehearsal?" Aaron pulled up his boxers, then held my hand, dragging me along with him toward the steps.

I whined. I sure as hell didn't feel like leaving him that day. I had spent damn near six months away from him. Basketball season had just ended in April, and I had just gotten my baby back. There were nights that I'd cry myself to sleep, missing him. I'd sneak off on the weekends to be with him in Miami every now and then. He'd be so happy, so surprised to see me each time. He held me each time like he was afraid to let me go. As soon as his season ended, he didn't go to training like a lot of players did; he was on the first flight to Atlanta. The next day, we were buying our first home together.

I didn't tell him that I had been in and out of the hospital a few times. Breathing was getting harder by the day, but it was manageable. I was taking all my medication, I was eating well, I made it to all of my appointments, but my heart still wasn't right. I felt physically and mentally broken. I was hoping that Aaron being with me for the next two months or so would be all that I needed to get my heartbeat back on track. Being without him was hell. I missed him. I needed him. We had just really gotten to know each other, and we needed to make up for years of lost time.

"Ugh, I don't feel like dealing with those bitches today, bae!" I moped, following him into the bathroom. "Aaron, you haven't seen these big booty Judy bitches at the club. You'll see today. They make me look like a little boy, I'm tellin' you. They have asses, hips, thighs, titties, and shit poppin' out everywhere!" I looked at Aaron, imagining those bitches poppin' their asses in front of him just to piss me off. "As a matter of fact, maybe you need to stay your ass here."

Aaron laughed out loud as he reached into the shower to turn the water on. "Heaven, you know I'm not even checkin' for that kinda trouble. You don't have to question where my attention is, you know that." He looked at me and grinned. Aaron searched my face before reaching for me, pulling me closer to him. "I'm loving this hair on you."

I looked at him, blushing a little. "Really? It's not too much?" Anastasia had her hair stylist put this long-ass, past-my-booty Brazilian weave in my hair. I mean, it was cute, but it wasn't mine.

"Naw, it's cute. I like it." Aaron gently kissed my lips. "C'mon, shorty, we gotta shower before we're late."

I sighed, getting into the shower. He was going to stop by my rehearsal for a little while and then he was off to a business meeting downtown. Even on his vacation, my baby was busy. I needed more time with him. Our brief encounters weren't enough. We played phone tag the entire time that he was away. Ashton even had a hard time trying to get up with him for Alisha's funeral as well. Aaron was a busy man. As much as he wanted me, he couldn't really give me the time that I needed. And it hurt. I needed him, more of him.

"No, no, no!" Anastasia shouted at me at dance rehearsals. "This is not the way I taught you this shit, Ne'Vaeh! Vinnie, start the record over. C'mon, boo, we got a show to do in four days, and you still can't get it right!" The deejay repeated 'Drankin' Patna' over the loudspeakers. "Jackie-O, 24-K, Deep Throated, Krystal, show her how we do this shit."

I sighed, rolling my eyes, embarrassed even, as I backed away and stood back against the mirrors of her dance studio down at Crunk Shakers. She was driving me hard as hell that day, and I knew it was because Aaron was there. He didn't like the way Anastasia was talking to me, but he kept his cool for that moment anyway. He sat on a stool, in the corner of the studio, watching. He'd seen enough strippers in his time. Anastasia's hoes were bad, but not bad enough to impress him. Aaron knew how uncomfortable they made me, which is why he stayed as long as he did. The fact that they made me feel insecure didn't rub him the right way. I really loved how our thoughts were always in sync.

Niggas were lined up at the door, drooling, watching those girls pop, twerk, and drop it. Like I told my girlfriend, Laysha, back at Howard University, I wasn't about that singing life. I tried to be, but it just wasn't me.

Anastasia promised me that no one would try and change me, but from the moment I stepped foot in Passion Productions, her image consultant was all over me. They changed my hair, changed my style of dress, changed the way I ate, changed the way I talked, even tried to change the way I laughed. They even had the nerve to suggest breast augmentation and muscle enhancer injections for my ass. Of course, when I told Aaron what they tried to do to me, he was pissed. He loves me just the way that I am and expected those muthafuckas to do the same.

I stood there, watching the girls gyrating. My heart beat hard in my chest, and sweat beads outlined my hairline. I felt lightheaded. The room started spinning under my feet. Aaron stood from his seat as he saw me slide from the wall and onto the floor. He made his way over to me as the Anastasia signaled the deejay to stop the music. She rushed over to me, but Aaron pushed her away. She placed her hands on her hips as Aaron helped me off the floor.

"Sweetie, are you okay?" Anastasia reached for my damp face.

Aaron pushed her away again, security moving closer. "Hell naw, she ain't okay! You been workin' her like a slave all muthafuckin' morning! How many times do you want her to do the same fuckin' dance? She did it fine the first ten times you made her do the shit!"

Anastasia was pissed, but she remained calm. "You need to lower your tone. This is the way we've been doing this shit since she moved here." She watched as Aaron unstrapped my heels, sliding them off of my feet. "She just needs some water. Someone get Ne'Vaeh some water!"

Aaron stood back up, getting in Anastasia's face. "She doesn't need no muthafuckin' water, yo! She needs to go home and get some rest! This is your husband's cousin, your family, and you're workin' the shit outta her like she's not sick, like she doesn't have a heart condition, like she didn't almost fuckin' die last year!"

Anastasia laughed to herself, her girls standing behind her, about to cosign and add to the drama. "Dude, you gettin' loud with the wrong one. You need to stay in your lane. This is my fuckin' territory, nigga, so respect it."

Aaron looked at her, temples twitching, before helping me up from the floor. "Well, this is my wife, and you need to respect her. I'm all about her, and you're all about yours, Anastasia! You don't give a fuck about her. I'm taking her home." Aaron's phone was going off on his hip.

I looked at him, my eyes growing weary.

"Yo, your phone's ringin' off the hook, shawty. Don't you have some meeting you have to attend to, my nigga?" Jackie-O rolled her neck and her eyes at Aaron. "We got Twinkie. She'll be a'ight."

I looked at her. 'Twinkie' was the nickname they gave me because they said that's what I needed to eat in order to gain some weight, to get a booty like theirs, to look as fly as they did. I hated all of their skinny jokes. I felt so out of place in Anastasia's world.

I looked at Aaron. I was feeling pretty bad. I needed Aaron, and he needed to go. His business meeting was pretty important. Little did I know, Aaron's mother's family owned several diamond mines in the South Africa. Ella's father decided to sign Aaron on as a partner in their family business. He was the oldest of fifteen grandchildren. Aaron never really told me how rich his family was. He didn't like to talk about a family that he hardly knew. Ella was happy when she found out that her father wanted her son to join the family business. Of course, Aaron couldn't care less, but I told him that he needed to get to know his mother's side of the family. I didn't have much respect for his mother, but she was his mother. And you only get one, no matter how fucked up in the head she is.

Aaron looked at me. "You need to get to the hospital."

"And you need to go meet your grandfather's attorney. You promised your mother you'd meet him." I held onto his arm, gripping his shirt in my hands. "I'll be fine. Just go."

"We'll get her to the hospital. Aye, Kalvin, come get Twinkie and put her in the car." Anastasia signaled Kalvin, the biggest security guard in the room to come and get me.

Aaron made an irritated face, then swooped me up in his arms, and I put my arms around his neck. "I got her, shorty." Aaron snapped. "I got my wife. And y'all need to quit callin' her fuckin' Twinkie, yo. Where's the car?"

Aaron carried me out to Anastasia's stretch Hummer, and carefully sat me inside. He handed my jacket, purse, and shoes to me. His eyes searched my face. He didn't want to leave me. His phone kept vibrating on his hip.

Anastasia and a few of her dancers got in the limo on the opposite side.

"Are you gonna be okay, Heaven? You know I don't wanna leave you." Aaron held my face in his hands.

I nodded, looking up into his face. "I'll be fine. I'm probably just dehydrated. Talk to you later, bae."

Aaron gently kissed my lips. "Call me when you get to the hospital. As soon as you get to the hospital. I'm for real, Heaven."

I watched Aaron hop out of the Hummer and stand alongside the limo as the driver closed my door. I waved good-bye to bae as the driver left the parking lot.

I was silent on the way to the hospital. I didn't have too much to say to Anastasia. She was showing her ass around Aaron, and it was really getting on my got-damn nerves.

"That nigga of yours, Heaven, he needs to stay in his place." Anastasia finally said.

I looked at her, feeling like I was back in Maryland with Renée again. Renée was a story all by herself. She wasn't Aaron's biggest fan. She was pissed more than anyone when she found out that we were married and that I didn't share that news with her.

"Stay in his place?" I scoffed.

"Yes, in his muthafuckin' place. He may be the king of your castle, honey, but at Passion Productions, I'm the queen. I call the shots. I don't tell him how to dribble out there on the court, so he can't tell me how to dance, something I've been doing a lot longer than he's been playing ball. He comes up in my spot again talkin' shit, and his ass is gonna get laid the fuck out. You need to tame your nigga before I do." Anastasia popped open a bottle of champagne. I was on the way to the got-damn hospital, and that bitch was poppin' bottles. Oh, she was pissed at me.

"Okay, let's be real. Let's be honest with one another." I turned to her. "Let's just put it all out there in the air, so there's no misunderstanding. You don't like my husband, do you? Just say the shit instead of throwin' all of this shade toward him!"

"No, I don't like the muthafucka." Anastasia poured her girl 24-K a glass. "Now, it was one thing when he came to rescue you from your depression, but it's another thing when he tries to come in my territory and change the way that I run thangs. At least that nigga Jamie let you do you. Aaron doesn't want you to do shit but sit home and be a fuckin' trophy wife."

I couldn't believe her. "Are you serious?"

"Yes, I am. With Jamie, you were strong, you were independent, and you had your guards up." Anastasia shook her head at me.

"That's because I couldn't trust the muthafucka!" I exclaimed.

"Well, at least you were doing you! With Aaron, you completely let your guards down. He takes you off your game. He makes you content. He makes you not wanna do shit but sit around him. You lost that spirit you had when you first came to Atlanta." Anastasia poured herself a glass.

"That spirit, Anastasia, was anger. I was angry all the muthafuckin' time! Yeah, anger makes for good music, but anger ruins your heart! I should know; I've been angry all my life! Aaron makes me happy! And if that's weak to you, then fuck you, okay?" I sat back in my seat, heart racing. "As a matter of fact, fuck all y'all!"

Anastasia and her dancers looked at me like I lost my mind.

"Okay," Anastasia lowered her glass, "I'll give you that one because you're on your way to the hospital. Don't start feelin' froggy just because your man is around, sweetie. Cuz if you wanna jump, you know I stay ready."

I sighed. "Anna, I love you, you're my family, but you're just like Renée, shit maybe even worse! Even she tried to look after my heart; you work me until I can barely feel my feet! You love money, and I get it. Money runs your life, but it doesn't run mine. I came from shit; more than anything, all I want is love. I thought you'd be able to relate to that! I wanna be around people who care about me and value my opinion. Aaron does that. Aaron wants what's best for me!"

Anastasia took a long sip from her glass, then looked at me, her brown eyes sparkling. "Well, what is that you want?"

I shook my head at her. "I want him. I've waited for him for so long, and I'm not gonna lose that boy. I left Maryland to leave the stress behind, and you just keep

building on more! If you really want me to do this, you're
gonna have to ease up. I can't hang with these strippers.
Shit, I'm not a stripper, and you can't turn me into one!
I'm Ne'Vaeh, take me as I am or take nothing at all,
Anastasia!"

Anastasia nodded. It was the first time that I'd spoken
up for myself to her. She was pissed that I disrespected
her in front of her people, but she understood.

Anastasia had her bodyguard carry me into the hospital. We all sat in the ER waiting room. You should have
seen the stares that the dancers were getting, all dressed
in crop tops, booty shorts, and heels. I had covered up
with my jacket, holding my heels in my hands. I refused
to let Anastasia and her dancers into the triage with me.
I told them it was fine if they left for a while, and I'd call
them when I was ready. Fortunately, my doctor was on
call, and we didn't have to wait too long for her to show
up to the hospital.

Dr. Leyland sat on a stool at the edge of my bed,
looking over the results of the lab work that came back.
She looked at me from over her Chanel glasses and
grinned. "How are you doing today, Mrs. Washington-
Whitehaven?"

I slightly grinned. "A little worn out."

"Girl, I told you what you were getting yourself into
last year when you told me you were signed under that
girl's label, but you wouldn't listen to me," Dr. Leyland
sighed, shaking her head at me. Dr. Leyland had to be
about twenty-six years old. She was married with three
kids. She couldn't have had a life because she worked
all the damn time. She was pretty with perfect teeth and
perfect skin. She barely wore her white coat, coming up
in the hospital dressed in skin-tight dresses and stilettos.
I'd see her flirting with the same handsome doctor just
about every time I saw her in the hospital. I even saw

her with that man on several occasions at the mall. She was definitely having an affair with that doctor, who also worked in her department, but I wasn't going to judge her. Though it was hard not to because she reminded me a lot of Charlie.

Dr. Leyland looked at me. "Sweetie, you're gonna have to slow down, and it's more important now than ever."

I looked at her. "Why?"

She grinned, "Because you're pregnant."

My eyes widened, and my heart immediately started skipping beats. Everything she said at that moment was tuned out by the sound of my heart beating in my chest. I was still mourning over the loss of little Sara. I couldn't take losing another baby. I was having Aaron's baby, and I should have been happy, but I was horrified.

"Ne'Vaeh, are you listening to me?" Dr. Leyland shook my arm.

I looked at her, my whole body going limp. "Dr. Leyland, I can't do this again. I just lost Sara, you know how difficult this is for me!"

Dr. Leyland held both of my hands, looking into my face. "Ne'Vaeh, you are a fighter. You have been through a lot this past year and a half. I'm not going to pretend that it's going to be easy, because it's not. But with some rest and maintaining a good diet, I believe you can do this." She let go of my hands, getting up from the stool. She went over to the counter to pick up her phone. "Now, let me find Dr. Uma's number. She is an awesome obstetrician who specializes in high-risk pregnancies. We will both help you get you through this." She searched her phone for the number.

I sighed, shaking my head to myself. "Anastasia works the fuck out of me, Dr. Leyland! How the hell am I gonna tell her this?"

Dr. Leyland looked at me, making a 'fuck that bitch' face. "Ne'Vaeh, sweetie, you have to give your body a rest. The play stuff might not be too detrimental to your health or the health of this baby, but you're gonna have to chill out on that international tour that Anastasia plans on dragging you into. Dancing, singing, and traveling aren't in your best interest. You and Aaron Whitehaven live very busy lives, but you're gonna have to slow down. Tell him about the baby and tell him about it now because you need him now more than ever. You don't need to do this alone. This is going to be a long nine months, sweetie. You're going to need all of the support that you can get." Dr. Leyland watched the tears begin to slide down my cheeks.

"Damn," I whispered to myself.

I didn't call Aaron, and he'd been blowing my phone up from the moment that I stepped foot in the hospital. I wanted to shout from the highest mountain tops that I was having his baby, but it hurt at the same time. I was afraid of losing the baby. Everything that I loved, I always lost. I called Anastasia as soon as Dr. Leyland signed the discharge paperwork. Anastasia was already at play auditions and sent 24-K back to get me.

24-K was the black light-skinned version of Pippy Longstocking. She had a honey-beige complexion with red hair and freckles. She was thick in all the right places and danced just as good as Anastasia. She worshipped the ground that my cousin's wife walked on. Kind of reminded me of how the dance squad used to follow Alisha's every move back in high school.

I didn't say much as we drove to the auditions in 24-K's black and chrome Jaguar. She glanced at me, looking out the window. "Twinkie, she doesn't mean to be so hard on you. You do know that, right?" 24-K spoke over my thoughts of Aaron.

I looked at her. "What?" I had heard her, I just couldn't believe she had the nerve to actually try to have a conversation with me. 24-K was one of the biggest haters in the crew. She really couldn't stand the fact that Anastasia was taking a chance on me. Cousin Darryl had to put her in her place on several occasions.

"Anastasia wouldn't push you so hard if she didn't believe in you. She knows you can't dance like us. The crowd she rolls with likes them teasers, girl, that's why she's just trying to bring out the sexy in you. Sex sells. No matter how pretty you are, boo, sex sells." 24-K looked straight ahead, fiery red hair blowing in the wind behind her.

I rolled my eyes. "So, who do we have for these auditions? Not really trying to be here all day; I have shit to do. And Aaron has been texting me for the past three hours."

24-K grinned to herself. "Oh, you'll see."

I looked at her, getting a horrible feeling in the pit of my stomach.

"Oh my muthafuckin' goodness, these niggas are awful!" Anastasia whispered to me at the judge's table that afternoon down at Passion Productions. She looked up at the young man on stage before us, who was trying his hardest to impress her. Everyone in Atlanta looked up to Anastasia. "Sweety, ummm, we have your information. We'll be in touch. Next!" Anastasia flashed the boy a fake smile.

The young boy, who had to be about seventeen, sighed, then walked off stage.

"Please scratch his name off my muthafuckin' list, OMG!" Kenya Love exclaimed, not even waiting for the boy to make it all the way off of the stage.

Kenya's assistant, Sandra, scratched the boy's name off of the list.

Kenya Love was one of the biggest black playwrights in the country. She had started to produce movies, and not to mention was about to have her own television station. She was big, and she wanted to work with me, someone who hadn't even been on the scene for a year. "Please tell me that we have someone else coming, P. Jones, cuz this line up you have coming up in here ain't hittin' on shit but my nerves!"

"Oh, my dude will be here, trust." Anastasia grinned.

I looked at her. By that grin on her face, I wasn't even about to ask what she had up her sleeve. I figured it must have been one of Kenya's ex-boyfriends. Anastasia was real messy. The more I got to know her over that year and a half, the more she reminded me of the chicks who I ran away from in Maryland.

Anastasia looked at me texting on my phone. She saw that I wasn't into any of the people who'd walked through that door in the last hour. I'd finally decided to text Aaron. He wanted to meet me for dinner at 6:30, and it was already 4:00.

"You okay, cuz? You still mad at me from earlier?" Anastasia asked.

I looked into her pretty face.

She poked her lip out, making the cutest pouty face.

"You're too pretty to be such a bitch." I rolled my eyes.

"Well, you can call me anything, just don't call me broke." She rolled her eyes back. "So, what did the doctor say?"

"That I need to slow down. That I won't be able to go on tour with you." I started to explain, but she cut me off, waving her finger at me as soon as I mentioned not being able to go on tour with her.

"What? Do you know how much we have invested in this tour? You're the main attraction, boo! How you not gonna be there? The entire theme is you!" Anastasia rolled her eyes at the big-boned dude who stood before her. "What'cha gonna sing, Mr. T? Can you even sing? Please don't waste my time."

The plump older gentleman, who was dressed very nicely, opened his mouth to sing. And before he could even get a tune out, a familiar voice was singing over our shoulders.

"Maybe this decision was a mistake. You probably don't care what I have to say." It was a voice I hadn't heard since the day I left Maryland.

My heart pounded in my chest at the sound of his voice, and I was afraid to turn around. Anastasia, Kenya, and Sandra turned around, all smiling from ear to ear. I could see all of the chicks around us jumping the fuck up and down, fanning themselves as he sang.

"I just wondered do you ever think of me anymore. Do you?" Jamie knew exactly which song would appeal to my emotions. What song by Ne-Yo doesn't leave your heart feeling some type of way?

I rose in my chair, slowly turning around to see Jamie walking down the aisle, looking like he just stepped off the set of a rap video.

I looked at Anastasia. Oh, I could've wrung her neck.

Anastasia winked at me. "Let the show begin."

Chapter 8: Money OverEverything

Ne'Vaeh

"Hell no, Anastasia!" I paced back and forth across Anastasia's office.

Anastasia sighed, sitting on top of her desk, dressed in a tight, green romper and matching green stilettos. Her hair was pulled up into a bun, long bangs swooped to the side. "Calm down, Ne'Vaeh! This is an awesome idea! He is perfect for this part!"

I looked at her, frowning, furious. "And you knew all day that he was coming? And your ass couldn't even tell me?"

"Well, actually, he called me last week on Tuesday," Anastasia cut me off. "And before you curse me out, he asked me not to tell you."

My eyes grew wider, "He asked you not to—" I stopped because I should have known she wouldn't do anything that Jamie asked her not to do. She had a weakness for them thug types, though she'd never admit it out loud. I was so disappointed in her total disregard for my feelings about Jamie. I had to say something about it. "Anastasia, you watched me cry over this muthafucka for damn near ten months! I almost died giving birth to his dead baby, and you wanna throw this shit back in my face by letting this dude try out for this play? How could you?" I exclaimed.

Anastasia shook her head at me. "Sweetie, you need to face him. You need to tell him about what happened. You have to! It was his baby, too! And don't go throwing that shit in my face when you came here, knowing you were pregnant and still decided not to tell me! If I would have known, your ass would still be in Maryland with that muthafucka! Not here, married to Aaron's high-yellow ass!"

I looked at her. Everything that Aaron was saying about her was starting to make sense. Everything was about money. Feelings didn't exist in her world. I almost never saw my cousin, Darryl. He stayed on the road. His life was his business and vice versa, when his life should have been about her. I knew she missed him, which was why she drove us so hard. He wasn't around, so she could care less if any of us had our loves around either.

Anastasia sighed, opening up a pack of Orbit gum, popping a piece in her mouth. "You need to talk to this nigga, seriously. You can't run from him forever. I knew you'd never confront him; this was the only way."

"Jamie is only doing this shit to hurt me! He hates reading in front of people!" I exclaimed.

"Shit, trust me, I'll find someone to help him rehearse his lines a *thousand* muthafuckin' lines if he needs to!" Anastasia laughed out loud, watching me roll my eyes. "You already know finding him the help he needs will *not* be a problem."

"Ummm, Mrs. Jones-Allan?" Anastasia's shy secretary, Lucy, tapped lightly on Anastasia's office door. "Kenya Love and Jamie Green, right this way."

I sighed, folding my arms, facing Kenya and Jamie as they walked through the door.

Anastasia smiled brightly, walking over to Jamie, shaking his hand, "Hey, boo, long time no see. You know Ne'Vaeh, don't you?"

"Aaron?" I called, walking through the front door of our new home that evening. Most of the boxes, which had been sitting in the living room, had already been unpacked. It smelled so good in the house, like cheese, pasta sauce, and chicken. The house was dimly lit by a few candles. The curtains were pulled back on the sliding doors that lead to our backyard. I saw candles, wine glasses, and a bottle of wine sitting out on the patio table. I grinned a little as I walked through the house and toward the kitchen. There my baby was, in a wife beater and sweats, looking so good. He grinned when he saw me.

"I thought we were going out to eat?" I smiled, putting my purse and jacket on the countertop.

"Why we gotta go out to eat when you got a nigga that can cook?" Aaron grinned, holding out his hand for me to come to him.

I walked right into his arms, pressing my face against his chest. He smelled so good. I loved the feel of that boy. Everything about him felt so good. I was so lucky to have him, and my own family was trying to drive us apart.

Aaron kissed my forehead. "What happened at the doctor? You alright, babe?"

I looked up into his face, shaking my head. "I may not be able to go on this tour. The doctor says I need to slow down. The play might be okay, but I'm not so sure that I wanna do it. So, what happened with your grandfather's lawyer?" I was trying to change the subject, and Aaron noticed.

He looked down into my face. "My grandfather wants to me to fly out to Senegal next month to meet him. He's sick. He wants me to take over Brightstone, his diamond mining company. I don't know the first thing about the business, so he wants me to meet a couple of his nephews. I'm not gonna have time for this shit. I don't even wanna be a part of this shit, but my mom wants me to do it. Taking over the company gives her control over her family, and you know she's a control freak. Dealing with this company is just gonna mean more time that I'm gonna be away from you."

I looked up in his face, unwrapping my arms from around him. "Why doesn't this surprise me?" I muttered.

"So, did you talk to your cousin's wife about you not going on this tour with her?" Aaron watched me get frustrated, rolling my eyes to myself. Aaron grabbed my hand, leading me out of the kitchen into the living room. He sat me down in the chair, then he started removing my tennis shoes, and then each sock.

I sighed as Aaron's warm hands rubbed my feet and ankles. "Yeah, I talked to her. She ain't even trying to hear it. She also took it upon herself to hire someone for the lead male role, despite the auditions that we'd been holding these past few weeks. She's always doing crazy shit, ugh!"

Aaron's eyes searched my face. "Who'd she pick?"

"Please don't trip." I exhaled deeply, bracing myself for the impact of Aaron's anger. "Jamie."

Aaron immediately stood from the couch. "The fuck?"

I sighed as Aaron made his way back to the kitchen where my purse was. I hopped up from the couch and rushed over to him. I knew he was about to get my iPhone and call Anastasia to curse her the fuck out. "Aaron, baby, don't, please!"

"Don't what?" Aaron exclaimed. "Fuck her! I told you, she's all about money! Having this dude in this play will have bitches lined up and down the street trying to get in to see this play! She doesn't give a fuck that the nigga left you in the hospital to die having his baby! She doesn't care that hearing that muthafucka's name still—" Aaron stopped talking when he saw me fighting back the tears. He grabbed me to him, surrounding me in his arms. "Baby, I'm sorry."

I buried my face in his chest, "Ugh, how could she do this to me? I don't know how I'm gonna do this. I really don't wanna see him, Aaron. Seeing him still hurts a little."

"Naw, it hurts a lot," Aaron whispered, knowing my heart.

I sighed, turned my head to the side, laying my head against his chest. "Yeah, it does. I know I should have told him about the baby, but I didn't want to talk about something that I couldn't change. "Anastasia says I need to move on. She says I need to just get over the past and focus toward my future."

Aaron held me tight against his chest, chin resting on the top of my head. "She doesn't care that you haven't healed from losing his baby. She's wrong, shorty. I'm pissed, I'm not even gonna lie, but I'm gonna play it cool until the muthafucka crosses the line. You know he's gonna try, and I'm gonna be there waiting when he does."

When I tell you that Aaron was at every rehearsal, he was at every rehearsal. There were several business trips that Aaron canceled just to stay with me in ATL. I'll admit, I was loving having him around, but I hated the fact that he was only sticking around because he felt threatened by Jamie's presence. I'm not going to pretend that it was easy to be in the same room as Jamie, because it wasn't. If it wasn't a line from the play, Jamie and I didn't say a word to one another.

The play was about a record producer, Katrina, who falls in love with the rapper that she manages, Cooper. Cooper came straight out of the streets of Compton to New York City. He escaped the gang life when he was discovered at a rap battle by Katrina. The play was supposed to have a lot of sex scenes, touching, kissing, fondling, but whenever the scenes were supposed to get steamy, I asked Kenya if she could have them close the curtain. Jamie felt the tension, and he tried to spark conversation from time to time, but I'd just roll my eyes and walk away. Whenever he'd get too close, Aaron was already on it, waiting for Jamie's smooth-talking ass to say something inappropriate. It was coming; it had only been a few weeks.

"Okay, ladies and gentleman," Anastasia stood in the center of the actors and actresses in Kenya's play, "Our first show is on July first—just two weeks. Our first show is here in ATL, and then we're off to Charlotte, then to Richmond, then the D.C., then Baltimore, then Manhattan, and so on and so on. We got a busy tour schedule, y'all. You all have been working extra hard, and you have done a phenomenal job. And must I say, the chemistry between Katrina and Cooper is awesome!" Anastasia winked at me.

I rolled my eyes at her, lightly clapping along with everyone else. I wasn't feeling all that well, and it was getting harder and harder to keep food down. Two weeks had gone by since I found out that I was pregnant. It was the second week in June. At my prenatal visit, I found out that I was just under eight weeks pregnant, and that my due date was January 13, 2017. I was trying my hardest not to get excited and tell Aaron. He was too busy watching Jamie watching me to notice that I'd been eating my ass off, snacking on shit all day to keep from being nauseous.

"Okay, I was gonna save this until after the documentation was notarized, but I think we should tell everyone the good news. This morning, at nine a.m., I met with my co-producers, and we signed Jamie Green onto Passion Productions sub-label, Swagga Kings. Give it up for Jamie Green, y'all, and welcome him to the family!" Anastasia whooped and whistled.

My eyes widened. I looked over at Aaron, who was sitting in the first row, leaned back in his seat, calm and cool. His temples twitched, but he was still calm. He planned on going to play some ball with these other basketball players that were home for their hiatus, but after hearing that bit of information, oh, I'm sure he was making plans with me that night.

Everyone loved Jamie. Groupies showed up to our rehearsals to see him. Shit, we were crowded damn near beyond capacity, and it wasn't even the real thing. The sound of Jamie's voice tickled every female's heart in the room. I'm not gonna lie; it was hard as hell getting through the love scenes with him. The sight of him, the sound of his voice, shit, even his smell still drove my heart wild. He knew he looked good as a muthafucka. I would have to go home every night and make love to Aaron for hours to keep from thinking about Jamie. Jamie's voice drove my heart crazy, but Aaron had the moves. He could dance his ass off, so you know his dick game was on point. Not saying Jamie couldn't put it down, but Aaron catered to my body in every way. Sure Jamie could lay the pipe, but Aaron could work his tongue, his lips, his dick, his hands, his fingers. Aaron touched me in ways that I can't even explain. When Aaron held me, I felt at home, where I was supposed to be. Being around Jamie only reminded me of the things that I hated about life.

"Y'all going out to the club with us tonight?" Jackie-O strolled past us, as I walked hand in hand with Aaron to our car.

I sighed. "Naw, Jackie, I gotta go home and go over this song that Anastasia gave me. Every time I turn around, she's got me coming up with melodies."

Jackie-O smiled, her diamond grill gleaming under the street lights. "Oh, you're talking about 'Love Spell,' your duet with Jamie? Oh, that single is gonna be hot when it drops, fo' sho'!"

Aaron and I both looked at her.

"Duet with Jamie? What?" I asked.

"See ya tomorrow at rehearsal, girl! I gotta get ready for this party tonight at Club Dip!" Jackie-O hurried off to her car.

I looked at Aaron, who was already shaking his head to himself.

"This bitch," he muttered to himself.

I'll admit, he was doing a really good job those two weeks keeping his cool, considering. As long as Jamie and I kept it straight business, Aaron was cool. As soon as Jamie tried to ask anything that didn't have to do with the play (I'm talking about anything as simple as "Shawty, can I borrow your pen?" or even "Shawty, what time is it?"), Aaron cut that conversation off where it started. I knew Aaron was feeling all types of pissed at the fact that Anastasia was trying her best to get me to talk to Jamie.

We got to his brand new Cadillac. It was clean, sharp, pretty, and white gold, just like him. I loved it. He opened the door for me, I slipped inside, and he closed the door behind me.

I sighed, watching him walk with an attitude, muttering to himself. He got in the car, cranked the engine, and then just sat there for a minute. I looked at him, eyes tracing his profile.

"Ummm, my cousin, Malik wants me to meet him in Senegal on Wednesday. He's gotta show me the family business, and we have to meet in person to sign some paperwork." Aaron didn't look at me; he just looked straight forward.

I looked at him, shrinking back in my chair. "And you're just now telling me this because?"

"I didn't tell you until now because I wasn't gonna go until next week, but I think I should roll out now so I can get back in time for your first show. You have a concert in a few days anyway, you're not gonna have time for me. Shit, you barely have time for me as it is. I only get to see you at your rehearsals, shorty. By the time you get home, you're too exhausted to spend any real time with me. Sure, we make love, but that's it. Baby, I'm not complaining about the sex. Shit, the sex is out of this world, but I want to spend some quality time with my wife outside of the bedroom and outside of business. I wanna get to know you. And my idea of getting to know you isn't seeing you with him." Aaron looked at me, his emeralds searching my face.

I just looked at him, not sure what to say. I wanted to curse him out, telling him that the only reason he stayed in town so long, canceling all of his important business meetings was because of "him." But I kept my mouth shut because Aaron was already heated enough as it was.

"I don't like this shit at all. Every time this nigga is around or anytime you're even thinking about this dude, I don't exist. I wasn't shit for years because of him, Heaven. I ain't trying to go back to that. Don't let your cousin's wife push me back to that shit, shorty. I'm tellin' you, if this dude tries me, I'm going to jail, yo." Aaron shook his head, putting the car in gear.

"Aaron," I called out to him. He didn't want to even look at me. I grabbed his hand, "Aaron, look at me."

Aaron looked at me, eyebrows knitted together.

"Baby, this is your ring on my finger," I assured him. "I told you last year when you asked me to marry you that I'd quit this music shit if you wanted me to, and you told me to stick with it. Do you want me to quit?"

Aaron shook his head. "Naw, I'm not sayin' that you have to quit." He sighed. "I don't know what I'm sayin', really. All I know is dude missed out. He's here to try to get you back; he's just waiting for the right moment. I'm not sayin' I don't trust you, because I do; I just don't trust that muthafucka. I have plans for us, Heaven, and you're letting Anastasia's goals ruin that shit. I'm proud of you, don't get me wrong, but you have to let her know that enough is enough. And when I want my time with you, she needs to give it to me. Play or no play, tour or no tour, at the end of July, I wanna take you to England to meet some of my father's family members. And you need to let shorty know that shit, too. She can't keep you from me."

I watched Aaron board his plane on Wednesday. I didn't want to see my baby leave me. You know he didn't want to leave me, let alone leave me with Jamie's ass, but he did. It hurt Aaron to see me with Jamie, and it hurt me to see Aaron hurting because of him. Aaron was signing on to a business that could have our family set for all the generations that followed us. Aaron wanted to take care of me in every way possible. My heart had a hard time convincing my mind that what was going on in my life was real. That Aaron was real. That the life he wanted for us was real. I guess that's why I had a hard time walking away from Passion Productions. I'd been taking care of myself for so long that I'd gotten used to the fact that all I had was me.

I decided to drown myself in my music while he was away. I sat alone, in my tank top and sweats, in Passion Productions lavish studio. It was around 11:30 that night, and I hadn't heard a word from Aaron. I had been inspired to write a song about Aaron for so long, and Anastasia was giving me the chance to do that. I had enough material in me to write an entire album about that boy if she let me.

I sat at the expensive equipment, just playing around with a few beats. All I could think of was the sound of Aaron's heart when I laid my head against his chest, hugging him good-bye that morning. The sound of him panting in my ear when he was on top of me, giving me the best that he had. The sound of pots clanging in the kitchen when he cooked for me almost every night. Aaron was the sweetest man I'd ever met, and I felt like I was losing him.

"Aye," Anastasia poked her head in the studio. Her hair was so pretty, long, wavy, and thick. She was dressed to kill in a sexy, black lace mini-dress and heels. "You're not headed out with us, Twinkie?"

I looked at her, shaking my head.

"Oh, I love that combination of beats." Anastasia grinned, walking into the studio. "What'cha doin'?"

"Working on that album I was talkin' to you about earlier," I responded as she sat down in a chair next to me. "I even have a title for the first single and the title of the album—'White Gold'."

Anastasia shook her head at me, grinning from ear to ear. "That bright-ass boy is everything to you, huh?"

I nodded, "Yes, he is. You already know what it is, Anna."

Anastasia laughed to herself. "I'm proud of your nigga, to tell you the truth. I know he wants to knock Jamie's head off every time he sees him singing to you during rehearsal. That has to be hard on any man, watching some other nigga—a sexy, singin'-ass nigga—sing to his wife. And Jamie is doing so great with his lines, not missing a fuckin' *word*. His memory is amazing. He doesn't let dyslexia hold him back. I love his drive, his ambition, his ability to never give up, no matter how hard shit gets. He's amazing."

I looked at her. I really wasn't in the mood for her rubbing-salt-in-your-wounds ass that night. "I'm really busy here, Anna. I can't go back and forth with you tonight about pointless shit. You want me to put in work, and I'm doin' it, so if you don't mind, sweetie, I got shit to do."

Anastasia laughed a little. "Okay, boo, my bad."

"Thank you." I turned back to the equipment. "I'll probably be recording all night. I have too much on my mind, and not enough hands to write. I'm just gonna freestyle, and see how it works."

"Well, call me if you need anything. I have plenty of producers waiting by the phone if you need 'em." Anastasia watched me turn a few knobs, and flip a few switches. "You're right about me, just a little."

"Right about what?" I asked.

"I am jealous of you," she whispered. "Just a little."

I looked up at her.

Anastasia shrugged, her big round brown eyes sparkling. "Darryl used to love me like that boy loves you. I'm not saying that Darryl doesn't love me anymore, but he doesn't have the time to love me like he used to. I put my mind into my music, into my dancers, into this play, this world wide tour, into you, so that I don't kill myself thinking about him and why he's not here with me. I miss him like crazy. I lose so much sleep because he's not here with me. Don't lose yourself in anybody, Ne'Vaeh. You're Aaron's little piece of Heaven now, but once he drowns himself into this diamond business, into basketball, into his fame, let's see if his love for you still remains the same." Anastasia got up from the chair.

I watched her as she left the room. And I sighed. I had to rethink everything in my life. When Aaron asked me to marry him, I jumped at the chance. He was wonderful. I had no business getting back involved with Jamie once I saw the type of lifestyle that he was living. My heart was so confused at the time. I wanted someone to love me, and I thought that he did. Being with him again helped flush out the fact that I could never be with Jamie. Everyone was right about Aaron—yes, he should have stepped to me in high school, but the fact that he came for me when Jamie didn't was the reason why I couldn't turn him down when he asked me to marry him. He nursed me back to life. When he walked in my bedroom at Anastasia's house that day, he made my heart beat again. The same way he did the first day that I saw him, walking into Mr. Porter's African American history class.

I stayed in that studio working until damn near four in the morning. I recorded five songs that night about Aaron. And just when I hit the last note to the last song that morning, Jamie walked into the studio. My heart raced in my chest as I removed the head phones from my ears. I slowly walked out of the sound-proof room.

Jamie smiled up at me, sitting down in the leather chair as I came into the room, stopping in the doorway. He was dressed in all black (including the black diamond and gold chain around his neck), looking like he just came from the club. "What's up, shawty?"

I folded my arms, trying to keep my cool. I leaned against the doorway. "What are you doing here?"

"I just left the club with your people. They're still out partying hard. I just wanna show you what I wrote to go with that song, 'Love Spell,' that P. Jones wrote for us. You know reading isn't one of my strong points, but I got this shit memorized. One of Anastasia's assistants helped a nigga out." Jamie reached into his pocket, pulling out a folded up piece of paper.

I rolled my eyes. "Yeah, I bet she did."

He looked up at me, grinning a little. "I can't believe Snow White actually left you here with me."

I looked at him. I didn't appreciate him calling my man a fucking female. I didn't have time for his shit. "Look, Jamie, I don't have time for your shit, I'm workin'. If it ain't about work, I ain't interested in shit you got to say."

Jamie leaned back in his chair, clearing his throat. He looked up at me, and then he sang, "You got me under your spell. Girl, you do it so well. I still remember your smell. Damn, you gotta nigga fiendin' like hell. Trying to drown my face in that cat. Girl, take the D, you know you like that. Girl, put that arch in that back. Take it all, girl, don't cha fight back. Blame my high on that skirt. Trying leave with you, put in work. Baby, you got me cravin' that body. Tryin' to make pleasin' you my hobby."

My heart pounded in my chest as Jamie rose from his chair and approached me.

I looked over my shoulder for Aaron, but he wasn't there.

Jamie grabbed my hand, pulling me to him. "I could care less about the man you left at home. He should've known better than to let you come alone. Just let me know when you're ready to leave. You don't need him, I'm the man that you need." He sang, his gaze glued to my lips.

I gasped, slipping my hands from his. "Umm, sounds good, but we're gonna have to lose that last part, Jamie." I walked past him, over to the chair behind him, to grab my jacket and purse. I really couldn't go there with him. He knew his presence made me uncomfortable, and he waited until Aaron left to try and flirt with me. I looked at him, "I know what we can replace it with." I cleared my throat, singing, "Nigga, you ain't shit. If I had one, you could suck my dick!"

Jamie nearly fell out laughing, sitting back down in the chair. "Oh, shit!" He laughed. "That nigga got you goin' hard, don't he? I gotta sit down for this one!"

I wasn't done. "You fucked up and let a real man get her. Now fall back, he'll show you how to treat her." I sang, neck roll, arms folded and all.

Jamie just leaned back in his chair, eyes low, hat covering his eyes a little, but I could still see the hurt.

"Why are you here, Jamie?" I shook my head at him, putting on my jacket.

"Why are you with him when you know you need to be with me?" Jamie looked up at me from his seat.

"I need to be with you? Okay, so tell me where the fuck you were when I was laying in the hospital last year? I haven't seen you in a year and a half, and you just pop up here out of the blue? What makes you think that I wanted to see you, be around you, know you, Jamie? Don't you have a son you're supposed to be raising?" I threw the straps to my purse over my shoulder. "Dude, why are you even talking to me? You waited until my husband left because you know Aaron wouldn't let you talk to me like this!"

Jamie laughed a little. "'Husband'? Man, that shit doesn't even sound right in the same sentence as his name. And he wouldn't let me talk to you? Shawty, ain't nobody worried about Snow White's ass."

I picked my water bottle up and slung it at him, but his athletic ass caught it without any problem. "Ughhhh, you make me fuckin' sick! Why do you have to be here? You know it hurts to see your face! You know I can't stand your black ass right now!"

Jamie laughed a little. I always hated the way that he was so fuckin' nonchalant about everything. "Shawty, how the fuck are you gonna be mad at me when you're the one that left?"

"You didn't deserve me, and you know it!" I exclaimed.

"I didn't deserve you, but he does?" Jamie was finally offended. "A nigga who doesn't know shit about you? A nigga who was too weak to approach you when he had the chance in high school? A nigga who was fuckin' you when he had a girl, your own best friend at that? At least when I was fuckin' around with shawty, it was before me and you got back together. You were fuckin' him when he was still with her, yet you wanna throw the blame on everyone else. You were just as wrong as we were. You gotta share some blame in this, shawty, for real."

Jamie was bringing the angry side out of me, and I hated him for that. I really didn't want to tell him about the baby, but he gave me no choice. "Okay, I was wrong, Fine. Are you happy? But there was no way that I was gonna stay in Maryland and watch Charlie chase after you! I had to leave! You think leaving you was easy? Well, muthafucka, it wasn't!"

Jamie just looked at me, brown eyes searching mine.

"I cried about you for months, Jamie! I was laying in that hospital, wanting to die! Wanting to end my life! Having no reason to live anymore! When they sent me home, I laid in the bed for three fuckin' months! You never showed up! You weren't there for me, but Aaron was! I pushed your dead baby out alone! I held your dead baby in my arms! Do you have any idea what I had to go through? Do you, Jamie?" I shouted.

From the word *baby*, Jamie rose to his feet. His eyes searched my face for answers, asking the questions that his brain couldn't get his mouth to say for a few seconds. He grabbed my arm, pulling me to him, but I pushed him away. "Ne'Vaeh, wh—what baby?" He was finally able to speak.

I didn't say anything.

"What baby, Ne'Vaeh?" Jamie exclaimed. "Ne'Vaeh, we had a baby?"

I looked up at him. "When I left Maryland, I was pregnant. I found out the day that Juanita went to the hospital. That's why I couldn't give her any blood."

Jamie's eyes searched my face. "What did we have?"

"A girl. I named her Sara. She—" I choked, "She was so beautiful, Jamie!"

Jamie's eyes glistened, but he didn't cry. "Why didn't you tell me? I deserved to know, Ne'Vaeh! How the fuck could you bury our baby, my baby, and not tell me?"

"Why didn't you come and see me? You never fought for me, Jamie! You just let me go and didn't come after me! You always abandon me! You always find an excuse not to come after me! I kept our baby a secret from you because she was the only part of you that I had left! The only part of you that no one, not even you, could take away from me!" I pushed him. "I dissed Aaron as soon as you came back into my life, Jamie! I told him he wasn't shit! I told him I wasn't anything without you! I told him that you were everything to me! He knew how much I loved you, but he still found it in his heart to be there for me when he knew I needed someone! You promised me that you'd never leave me! That I was everything to you! That only God could keep you away from me!" I pushed him again. "And as soon as I hurt your pride when you tried to give me a ring that you had no business giving to me in the first got-damn place, I wasn't shit to you!"

Jamie grabbed my hand, pulling me to him. "Baby, I'm sorry. What can I do to fix this? I'm here now, so just tell me what I gotta do, and I'll do it."

My lips trembled. "Go to Hell, Jamie! That's what you can do!" I slipped my hands from his and darted out the door.

You should have seen the look on Anastasia's face when she saw me standing beside her car, outside of Club Fire, at 5:00 in the morning. She looked at her Marc Jacobs watch before looking back at me. "Twinkie, it's five in the morning! You been in the studio all night, seriously?"

I looked at her, then at the rest of her drunk entourage. "Anastasia, you're gonna have to find someone else to play the lead, 'cause I can't do this shit!"

"Can't do what, Ne'Vaeh?" Anastasia sighed, really not in the mood for my whining at that time of the morning.

"It's really too early in the morning to be dealing with your whining ass. Go home. Get some sleep. Let's talk at eleven o'clock at rehearsal."

"Anna, I'm not going to rehearsal, do not you hear me? I can't work with Jamie! I can't be around Jamie! He's too much! You're too much! Where's my understudy? Call her!" I exclaimed.

24-K folded her arms. "I'm your understudy."

I rolled my eyes. "Well, there you have it, Anastasia. You got your Katrina."

Anastasia shoved 24-K. "Ne'Vaeh, she's just joking. She's too sexy to play your part!"

I scoffed. "Okay, so now I'm not sexy enough for this shit?"

Anastasia sighed, trying to take me by the hand, but I pulled it away. "Cuz, you know I didn't mean it like that. 24-K looks like a got-damn stripper because she is a got-damn stripper! She doesn't look the part of a record executive, but you do!"

24-K shoved her friend back, offended. "Bitch, you don't look like a record executive, but you are one! And you're a stripper, too, ho. Don't try to play me!"

Anastasia rolled her eyes at her friend, then looked at me. "Cuz, what happened?"

I exhaled deeply. "Jamie showed up to the studio at four o'clock this morning, talkin' all this shit about Aaron, calling him Snow White and shit!"

The girls giggled. Anastasia tried not to smile.

I looked at her, offended.

She smirked, unable to hold it back. "I'm sorry, boo, but that shit is so Jamie! He would say some stupid shit like that!"

"Well, I can't work with him, so you have to find some-body else!" I replied.

Anastasia shook her head at me, laughter subsiding. "You gotta let your feelings for this dude go and move the fuck on. It's over between you two. You have Aaron, and I know that after what Jamie did to you, your husband doesn't have to worry about him stepping back into your life. Aaron knows that you love him, doesn't he?"

I sighed. "Yeah, but—"

"Then tell the nigga that shit, and stop stressin'." Anastasia walked past me and got into her new, royal blue Mercedes Benz. Her entourage hopped in, too. Anastasia rolled down her window, looking at me standing there, pissed, arms folded, emotions going every which way. "Go home, get some rest. I'll see you at rehearsal in a few hours."

Chapter 9: Emotions on Display

Ne'Vaeh

It was so hard being around Jamie from that day on out. I wasn't on my A-game at all, and everyone around us felt it. I'd show up late to play rehearsals and almost never showed up to rehearse for my concert tour. I was stressed, sick, depressed, and didn't feel like being around anyone but Aaron, and he wasn't there. I think he only called me once the entire two weeks that he was gone. And on the day he was due to come back home, the day right before the first showing of *Thug in Love*, I collapsed on stage. And who rushed to my side to pick me up off of the floor? Jamie scooped me up in his arms, and I was too weak to fight him back.

Anastasia and her damn entourage had to follow us to the ER. Dr. Leyland shook her head at me, looking at me lying on the hospital bed of the triage. "I told you a few weeks ago that you needed to take it easy because you're—"

"Because of my heart condition, right?" I interrupted her, giving her the I-didn't-tell-Anastasia-or-*anyone*-that-I'm-pregnant-so-let's-keep-it-that-way look.

Dr. Leyland nodded, looking around the room at all of the ladies standing around me. And then she saw Jamie, leaning back, sitting in a chair in the corner of the room.

She gasped a little, "Oh, my!" She fanned herself a little. "No wonder you have a heart condition! Is this—"

"Jamie Green!" Anastasia's dancers swooned in unison.

I rolled my eyes, as the doctor made her way over to shake his hand. "Lawd, help these fools."

Jamie stood from the chair, shaking her hand. "What's up, shawty?"

Dr. Leyland looked him over. "I have been dying to meet the man who didn't bother to come see my patient in the hospital when she had his baby last year."

I looked at her. By the way she was gawking at him, you would have thought she was going to eat him, not throw judgment.

Jamie cleared his throat, sitting back down in the chair.

Dr. Leyland looked around at everyone. "Though Mrs. Whitehaven doesn't want to speak on her condition, she is very fragile. My sister used to dance for you, Anastasia, so I know how hard you push them."

Anastasia rolled her eyes at Dr. Leyland. "Girl, I'm gonna tell you now like I told you and your sister back then: if your sister couldn't take the heat, then why the fuck did she step her ass in the kitchen? You need to stay in your lane, Dr. Leyland. Your sister was a drug addict, and that's why she couldn't hang. You wanna throw shade, I can throw some, too."

Dr. Leyland cleared her throat. I could tell she wanted to dig in Anastasia's ass, but she didn't. She removed her Prada glasses, looking Anastasia in her face. "You're gonna have to let Ne'Vaeh go. She can't handle a worldwide tour, let alone traveling for this play. If you care about your cousin, you will take it easier on her, and you will take her off of both tours."

"My cousin is stronger than you and her punk-ass husband think she is!" Anastasia was getting agitated with everyone's opinion about my health and her drive for greatness. "You and Aaron are only hurting her by always limiting her!"

"No, you're hurting her by pushing her beyond her limits and hiring this man, who though he brings you in massive amounts of revenue, has caused this girl massive amounts of pain!" Dr. Leyland spoke beyond her duty as my doctor. She was then speaking to Anastasia as my friend. "You want to hurt this girl? She just lost a baby by this bastard, and you're gonna hire him to work side by side with her?"

Everyone in the room just stared at the doctor like she was speaking a foreign language. Jamie laughed to himself. I'm pretty sure he was tired of people throwing shade at him as if he wasn't in the room listening.

Anastasia laughed a little to herself. "Doc, you're really overstepping your boundaries. You must wanna lose your license talkin' to me like you don' lost your muthafuckin' mind. My cousin needs to grow up and face reality instead of running from it. Putting these two together was the only way to make her realize that she really can get over him. I put them together so she could see that she doesn't need him. That she doesn't need him to breathe, to eat, to sleep, to drink, to live! I watched my cousin dyin', missing this nigga. I saw it all! Since she's been with Aaron, she's been happy, alive, breathing, and well! I wanted her to see this nigga again so she can see how strong she's really become without him! That Aaron made her stronger." Anastasia looked at me. "You can do this; you need to do this."

I just looked at her, tears streaming down my face from the moment she mentioned my state of mind those months after losing my daughter.

Anastasia shook her head at me, signaling her crew to get up out of their seats. "We gotta get back to the studio to rehearse. Our first show is tomorrow. Like I told you before, there are plenty of bitches willing and ready to take your spot. You're good, but no matter how good you are, there is always someone better. You wanna make a name for yourself, you gotta work for it. You have something special, Ne'Vaeh. I wouldn't push you if I didn't think you did. So, you gonna be the star of this show or not?"

I looked at Jamie, then at my doctor, who was shaking her head at me. I looked back at Anastasia. "Yeah, I'll be there," I sighed.

Anastasia looked at Jamie, "You gonna give shawty a ride home, or what?"

"You trippin', shawty." I heard Aaron's voice before I looked up and saw him in the doorway.

My heart pounded in my chest at the sight of him. Oh, he looked so good, dressed in a plaid blue and white short-sleeved flannel shirt and baggy dark blue jeans. It didn't take much for him to look delectable. He was fly effortlessly.

Jamie stood from his seat, temples twitching like he didn't expect Aaron to make it back from Africa in time.

Aaron glanced at Jamie's stance and then looked at Dr. Leyland, who looked relieved to see him. She knew that whatever she said, Aaron would back her up.

"Doc, what's the status? How is she?" Aaron asked her. "Seeing that y'all got her hooked up to another IV in a few weeks' time doesn't look good to me."

Dr. Leyland shot Anastasia a quick glare. "Like I was just telling your wife's manager, producer, and choreographer, Ne'Vaeh needs her rest. This whole lifestyle isn't for her. Ne'Vaeh needs a break for a long time, at least for the next year. You need to convince her that she needs to go home and stay home and that if she doesn't listen to my advice, I can't continue to treat her. She'll have to find another doctor." Dr. Leyland patted Aaron on the shoulder, then left the room.

All of Anastasia's dancers rolled their eyes and smacked their lips at her as she left the room.

"Funky bitch." Jackie-O rolled her eyes, smacking the hell out of the gum she was chewing. Oh, I hated the way she was always popping that got-damn gum.

"Oh, my goodness, can you stop poppin' that got-damn gum like that?" I muttered under my breath.

Aaron approached my side, pulling up the doctor's stool, sitting down beside me. He leaned over, gently kissing my lips, giving me that I-wanna-fuck-right-now kiss again. He knew Jamie was watching, and he didn't give a fuck. "You gotta listen to your doctor, Heaven," he whispered. "I care about you. I need you."

I looked into Aaron's eyes as he sat up straight.

"Like I just told that bitch who just walked up out of here, Ne'Vaeh can do this. She's not as weak as y'all are making her out to be. My cousin is strong. She's been through worse than a few IVs. Shit, IVs and a few hospital stays ain't got shit on what you and Jamie have put her heart through these past few years!" Anastasia scoffed. "Don't get me started, nigga, 'cause I can go all fuckin' night!"

Aaron shook his head, looking me in my face. "Anastasia can talk all the shit she wants, but they call you 'Twinkie' for a reason, shorty. They don't think you can dance like them, look like them, talk like them, walk like them. They treat you like you ain't shit, and when you're on stage with these girls, who do you think the people see? They don't see you, because Anastasia has the dance routine centered on their fuckin' strip tease and not your voice. She's using your voice to get her girl's the attention they need to draw more attention to that fuckin' strip club!"

My lips trembled. I hated having everyone in my ear telling me what to do. I knew Aaron cared about me, but at that moment, all I could hear was him criticizing me for not being as sexy as my cousin and her bad bitches. I wanted to look like them, be like them, act like them, talk and walk like them, and I hated the pressure of not being able to. The whole reason why I quit the dance team in high school was that I was tired of everyone judging me about how skinny I was. Dancing with Anastasia reminded me of being on a cheerleading squad with Charlie. Charlie had the looks, the sex appeal, and the confidence. She exuded sex without even trying, just like Anastasia. I, on the other hand, had to pretend to be something that I wasn't, just to sell an album. Sure, I was cute and talented in a gospel choir. But to a record executive that was once one of the baddest strippers known to man, cute and talented wasn't enough. I had to represent her, and she was all about sex appeal. Yes, the fact that Aaron thought I was sexy should have been enough, but at that moment it wasn't. He hadn't called me all week because he was upset about my duet with Jamie. I wasn't sure if he was just mad because Jamie was around, or if he really wanted me out of harm's way.

"You don't think I can do this? You think that I'm not sexy, that I don't fit in with this group. Is that it, Aaron?" I shook my head at him, drying my tears.

Aaron made a face at me. "What? How could you even ask me some shit like that when I barely notice any of these females? I've seen strippers before, shorty. You see one ass, you've seen 'em all."

"Aye, shawty, I think you're sexy," Jamie spoke up.

Aaron looked over at Jamie, ready to jump across the bed on his ass.

Jamie grinned, looking straight at Aaron. "I think when you're on stage, all the niggas see is you. Anastasia put these girls with you on stage to show the world that no matter your size, you can be sexy and draw a crowd. You're a crowd pleaser. Don't let anyone tell you different, not even your nigga. Especially not your nigga."

Aaron stood from his stool, about to pop off, but I grabbed his arm. Aaron looked at me.

I looked up at him, shaking my head. "Aaron, baby, I'm fine."

No, I wasn't fine. I was so upset that night, sitting in my kitchen, at the bar. I was so tempted to drink the entire bottle of Hennessey that was staring me in the face. Aaron was trying to play me like I was the only girl that he noticed when he said himself that all people saw on stage was those strippers and not me. And there Jamie was, trying to pull at my heart strings, telling me that I was the sexiest girl in the room no matter what. Maybe Anastasia was right, maybe Aaron was trying to hold me back. I wasn't so sure at that moment, but I did know that I wasn't ready to give up singing or acting in the play just yet. I should have quit that play the day my doctor quit me, but I didn't. And I regret it to this day.

I sat there, listening to the songs that I recorded about Aaron. The song playing was called "Workout Sex." The title wasn't mentioned anywhere in the song, but the beat and the vibe of the song made you feel like you were having sex in the weight room. My next album was going to be centered on Aaron. I hated the way my cousin worked me, but she gave me the opportunity I would have never had otherwise. Other artists that I know had to fuck their way to stardom. With my cousin, all she wanted me to do was learn to stand on my own two feet. She thought I was stronger than I thought that I was, but I wasn't so sure.

"Babe, you still mad at me?" Aaron walked into the kitchen with nothing on but a pair of boxers. Oh my goodness, if muscles, chests, and abs could kill, boy.

I sat at the bar, in sky-blue lace panties and a matching bra. I looked up at Aaron, trying to be mad at him, but that body and my hormones weren't playing fair at all.

I sighed, shaking my head at him, eyes tracing his abs, then his muscular arms. "Why are you trying to make me feel special when you know I'm not? You don't think I'm sexy enough to be with Anastasia and her crew, and that hurts a little. It hurts a lot." I looked up into his face.

Aaron sighed, sitting at the bar with me, pulling my stool closer to his, in between his legs. His eyes traced my face. "Heaven, you already know what you mean to me. You ain't no stripper, and you don't have to be. You're the most adorable thing that I've ever seen. I don't want that type of girl. If I wanted that type of girl, I would be with that type of girl. I love you for who you are, Heaven, I told you that. Don't let these people trip your head up. Stay my sweet little girl, please. You're sexy as a muthafucka, at any size. I know I told you not to quit singing, but your doctor quit on you because she thinks you're hurting yourself. She told you what to do to take care of yourself, and you're not listening."

I sighed.

"And then you got your ex in the hospital room, cosigning with Anastasia. I'm outnumbered by your people, and I'm starting to think that their opinion means more to you than mine. I understand that I'm not around much, but I'm here as soon as I get some free time. I should be training for the next season, but I'm here with you." Aaron held my thighs in his hands.

I looked into his face. "Yeah, but you're only here because he's here. If he wasn't, you'd be gone for days at a time. Don't try to play me, Aaron, I know you. You're jealous."

Aaron disagreed. "What I got to be jealous for? A person is only jealous when they don't have something. I'm being protective of what's mine. There's a difference." His eyes searched mine. "Okay, I can't lie, I don't like him around you. I'll admit that yeah, I canceled some business trips to keep an eye on you because I wanna protect the heart that this nigga gets joy out of breaking. But don't mistake my reason for being here just because he's here. I love being around you. Heaven, nothing feels better than being with you. It took me forever to get you, and I'm not trying to lose you."

I looked up into Aaron's face. His hands felt so good gripping my thighs. I shook my head at him, "Baby, I put some thought into this, and I can't just quit on Anastasia. When I needed to get away from Maryland, she brought me back here with her. I felt like no one else cared about or loved me. I needed an outlet, and she gave it to me. I can just sit on stage and sing on a stool; I don't gotta dance. I can continue to act in this play as long as I stay hydrated and rested. I can do this for a little while, Aaron. When it gets to be too much, babe, I promise you, I'll give it a rest."

Aaron began kneading his hands into my thighs. "I hate that that nigga is near you. I don't even want him fuckin' lookin' at you, let alone talkin' to you, singin' to you and shit."

I gasped. His hands were so strong and passionate. It made my clit tingle. He pulled me closer to him by my thighs and gently kissed my lips.

He started bobbing his head to the music. He grinned, eyes tracing my lips. "What's this song you're playin'?"

I grinned at him, reaching for the remote on the countertop to turn the song up.

Aaron looked into my face, listening to the words. "I like it. It sounds like a seductive workout."

I couldn't stop smiling. "I worked on this song all night the day that you left me to go to Africa."

"You wrote this for me?" Aaron kissed my lips again.

I stood from my chair in between his legs. I backed up a little so he could get a better view of my body. I stared into his eyes as I danced slowly and seductively to the music. I was very flexible, contorting my body into all types of sexual positions. I could tell that my shifting curves were driving him wild. He rose from his seat, tilting his head, watching me as I bent over, touching my toes. Aaron held my waist in his hands, watching my booty slowly twerk. He'd never seen the entire dance routine that Anastasia had me perform for our dance break during our concert tour. I had to show it to him, because apparently, he didn't think that I could hang.

I had him pinned up against the bar. I popped my booty on him.

"Shit, hold up. Got-damn." He whispered, an erection forming in his boxers.

I grinded on his dick so hard, his dick bust straight through the opening in his boxers.

I stood up straight, turning around, facing Aaron, and looking up into his face, grinning, holding his dick in my hands, sticking it back inside his boxers. "Didn't think a girl as little as me could pop it like that, huh?"

Aaron looked down into my face. "This is the shit she has you doing at y'all concert?"

I grinned, nodding, looking up at him. "You like it?"

Aaron scoffed, looking my body over, still picturing me dancing in his head. "Like it? Man, I am in love with a stripper. Naw, Heaven, you can't do this dance outside of the house, a'ight? Hell naw, fuck that."

I laughed out loud. "Naw, bruh, you said that I wasn't a stripper, that I couldn't hang, remember? Now you claiming me?"

Aaron grinned, pulling me closer to him, kissing my lips. "Naw, you was playin' or something in the studio, because you didn't show a nigga this shit!" He slid his hands up my back, pulling my sports bra over my head.

I gasped as he gripped my hips, then lifted me on top of the countertop, standing in between my legs. I wrapped my arms around his neck, looking into his face.

"I've been waiting on all of this to be mine since high school. I'm still trying to wrap my heart and mind around the fact that you're really mine, Heaven." Aaron's eyes gazed into mine. "So you have to forgive me if I'm a li'l overprotective, a'ight?"

I nodded. "It really feels good to have someone finally really protect my heart. It feels strange, but it feels so good."

Aaron held my face in his hands, kissing my lips. "Aye, do that dance for me again, only this time, take your panties off."

"Good luck tonight!" Renée made her way into my dressing room the next night, for the first showing of *Thug in Love*. She looked so pretty in her Christian Louboutins. Her newly-dyed platinum blonde hair was pulled up into a ponytail. She looked like she was at the GRAMMYs instead of a play.

I bit my lip nervously as the makeup artist dusted blush over my cheeks. "Thank you for coming!"

Renée waved her hand at me, sitting down in the chair next to me. "Girl, you know I wouldn't miss this for anything." She looked around the room, seeing all of the roses scattered about, and then at me. "Where's bae?"

I looked at her, surprised she didn't call him "the bastard who stole me from her" or "the nigga who didn't ask her permission to marry me." I sighed. "Girl, he's out there with Anastasia, making sure the sound is perfect for the play. I think he's just as nervous as I am."

I was sweating bullets. Not just because I was nervous performing in front of thousands of people that night, but because I was going to have to be alone onstage with Jamie. He was looking so good that night. He passed me in the hallway earlier that night, winking at me, and my heart fluttered in my chest. Of course, I had rolled my eyes, giving him that "I don't give a fuck about you or anything that you do" look, but y'all know my heart was on fire seeing him again. Yes, I loved Aaron and could not have asked for a better man than him, but a part of me was missing, and I knew it was Jamie. I really needed closure, even though I was afraid to get it.

"Girl, you got everybody in the family back at home talking about you and this play. You know they got something to say about you and Jamie. Did you know there's a 'Behind the Movie' for this shit? It's been on VH1 all week!" Renée exclaimed.

I rolled my eyes, then closed them as eyeliner was applied to my eyelids. "Lawd, Anastasia needs help. Now she's airing shit without people's permission? That is so like her. I'm telling you, this chick is a hundred times worse than you!"

"Well, all I can say is that she be gettin' that gwap," Renée replied.

I opened my eyes, looking at her. I didn't expect her to say anything bad about Anastasia as long as she was supporting Jamie. "But at my heart's expense? Can you really put a price on heartbreak?"

Renée sighed, crossing her legs. "Evidently your heart ain't too broken; you married Aaron, didn't you? Or was that just on the rebound?"

I shook my head. I really wasn't for her shit that night. "Rebound? When I needed Jamie, where the fuck was he? When I lost his daughter, where the fuck was he and what was he doing? Somewhere fuckin' hoes and gettin' his dick sucked! He never called me once, Renée! I know I left him, but that was no reason to just totally cut me off! I sent him an invitation to come to the BET awards to see me last year, but did he show the fuck up? No, as a matter of fact, he had his agent call to tell me that he couldn't make it! Every time I think about Jamie, I see my little girl's face. If Aaron is anything, he is my angel, not a fuckin' rebound!"

Renée threw her hands up surrendering. "My bad. I'm sorry, boo. I just know how much Jamie means to you. I know he hurt you, but seeing his face again still has to have some effect on you. You can't tell me it doesn't feel good to have him back around."

I shook my head at her, then looked up at the makeup artist. "Paula, can you leave us alone for a minute?"

She nodded, then left the dressing room.

I looked at Renée, then sighed. I had to tell someone about my secret. I was tired of holding it in, and I know she was the only person who wouldn't tell anyone. "Renée, I'm pregnant."

Renée's eyes grew big, and her mouth dropped open, but no words came out. She scooted her chair closer to mine, then placed her hand on my stomach, as if I already had a baby bump. Surprisingly, she seemed happy. But a worried look quickly swept across her face. "Wait, is this safe? Will you be okay?"

I shrugged. "The doctor is telling me that I need to get off this tour."

"Then maybe you should listen to her. You don't need the money. Shit, Aaron's got enough bread to take care of his bae." Renée's eyes traced my face. "You haven't told him about the baby, have you?"

I shook my head. "Girl, no. I am scared that if I get too happy about this pregnancy, I might lose little Aiden or Aerial or whatever he wants to name her."

Renée grinned, her eyes glistening. "Well, you need to tell him. I'm sure he'd love to hear the news. And you already know he's pulling you off of this tour, like it or not. He's not my favorite person, but I can say that he's showed and proved that you are the girl for him. He may not be able to give you all of his time right now, but you know he's in love with you. Whatever you did to the nigga has got him sprung! Ol' pussy-whipped ass!"

I laughed a little, trying not to cry.

There was a knock at my dressing room door before it opened without an invitation.

Both Renée and I rose quickly to our feet as Jamie entered the room with a bouquet of sunny knockout roses. When we were kids, he would always pick those yellow roses, and leave one for me on my desk at school. To see him standing there with a whole bouquet of them was heart-wrenching.

Renée looked at me, watching me fight my hardest to fight the tears. "Ummm, I'll leave you two alone."

I quickly grabbed her arm. "No, please don't."

Jamie laughed a little walking up to me, handing me the roses. "Naw, Renée, you don't gotta leave. I'm not gonna take up too much of her time. I see shawty still has to get dressed."

I looked up at him, lips trembling, taking the roses in my hand. "Th–thank you," I stuttered.

Jamie cleared his throat, looking down into my face. "I swear I didn't come here to fuck up what you got going on with Aaron. Okay, I'll admit, I did come here to be nosey, but I also came because I needed to expand my career. I had no idea about Sara, shawty. If I would have—"

I put my hand up, stopping him from talking. The roses were hard enough to handle; talking about Sara would be unbearable. "Jamie, I really don't wanna talk about this, okay?"

"Shawty, I couldn't handle you leaving me. That shit hurt like a muthafucka. It's hard watching this nigga take care of you when you're supposed to be mine. I'm not gonna stand here and lie to you, sayin' that I don't regret letting you go, because I do." Jamie held my hand, pulling me to him, digging into his pocket with his other hand. He turned my hand palm up, placing the key-charm necklace that he'd given me Christmas Day, 2014, in my hand.

My lips trembled, looking up into his face, shaking my hand. "No, Jamie, I told you before that I can't take this!"

Jamie nodded, "Take it. It's yours. It always has been, probably always will be. Man, you fucked me up when you showed up to Alisha's funeral with that nigga, I'm not even gonna front. Seeing you with someone else made me realize that I should have fought for you."

"Well," I fought back my tears, "Aaron realized my worth a little sooner than you did." I glanced back at Renée, then looked back at Jamie.

And just like that, Jamie snuck a kiss from me, catching me totally off guard. It was so sweet, so gentle, so wrong, enough to make me nearly jump out of my skin.

"Good luck tonight." Jamie turned and walked away before I could take a swing at him.

I turned to Renée as Jamie left out the door, closing it behind him.

Renée was blushing harder than I was. "That smooth mulhafucka! Okay, sweetie, don't cry!" She held my face in her hands, seeing my eyes already welling up with tears. "You look so beautiful tonight. Try focusing on your future and your baby tonight, okay? I'm here for you."

"Oh, I need Aaron. Please, go get Aaron." I sighed, sitting back down in my chair.

I'm not going to pretend that being in that play, performing on stage with Jamie, wasn't difficult, because it was. Anastasia sat in the first row, watching us from the audience. Renée and Aaron stood alongside the stage, backstage, watching me throughout the entire play. Aaron looked so proud of me, watching me on stage. I was so nervous that I would hit the wrong note or forget my line. I had to say, we had a fantastic cast. The music for our play was phenomenal, written by Anastasia and Jamie. Jamie was a natural, I hate to admit. He was never into academics. Pen and paper weren't his best of friends, but the way that he wrote those songs, you would have never been able to tell. He kept it all in his head. He was good at just about everything that he did, which made it hard for anyone to not give him his props. As arrogant as he was, he was the best at whatever he set forth to do. Except loving anyone other than himself.

We were right at the end of the play, the part where I was telling another character, Holly, that I was firing Cooper because he never showed up to rehearsals and that I heard that he "was back out on the block slangin' rocks." We were just about to break out into a song called "Fallen Angel," when Jamie entered the scene.

Both myself and Tiffanie, the girl who played Holly, looked at each other, then at Kenya who was looking back at us, eyes wide as saucers. I looked down off the stage at Anastasia, who sat there, chin in her hand, shaking her head to herself. Jamie wasn't supposed to be in that scene, but there he was, walking out onto the stage, walking straight up to me.

My heart pounded in my chest as Jamie held my hand, pulling me closer to him.

"Shawty, why didn't you tell me about the baby?" His eyes searched mine.

I gasped, looking out at the crowd who was staring straight back at us. Everyone thought it was a part of the play, but everyone on that stage and behind it knew that it wasn't.

"Oh, shit!" Tiffanie muttered under her breath.

I tried to pull my hand from Jamie's but the more I pulled away, the closer he pulled me to him. "This isn't the right time to talk about this, *Cooper*." I tried to play it off. I looked back at "Holly."

"Could you please escort Mr. Cooper out of my office, Holly?"

Tiffanie removed herself from character, shaking her head at me. "Naw, girl, I'ma stay out of this one." She walked off the stage, and the audience giggled.

I looked at Jamie, nervous out of my mind as to what he might say. "Don't do this," I begged him, looking back at Aaron. Renée was holding his arm, struggling to pull him back. You should have seen his face, his light skin turning bright red. I looked at Kenya, who was signaling us both to just keep talking. I looked at Jamie. "Why are you doing this now, here, today?"

"You wouldn't talk to me any other way. You won't listen to me, shawty." Jamie responded, holding the hand that displayed Aaron's ring, which I had forgotten to take off for the performance. He looked down at it. "This ring doesn't even matter, and that marriage license is just a got-damn piece of paper. You and I both know that this nigga will never have all of you."

I was finally able to snatch my hand away from his. "He does have all of me! I don't know why you came here, but if you came to try to win me back, you already lost the fight. It's over, okay?" I backed away from him a little.

Jamie shook his head at me. "Do you remember the day you had your first heart surgery? It was me who sat with you all day and all night for a muthafuckin' month. When your brother was killed, who was there holding you at night? When your mother used to beat the shit out of you for stealing food from the corner store, who was there to nurse your wounds? When you needed clothes, food, soap, money, anything. Who was up all night, workin' the block, making sure you, your sister, and your brother had what y'all needed? Was he there for you when your mother used to beat the shit out of you? Was he there for you when your mother's boyfriend tried to rape you? Was he there for you when your mother was so strung out she tried to sell all of y'all for drugs? You and I have history, shawty. I protected you! Me, not this muthafucka! He doesn't deserve you, Ne'Vaeh! He didn't earn you; the nigga hasn't paid his dues! This nigga you fuckin' with ain't shit!"

He really pissed me off with that last statement. I couldn't take anymore, I had to do something to stop his mouth from running. I smacked Jamie dead in his face.

The crowd gasped.

Jamie looked at me, eyes sparkling.

"Not shit? Didn't earn me? Muthafucka, if you were so good at 'protecting' me, why couldn't you protect my heart? Why did my own sister have your baby? Why did you let me hold our dead baby in my arms alone? Aaron was there for me when you forgot how to be! That's how he earned me, and that's how you lost me!" I pushed him in his chest. "You never give a fuck about me until you see someone else is interested in me! I'm happy with him; leave us alone!" I broke down and cried.

"Shawty, you have to forgive me. I know I fucked up, I know I should have been there, I know you shouldn't have had to go through that type of pain alone." Jamie reached for my hand, and I pulled away. "Baby, I'm sorry."

I pushed him. "No, I don't wanna hear this! Leave me the fuck alone! Go back to her! Spend time with her! Go live your life with her and leave me the fuck alone! It's your fault that I love him! I had to find someone else! You left me! I needed you, and you left me! And even when you came back, you still managed to abandon me again! You pushed me to him when all I ever wanted was you!"

It was too late to stop the words from coming out of my mouth. It was too late to take them back. It was too late to unbreak Aaron's heart.

I gasped, turning around, seeing Aaron standing there, temples twitching, eyebrows knitted together. "Aaron, I didn't mean it, I—"

And just when I tried to take the words back, Jamie grabs me back to him, kissing me, lips stroking mine. The crowd rose to their feet, whooping and hollering.

"Close the curtains!" Kenya shouted at the stage hands, because she already knew some shit was about to go down.

I tore my lips from Jamie's, pushing him off of me just as the curtain closed. In an instant, before I even had a chance to react to what Jamie had just done, Aaron raced across the stage, darting straight at Jamie.

I screamed out, rushing toward the two on the floor, but Renée and Kenya held me back. By then, all of the actors were on stage, eying the fight, but no one jumped in. You should have seen the way they were jacking, but no one was stopping the fight. Jamie had Aaron fucked up if he thought just because he was a rich boy from privileged parents, he didn't know how to throw blows. I'm not saying Jamie got his ass beat, but I can say that Aaron gave him a run for his money. Blood splattered everywhere, and pools of blood were on the floor before the fight was finally broken up.

Anastasia rushed back stage with two of her biggest bodyguards to pull them apart. Aaron was still swinging in Kalvin, the body guard's, clutch. Kalvin had to damn near put Aaron in a headlock to stop him from trying to charge at Jamie. Aaron had completely lost his cool. Jamie, on the other hand, thought the situation was hilarious.

Jamie held his wrist, laughing at Aaron, still taunting him. "Nigga, it doesn't matter what the fuck you try to do; her heart is mine, nigga!" Jamie spit blood from his mouth. "She's only with you temporarily, my nigga. It's only a matter of time! You're wastin' your time, muthafucka! Don't act like you don't know that every time she's with you, she's wishing it was me, nigga!"

Kalvin gripped Aaron's neck tighter as Aaron tried to fight his way out of his chokehold.

I broke away from Renée, rushing over to Aaron. "Get off of him! Let him go!" I screamed at Kalvin.

Kalvin looked to Anastasia for instruction.

Anastasia sighed, nodding for him to let Aaron go.

Aaron pushed the bodyguard off of him once he loosened his grip enough to set Aaron free. Aaron stood there, chin bruised, left eye scratched a little, blood dripping from his lips. Aaron looked at everyone and then looked at me. "You dissed me for this nigga and every time he's around, I ain't shit!" Aaron's chest heaved in and out.

I shook my head at him, crying, "Aaron, baby, that's not true!"

"You wanna be with him? You wanna go back this dude? Then go, shorty. I'm not gonna try and stop you if that's where you wanna be!" Aaron tried ignoring Jamie and just talking to me, but Jamie kept running his mouth.

"Muthafucka, there's no question of her love, I got it. You ain't got shit but my leftovers!" Jamie laughed, Anastasia examining the hand that he was holding.

Aaron attempted to charge at Jamie again, but I pulled him back. Aaron pulled from me, pushing me off of him.

"Aaron, please, don't listen to him!" I screamed. "You already know that I love you! It's over with him; it's been over!"

"Then tell dude that shit because apparently, he seems to think different!" Aaron shouted. "And you just told him that loving me was a muthafuckin' mistake! That if the nigga didn't leave you here to fuckin' rot, you'd still be with him! The only reason I'm here is because he fucked up! The nigga left you for dead, I came to rescue you, and you're still in your feelings about dude? Where the fuck was he when you were trying to overdose on pills and shit? Where was he when you were barely sitting at ninety pounds? Where is he at night when your ass still cries yourself to sleep over him?"

My heart jumped at the sound of Aaron's angry voice. He'd never yelled, never screamed, and never raised his voice at me. It hurt like hell. I wish I could take back what had just happened with Jamie, but I couldn't. And I was going to lose Aaron because of it.

"I'm sick and fuckin' tired of competing with this dude, yo. He had his chance. He missed out. End of story." Aaron spit blood from his mouth. He looked over at Anastasia and another actress wrapping Jamie's wrist with an ace bandage. Jamie grinned at Aaron, still taunting him, rubbing in the fact that he was more important than Aaron was to everyone around him.

And right then, two police officers came backstage. Anastasia approached them, whispering. Both of them looked at Aaron, and then back at Anastasia. They recognized Aaron apparently and were baffled as to why she wanted him arrested.

My heart was doing a high-speed chase in my chest as the officers approached Aaron. I looked at Anastasia. "Anastasia, no!" I wailed.

"Mr. Whitehaven, you're going to have to come with us." One of the officers removed his handcuffs from his belt.

Aaron laughed a little as the officer stood behind him, pinning his arms behind his back. "This nigga is trying to steal my wife, and you have me arrested?"

The officers could care less that he was the son of a multi-billionaire and a star player on an NBA team. Anastasia ran Atlanta, and what she said was the law.

"From what everyone saw here, you attacked my actor. I'm responsible for my actors, not for you, boo-boo." She blew Aaron a kiss as the officer struggled to remove Aaron from the room. "Don't drop the soap."

Aaron's feet were planted on the floor. "Muthafucka, she's mine!" he shouted at Jamie. "She was made for me, you remember that shit!" It took both of the police officers to drag Aaron from backstage.

I tried to go after them, but Renée held me back.

The police department refused to let me speak to Aaron that night. They refused to tell me anything about the charges that were filed against him. They refused to let me pay his bail. After four hours of waiting outside of the detention center with Renée, she decided to take matters into her own hands. She suspected that maybe they were purposely not telling me anything because Aaron might have not wanted them to. She called the front desk herself, asking information about Aaron's bail. She was informed that he'd gotten out of jail three hours earlier, that they let him go as soon as he went to visit the commissioner. The charges had apparently been dropped the moment that he made it to the detention center. It was then that I knew that Aaron asked them to stall me. It was then that I knew that Aaron was through with me.

Renée zoomed down the highway, trying to get me back home to see if my instincts were correct. Aaron's car wasn't in the driveway. I got out of Renée's car, racing to the front door of my house to unlock the door. I walked into the house and called out his name. Nothing. I raced up the steps and into our bedroom. He wasn't there. And I walked slowly to Aaron's walk-in closet to open it. I gasped at the sight of the empty closet. I shook my head, backing away from the closet. And to put the icing on the cake, when I looked back at our empty bed, I caught sight of Aaron's wedding ring sitting on his pillow.

Chapter 10: Be Without You

Ne'Vaeh

Renée stayed with me the night that Aaron left. She knew my heart couldn't take it. I was barely breathing as it was. I couldn't take any more sleepless nights. I couldn't take any more heartbreak. I couldn't handle Aaron leaving me. I needed him back; I couldn't live without that boy. He was the only reason why I had survived for as long as I did.

Renée tried staying up with me that night, but she fell asleep with her head on my lap. I sat there on the couch, twiddling Aaron's wedding ring in my fingers. I'd tried calling him all night only to get his voicemail. The next available flight to Miami was at 10:00 the next morning, and I planned on jumping aboard that bitch. I wasn't losing him because of Anastasia or Jamie. No one wanted to see me happy, it seemed.

At 2:00 in the morning, there was a faint tapping at my front door. I rolled my eyes. I left my door unlocked because I already knew he'd show up when he did. Whenever Jamie would hurt my feelings as a kid, he would always show up at 2:00 in the morning, tapping on my window. He knew that I couldn't sleep, that I'd be up waiting on him.

"Come in, Jamie." I scooted away from Renée gently, laying her head on the couch.

Jamie walked into my house, head hanging down, closing the door behind him. He was dressed in a white tank top and dark blue sweat pants. He looked like he was on his way to go work out.

I stood from the couch, dressed in a tank top and sweats, damn near wearing the same thing that he was. I walked over to him, looking up into his face. His face was scratched up a little, and he had a cast on his arm. His eyes sparkled a little, his temples twitching.

"Renée is asleep, so we need to step out on the back porch to talk, Jamie," I whispered, rolling my eyes and turning around, walking through the house to the back sliding door.

Jamie followed behind me.

I sighed, sitting down at the umbrella table that sat on my patio.

Jamie shut the door behind him, and then sat across from me, looking me in the face.

"I knew you wouldn't take that necklace back, so I had Anastasia's assistant UPS it back to your house in Maryland," I said, watching Jamie laugh a little. I sat Aaron's wedding ring on the table.

Jamie's laughter subsided. He shook his head to himself. "Shawty, I had Anastasia drop the charges as soon as he got to the station last night."

I shook my head at him. "Why did you kiss me like that? Why did you come out on stage the way that you did? You put on this show in front of that crowd, and they fuckin' loved it like it was a part of the got-damn play! This was my career, this was my life, that was my fuckin' husband! It hurt him seeing you here with me! That boy loves me and only me! I don't have to share his heart with anyone else, and it kills him to know that he has to share my heart with you!" I broke down and cried. "Jamie, it's over between me and you! I was sick as fuck, and he brought me back to life! He cooked for me, cleaned for me, bathed me, massaged my feet, combed my hair, shaved my legs, ironed my clothes, warmed my towels, opened up car doors; he *worshipped* me! I never had to ask that boy for anything, he just did it!"

Jamie's eyes traced my face. "Shawty, I didn't mean to fuck dude's head up the way that I did. I was just mad. I hate seeing you with someone else, shawty, you know that."

"So once again, you come at me with that dumb shit! You can fuck whoever, but you don't want anyone to step foot near me? Get the fuck out of here with that bullshit! You sound so stupid!" I rolled my eyes, drying my face. "What you did was stupid! Look at your face! Look at your wrist! You knew as soon as you kissed me what Aaron was gonna try and do to you! Y'all would have killed each other on stage if those bodyguards wouldn't have pulled y'all apart! Aaron is gone because of you, Jamie! I hope you and my bitch-ass cousin are happy now!"

Jamie just sat back in the chair, looking at me. "Shawty, he's coming back."

"No, he's not! He left his got-damn wedding ring, and he took all of his fuckin' clothes with him!" I cried out. "Jamie, you know I love you! Why did you have to remind him of that shit? We were doing so good, Jamie! It felt so good to have a man holding me at night again, kissing me again, cherishing me again, touching me again, and loving me again. He made me feel like I was the only woman that existed in the world. Even when he was with Charlie, that boy wanted only me! You are not worth losing that! You are not worth losing him!"

Jamie nodded to himself. He was upset with the entire situation; with himself more than anything.

"Jamie, I really love him. He's not some rebound! He makes me happy. He makes me forget the pain that I've been through because he brings me so much joy. Don't I deserve that?" I cried.

Jamie looked at me, watching the tears slide down my face. "Of course you deserve that, shawty. I'm sorry that I couldn't give it to you. Shawty, don't cry. I'm sorry. What do you want me to do? Just tell me and I'll do it."

I looked at him. "Just leave us alone, please."

Jamie nodded. He knew there was no point fighting for me. I had made my choice, even if my choice had given up on me. "So what'cha gonna do now, shawty?"

"Quit. Quit it all. Then try to get Aaron to take me back. I need him. I can't–I can't have this baby alone." I had to tell him before he found out from someone else. "I'm ten weeks pregnant. I haven't told anyone but you and Renée."

Jamie looked at me. He looked like his heart had stopped. Jamie just stared at me for a few seconds before standing from the table.

I looked up at Jamie, as he walked over to me and kissed my forehead. He was so hurt, he was speechless. He couldn't be angry, he had no right to be. But he was hurt. "If you need anything, shawty, don't ever hesitate to call. I never meant to hurt you. You were everything to me. You will always be my girl, no matter who you're with. I know Aaron will take care of you, so I don't have to worry about you. But I'm here when you need me." His hand brushed against my chin.

I stood from the table as he started to walk away from me. I grabbed his arm, pulling him back to me, throwing my arms around him. I cried, burying my face in his shirt, as he wrapped his arms around me. "Jamie, I love you, but I need him." I cried.

"I know," Jamie whispered. He gently kissed my forehead again, before letting me go. The hardest moments of my life were always watching that boy walk away from me.

***

I walked into Passion Productions' dance studio the very next morning, dressed in a cute turquoise wrap-dress and flat sandals. I wasn't even three month's pregnant and my feet had already started to swell. When I walked into the studio, Anastasia and her girls were doing their usual seductive dance routine. When Anastasia saw me, she stopped in her tracks, signaling the deejay to stop the track. She saw me carrying a folder in my hands.

"You're not dressed to rehearse." Anastasia grinned. "Our contract states that you will be here at the time of rehearsal, dressed and on time. You're late, and you're not even dressed."

I opened the folder, taking out the contract I had with her record label. "Oh, about that contract—" I tore the contract right down the middle, then into tiny pieces, and flicked the pieces out onto the floor.

Anastasia's dancers looked at me, folding their arms and clicking their teeth.

Anastasia watched as the pieces float to the floor. She looked back up at me as I took out the contract I had with both her and Kenya for our stage production. And I ripped that shit up in her face, too. Anastasia's bright brown eyes widened, "Ne'Vaeh, you can't—"

"I just did!" I snapped. "You wanna take me to court, go ahead. Sue my ass then! I could care less. But don't you think that fuckin' up my marriage is payment enough?"

Anastasia sighed, flipping her hair over her shoulder anxiously. "Honey, we got your bae out of jail. He's out. The charges were dropped."

"Anastasia, that's not the fuckin' point!" I screamed. "I nearly died giving birth to Jamie's baby, and you brought him here only because you wanted to drive a wedge between me and Aaron! All I want is Aaron, and all you want is money! I work my *ass* off for you, Anastasia! I stay up all night writing songs, stay up all night going over my lines, and stay up all night trying to twerk like these got-damn strippers you got around you, sniffing your ass!"

24-K stepped forward to step to me, but Anastasia pulled her back.

"I am ten weeks pregnant, Anastasia!" I exclaimed.

Anastasia looked at me. They all looked at me.

"I–I didn't know." Anastasia shook her head, her eyes sparkling.

"You didn't take the time to ask me! You're so hung up in keeping Aaron from me that you didn't realize that he's my husband, that we want a family! I just lost my baby last year, and I'm pregnant with another one! I am scared out of my mind right now, Anastasia, and I need him, but he's gone!" I tossed the folder I had in my hands onto the hardwood floor. "Jamie, you, singing, dancing, acting, money, cars, clothes, houses, fame, fortune—none of this bullshit is worth more than Aaron!"

Anastasia felt really stupid. They all did. "Ne'Vaeh, I'm sorry."

"Well, sorry isn't gonna bring my baby back. Tell Darryl thank you for everything. I appreciate you both for giving me the opportunity of a life time, but I can't do this shit anymore. My place isn't here; it's with Aaron. Y'all can have whatever rights to whatever you want except my 'White Gold' album. That shit is mine. Everything else, do whatever you want with it. Like I said, Anastasia, if you wanna sue me, go ahead—see you in court." I turned around, walking out of the studio.

I placed Aaron's ring on a gold necklace and hung it around my neck that morning. I packed my clothes into three suitcases and placed the suitcases at the front door, just when the doorbell sounded. I answered the door to see Renée and my sister, Autumn, standing at the door.

I broke down and cried as Autumn threw her arms around me. "Hey, sis. I heard you needed back up." She whispered in my ear. "Let's go get your dude back."

I was a nervous wreck once we stepped off that plane in Miami. I was scared to face Aaron. I knew he was upset with me. He had his number changed and everything, making it impossible to get in touch with him. When we got to Aaron's beautiful beach house, two of Aaron's cars were parked in the driveway, and another two cars were parked right alongside his.

We got out of the taxi and walked up the side walk to the house. My hands shook as I unlocked the door. I was surprised he hadn't changed the locks, but then again, he probably wasn't expecting me to fly to Miami either.

When we walked into the house, we ran straight into Aaron, his mother, his father, and another pretty young girl who sat on the couch, wearing a lovely, tight Dolce and Gabbana floral dress. I wasn't sure what was going on, but it looked like they were all planning something.

"Good afternoon." Renée spoke first, pulling me by the hand to meet Aaron's family, sitting there, staring at us from the living room.

Aaron stood from the couch, eying me, standing there in my cute wrap-dress. "What's up?" He asked, face looking better than it was the night before. He frowned at me, seeming very irritated to see me. "Why are you here, shorty? Don't you got a show to do? Or an album to record?"

I turned around, ready to leave the house, but both Autumn and Renée stopped me. I shook my head. "He's so cold!" I fought back crying. "He doesn't wanna talk to me!"

"Cuz, we flew all the way here from Georgia to get this dude," Renée whispered. "Tell him what you have to say. Make him listen to you!"

I took a deep breath, turning back around to face Aaron. I stood there alongside my family, in the center of the living room. "Aaron, I love you," I whispered.

The expression on Aaron's face softened a little.

"Aaron told us what happened," Aaron's father, Avery, spoke up.

I looked at Aaron's mother, who sat there looking so elegant, like a brown-skinned Dorothy Dandridge. Her lips were pursed together, and her arms were folded across her classic beige Chanel dress.

I looked back at Aaron, "Aaron, I quit. I quit everything."

Aaron looked at me, shaking his head. "Heaven, you didn't have to do that for me."

I shook my head back at him, walking up to meet him at the couch. I stood before him, "Aaron, you are everything to me. The fame, the fortune, the money, none of that means anything if I don't have you. She can take me to court if she wants; I could really not care less."

Aaron shook his head. "She just called about an hour ago, trying to apologize. She was pissed that you walked out on her, but I don't think she's gonna sue you. She says she had to talk Jamie out of quitting on her, too."

"So, about this Jamie—" Ella stood from the couch, straightening her dress. "What role does he play in your life? And what use is my son to you if you're still pining away over him?"

Avery sighed. "Honey, stay out of this. We already had a long conversation with our son about leaving her the way that he did. Just sit down and let these young people handle their own situation."

Ella sat back down on the couch. "I don't appreciate my son fighting and almost going to jail over some nonsense, but okay, I'll just sit here and say nothing, like a good wife." She even looked classy rolling her eyes.

I looked at Aaron, "I would never ever go back to Jamie. You're my life, my heart, my soul, my air, the only reason I exist! I didn't mean for any of this to happen. I didn't think my own cousin would set me up the way that she did. She knew what would happen if she put Jamie in the same room with me. She knew it would upset you. Please don't question where my love is, Aaron. I'm not confused about the way that I feel. You didn't have to leave me." Tears trickled down my face.

"It doesn't feel good sharing your heart with another man, sweetheart," Aaron finally spoke from the heart.

"I know, but I can't help how I feel. I have known him all my life, Aaron. He was my best friend for a long time, and though I still care about him, I'm in love with you, and I would never purposely do anything to hurt you. He is not worth losing you, Aaron! I wanna be with you! I have been in love with you since the first day you walked into my life. I hate the fact that we have wasted so much time apart when we should have been together. Quitting Passion Productions is probably the best decision that I've made in my life, outside of deciding to venture into a lifelong partnership with you." I looked into his face.

The young lady in the floral dress cleared her throat. "I'm sorry to interrupt, but I really have to get going if y'all want me to get started on this list."

I looked at Aaron and his parents. "I'm sorry, who is this?"

"Oh," Ella stood up, looking at her husband. "Can I speak? Is it okay for me to interject now, Avery?"

Avery nodded.

Ella looked at me. "I am not going to stand here and pretend that I wasn't upset when you decided it was okay to get married to my son without my approval. What mother doesn't want to see her child get married? You two snuck off to another country to get married without inviting me and—and I was hurt." His mother choked back tears.

My eyes searched her face. I looked at Aaron and then back at her, my intestines in bunches. "I know you love your son very much. I know you don't like me, but I have never disrespected you, Miss Ella. I don't always agree with some of the things that you do, but I will admit that I wished my mother put as much effort into my life as you put into your son's life. I'm just getting to know Juanita. I don't want to come between a mother and her child. I didn't mean to marry Aaron without letting you know, but I didn't want any problems out of anyone. I love him, Miss Ella. More than words can express. You have a wonderful son, and I can see why you want to protect him."

Ella composed herself. "I'll admit that I was ignorant and judged you off of your appearance. I just wanted what I thought was best for my son's future. The color of my skin has never gotten me anywhere. Though I come from a rich family, all anyone sees when they look at me is a little black girl. My son, in my opinion, was blessed with light skin and white features, so of course I wanted him to marry a woman similar to him. I apologize if I ever offended you."

I was speechless. I couldn't say anything at the moment; I just stood there staring at her.

Ella grinned, holding her hand out, presenting the girl in the floral dress. "This is Miss Bridget Good, the wedding planner that I hired."

Renée and Autumn both gasped behind me.

"If it is okay with you, I would like to have sort of a wedding celebration, kind of like an extended wedding. I know you and Aaron are already married, but you didn't have a ceremony in front your family or friends. I really think people would like to see you two get married." Ella's eyes glistened. "I would like to see you and my son get married. Please. I have a dress picked out for you and everything. All you have to do is get fitted for it. What do you say?"

My knees grew weak. I felt like I was about to faint. Just when my knees gave out, Aaron caught me.

I balled my eyes out in his arms. Ella patted my back. She knew that her blessing meant everything to me. I didn't have my mother in my life, and I needed her. The fact that Ella found it in her heart to get over her prejudice and accept me into her family meant more than words could express.

I looked up at Aaron.

Aaron looked down into my face, holding my waist in his hands.

"You both are young, and you have a lot of growing to do," Avery spoke up. "When situations like these arise, you have to talk to each other. You can't just pack up and leave when times get tough, Aaron. It's obvious that this young lady loves you. You both have been through a lot over the years. Young lady," Avery looked at me, hugged up with his son, "we were just about to send Aaron back to you. My son needs you. I think that you deserve this event that my wife wants to coordinate for you. Weddings are her specialty. It'll be phenomenal, trust me." Avery grinned, ocean blue eyes sparkling.

"What do you think?" Aaron looked down into my face.

I nodded, letting go of him, looking back at my sister and my cousin. "Let's do it."

Renée winked at me, tears already sliding down her face.

Autumn was so happy, jumping up and down like a little kid in a candy store. "Bachelorette party, whoop!" She squealed.

Everyone laughed a little.

"Baby, I didn't mean to leave you." Aaron held my chin, turning my face back around so our eyes could meet. "I couldn't stay around and watch you with that dude. It hurt too much. I just needed to get away from all that for a while. Fighting muthafuckas isn't my style, and you know it. I know you love me, and I know it was hard as hell for you to work with him. Your cousin was wrong about me, I'm not trying to control you or run your life. I just want what's best for you, what's healthy for you. You're my wife, and yes, you belong to me, so I just figured that I at least had a little say so in what goes on in your life. Being around that dude was unhealthy for you, and it was unhealthy for me, too. I couldn't stand by and watch him hurt you anymore."

I sighed, feeling the urge to tell everyone about the baby. "Ummm, since everyone is here right now, I think I should just say this."

Aaron looked into my face, preparing himself for the worst. He sighed.

"I love this house, but I am not sure that it's big enough. We have one bedroom, your weight room, your library, and the guest room. I think we need a five-bedroom house unless you plan on turning one of those rooms into a nursery." I braced myself for everyone's reaction.

Aaron and his parents just looked at me for a few seconds before it actually registered to them what I had just told them. Ella was the first to catch on, screaming, grabbing me, and squeezing me as hard as she could. "Oh my God!" she squealed. "Oh my goodness, a baby?" She let go of me, watching the look on her son's face.

Aaron held my hands, his light eyes glistening. He had the same reaction that my cousin had when I told her. He placed his hands on my stomach, his light eyes searching my face. "Baby, is this safe? Are you gonna be okay?"

I nodded, looking up into his face. "I think so. I was just afraid to tell you because of what happened to Sara. I'm so scared, Aaron, of losing this baby. I can't go through that again."

Aaron held my face in his hands, kissing my lips. "Your loss matters to me, Heaven. I'm here with you, baby, you know that. Whatever happens, we're in this together. Let's just hope for the best and not think about the worst."

I looked up into his face. "Aaron, are you happy?" I whispered.

Aaron kissed my lips again, "Hell yeah, I'm happy."

I unhooked the necklace from around my neck and removed his ring. I held his hand, looking up into his face as I slid his ring back onto his finger. "Never take this off again, Aaron."

Aaron grinned. "I won't. I promise." He looked back at his father. "Dad, my baby is having my baby, did you hear that?" Aaron let go of me and went over to hug his father.

"Congratulations, son." His father was teary eyed, wrapping his arms around his son.

Ella hugged me again. "Wait." She let go of me. "You are sure this baby is my son's, right?"

We all looked at her.

"Mom, really?" Aaron shook his head at her.

Ella shrugged. "Well, given past circumstances, you know I had to ask!"

I can't begin to tell you how happy that I was. The events that happened prior to that day didn't even exist at that moment. Of course, a part of my heart would always belong to Jamie Green. He taught me how to love, but Aaron taught me the definition of what love truly was.

It was about sacrifice, honesty, and commitment. I finally had someone who valued me. I had a family, and for the first time in my life, a mother. I couldn't have been happier. I guess fairy tales do exist after all.

Chapter 11: Mama's Baby, Daddy's Maybe

Charlene

I woke up to the sound of Ashton's heart beating in my ear and breath blowing through my hair. I looked up into his face, gently kissing his lips. I hated to admit, it but it felt good waking up next to someone who I actually cared about every morning. I know I had told Ashton two months before that we weren't exclusive, that I wasn't his girl just because we had sex, but somehow, from the moment he touched me in that closet, my body belonged to him. I deleted every contact in my phone that wasn't family. If it wasn't about modeling or Alisha's dance studio, I had nothing to do with it. From the moment I left work, from the moment I left Alisha's dance studio, I was with Ashton. But even though Ashton had me feeling some type of way, I still couldn't shake the fact that it all felt so familiar, that we'd slept together before. Though I couldn't see how that was possible, the more I slept with him, the more apparent it became.

We got up that morning around 7:30. The cook fixed us a nice breakfast, and Ashton was off to work. I sat there in the kitchen waiting for my sister, Heather, to stop by to pick up little August. I sat at the island in my kitchen drinking a cup of coffee, when Lilia came into the kitchen, removing her apron. She looked at me, lips pursed together.

I looked up as she stood beside the doorway, letting Jamie into the kitchen. I stood from the stool, watching Jamie walk in, dressed in Giuseppe from head to toe. I rolled my eyes, folding my arms across my chest. I hadn't heard from Jamie since June, and it was August 8. I saw clips from his stage play on VH1. I also heard over the radio that his reckless actions during the stage play caused Ne'Vaeh to end both her contact with Anastasia and her contract with Kenya Love. He never could follow directions.

Jamie grinned, "Sup, shawty?" He approached me at the island, sitting down on a stool just as I sat down beside him, facing him. "What's good wit'cha?" he sat the bag that he had in his hand on the floor, and then removed his cap.

"Oh, I'm good. How about you? You're the one who's a star." I picked up my coffee mug and started sipping from it. "How was the tour? I heard you were a showstopper."

Jamie's eyes searched mine. "I did about ten shows. Once shawty quit, they had a hard time finding an actress who could bring it like she could. I spent a lot of time in the studio, though."

I shook my head at him. "What did you do to her? Why did she quit the opportunity of a lifetime?" I took another few sips

Jamie shook his head at me, "Naw, shawty, it wasn't just me. Her cousin's wife was driving her hard, doing whatever she could to piss Aaron off. Hiring me only made it worse. Not to mention shawty is pregnant."

I spit coffee all over him.

Jamie just looked at me as I hopped up off the stool to grab a towel.

"Oh my goodness, Jamie, I'm sorry!" I ran a dishtowel under some water. I came over him and patted his shirt.

"I'm sorry; I'll fix this. Oh my goodness, you just threw me with that information." I looked up into his face as I dabbed his shirt. "Pregnant? How is she?"

Jamie shrugged. "Fine now, I guess. She left Atlanta and went to go get dude after he was arrested."

My eyes widened. I shoved the towel into his chest, nearly pushing him off of the stool. "Jamie, what the fuck did you do? You know what, I don't even wanna know. It was my fault; I should've known better to give you the idea of going to Atlanta. I told you to get an acting career started, not fuck up a marriage."

Jamie just looked at me as I sat back down on the stool next to him. "I didn't do anything but bring the two closer together. She left Atlanta and went to Miami to be with the nigga, yo. She's happy with him. She's finally getting the life she deserves. It's not with me, but it's what she deserves regardless."

I just looked at the hurt expression on Jamie's face. "She told you about the baby she lost, huh?"

Jamie nodded, "Yeah, she hates me for letting her go through that alone, too, yo. Shawty hates the fuck out of me right now. I don't exist anywhere in her world anymore. I tried apologizing to her, but she wouldn't listen. So I had to do that shit in front of thousands of people, during our first performance. I know I was out of line when I kissed shawty, but I had to do something to get her to listen to me. Once they closed the curtain, it was on. Next thing I know, me and her nigga were on the floor, throwin' blows. The nigga can fight, too." Jamie laughed a little. "I tried to block one of his punches, and the nigga broke my wrist. The shit still hasn't healed all the way."

I shook my head, getting up, going over to the counter to pour another cup of coffee. Jamie was always about the drama. He loved being the center of attention. He loved when the spotlight was on him, which is why being in the acting industry was the perfect career for him. I had no idea he was going to bring his personal life out in public. I am pretty sure that little stunt of his cost Anastasia and Kenya hundreds of thousands of dollars. Just when I started to pour another cup of coffee, I noticed Ashton's work badge sitting on the counter. "Shit!" I muttered to myself.

Jamie looked up at me, "You good?"

I hesitated. "Uhhh, yeah, Ashton left his work badge over here is all." I continued pouring my cup of coffee.

Jamie just looked at me, not even sure what to say to me. When he left, I was sleeping with Ashton, and when he came back, I was still doing the same. I had been seeing Ashton for two months. We never verbally said that we were a couple, but we were always together. We were best friends who had sex, and it felt awesome. I could be myself with Ashton. I didn't have to get cute, put on makeup, wear expensive clothes, try to impress him, or lie about who I was. He accepted me, flaws, past, and all, and it felt so good. He was spending time with little August, and the more they played together, the more it became apparent that I had to find out whether or not we'd slept together. Little August looked just like me, so I couldn't go off of his looks, but the way they both laughed together gave me chills.

"So, you and Ashton, y'all are seeing each other now?" Jamie watched me drip French vanilla cream into my coffee.

I rolled my eyes to myself, stirring my coffee. "The last time I checked, I could do what the fuck I wanted. And unless you're wifin' me, you have no say-so in what the fuck I choose to do with my time."

"Is this exclusive?" Jamie asked, ignoring my smart-ass remark. "Are you seeing this dude, Charlie?"

I looked at Jamie. "What does it matter to you? Ashton is my friend. Do you know he has nightmares at night about Alisha? If someone died in your arms, how would you cope with that? You'd need someone to hold you at night, too. He needs me, and whatever way I can help, I will."

Jamie shook his head at me. "You're not helping him by leading him on. You know that boy is ready to settle down wit'cha. And you're not ready to settle down with anyone, shawty."

"Well, what if I am?" I looked at him.

Jamie grinned. "Not with him you're not."

I looked at Jamie. I needed Ashton just as much as he needed me. In a way, we were each other's crutch. I needed someone to care about me and so did Ashton.

"You keep fuckin' with this dude's head, the next thing he'll be doing is bending down on one knee. Just watch, shawty." Jamie warned me. "I bet dude already has the ring picked out. Shit, it's probably in the gym bag I'm sure he brings over here every night. When dude comes home tonight, check his bag, I'm tellin' you, shawty, it's in there!"

"You need to mind your own damn business. You can't even get your own problems right, yet you miraculously know the solutions to mine." I rolled my eyes, really not feeling like hearing Jamie's opinion about my life or what I decided to do with it. "Ashton can get whatever, whenever, wherever, how the fuck ever he wants it. And you can take that whatever, whenever, wherever, and how the fuck ever you wanna take it. You always wanna run everyone. Nigga, you don't run me! You always want your pie, cake, and ice cream, and think the next bitch don't want the same thing."

Jamie just shook his head at me, placing his cap back on his head. "Yo, I need you to come to this White Party with me tonight. It's a benefit for cancer survivors. My sister is gonna be there. You know she had cervical cancer a few years ago. I think it would be a good look if you came to show your support to the women still battling cancer."

I sighed. "Jamie, I really got a lot to do tonight."

Jamie knew I was really fragile when it came to the cancer stuff. I watched Alisha remain strong through her entire ordeal. I tried to keep a positive state of mind about life, but it wasn't easy.

Jamie still kept picking at my wounds. "Shawty, some of them are girls as young as three and four, shawty. What if we had a daughter? What if that was our little girl? Some of these girls don't have parents who are there for them. They don't have anybody. They need to know someone cares."

I just looked at him, lowering my cup. He always played on my guilty conscience. He knew if he brought up the fact that our child could have been suffering from that fatal disease that I couldn't just say no.

Jamie picked up the little white gift bag that he brought in with him from off the floor, then set it on the countertop.

I sat my coffee cup down, looking at the bag and then looking back at him.

He grinned a little.

I hesitated before walking back over to the island where he sat. I looked at him as I dug through the paper to get to whatever was in the bag. And I felt it before I grabbed it out of the bag. It felt so soft and smooth in my hands. I pulled out the nicest, prettiest, sexiest little white dress I'd ever seen. It was a form-fitting silk Versace dress. I could picture myself in that dress. I knew it would look like it was painted on my skin. I loved it, and I just held it tight against my chest.

"Oh my gosh, I love this!" I wanted to say that I loved him. I should have put that shit back in the bag and gave it back to him, but I didn't. All that trash talking I did to Ne'Vaeh for taking that dress from Aaron, now I know how she felt. There's nothing like a man who knows your taste.

"You got plans tonight, shawty?" Jamie grinned, watching me eyeing the dress.

I looked at him, "I do now."

No, I shouldn't have gone out with Jamie that night, but you know every bit of attention he gave me soothed my soul. The cancer benefit was an emotional one. There were so many little girls there who had little to no hair. I cried as I talked to them, and most of them played in my hair, admiring it. Jamie and I both gave a huge donation to the National Cancer Society that night. I also paid to have wigs custom made for all the little girls there who suffered hair loss. It broke my heart to hear them crying and thanking me for caring about them. If it hadn't of been for Jamie, I would have never gone. That boy was seriously playing with my heart.

I did a lot of mingling and saw a lot of familiar faces. There were so many women there who I knew but had no idea of the disease that they were fighting. I even ran into Misty Daniels. You know when I saw that girl I had to pull her to the side.

"Misty Daniels?" I squealed behind her.

She turned around from the circle of people that she was talking to. Her eyes lit up when she saw me. She came from a rich family. She was pretty and country as hell, straight out of Arkansas. She was the loudest white girl I'd ever met in my life, outside of my mother and her sisters.

"Hey, bih! What up, chick?" Misty threw her arms around me.

We ended up outside of the hotel, smoking some medicinal marijuana that Misty brought with her in her Marc Jacobs purse. Turns out, she had retinoblastoma, cancer of the retina. She lost vision in one eye, and could barely see out of the other. No wonder her damn medicine cabinet looked like a pharmacy back when we were in high school.

Misty passed the blunt to me, sitting on a bench outside of the Hilton. "Girl, what the fuck you doing here with Jamie Green?"

I looked at her, inhaling as much of that good shit as I could. I held it in before exhaling it through my nose, little by little. "Girl, it's a long story. Trust me."

Misty shook her head at me while taking the blunt out of my hand. "I see. I saw li'l Ne'Vaeh on TV with Aaron a few weeks ago. Did you know his grandfather is passing down his diamond mine business to that boy? Ne'Vaeh doesn't ever gotta work another got-damn day in her got-damn life! You must've been out your mind to let that boy slip through your fingers!" She took a few puffs in. "But then again, he was never yours to begin with. Everyone but you knew he liked that girl."

I shook my head at her. I sighed. I didn't feel like discussing Ne'Vaeh or Aaron's ass. I looked at her. "When is the last time you had one of your parties, girl?"

Misty laughed a little. "Girl, since the time my brother's friends robbed my house lookin' for my stash. The last party I had was in 2014. Girl, you don't remember my party in 2014? Y'all muthafuckas drank up every got-damn bottle of alcohol in my house, that's probably why you don't remember! Or should I say can't remember! Everybody got fucked up, especially when my brothers spiked the green punch with all types of shit. You and a few of your friends were gone, I'm tellin' you."

I looked at her, "Few of what friends?"

Misty looked at me, giggling at my memory loss. "Girl, half the got-damn dance squad! My brothers put Molly, liquid morphine, Rohypnol, Ecstasy, e'ry got-damn thang in that drink! Y'all know better than to drink anything my brothers make! I don't even know how y'all made it home safe! Come to think of it, I think Ashton's ass took you home. He had drank some of that green punch, too, but I'm pretty sure it didn't hit him until he got you back to his place."

I exhaled deeply, "Misty, what night was this?"

"The night before y'all left to go to Miami." Misty watched me damn near choke from inhaling too much smoke. She patted my back, "Girl, you a'ight? This shit is too strong to take to the head like that!"

I shook my head, standing up from the bench, just when Jamie made his way outside. It was about 11:00, and after hearing that bit of information from Misty, I was definitely ready to go home.

"Shawty, y'all can't smoke that shit out here." Jamie shook his head at the both of us.

Misty rolled her eyes. "Boy, bye. My dad is the one sponsoring this banquet. He owns this hotel, remember? And hello to you, too, Mr. Star Quarterback. How you been?" She hugged Jamie around his neck.

Jamie hugged her back, looking at me over her shoulder. "I'm good. Yo, let me holla at shawty alone real quick."

Misty grinned at me. "Okay. See you later, Charlie. It was really nice seeing you again, boo. Don't be a stranger! You got my new number now, girl, so dial it!" She winked at me before walking back into the hotel.

I looked up at Jamie. My heart pounded in my chest. Ashton's dreams were a reality. We did go to Misty's party back in 2014, and the worst part about it all is that it was right before the day we went to Miami. Right before I spent that week with Jamie in that beach house. I was fucked.

Jamie's eyes searched my face. He sensed something was wrong. "Shawty, you good?"

I faked a smile, shaking off my guilt. "Oh, yeah, I'm good. Just a little buzzed."

Jamie laughed a little. "I know you got somethin' from her for a nigga."

I grinned, "Oh, you know I did. I got you." I patted my purse.

"Seriously though, I never got the chance to thank you for that contract. I'm not saying that I agree with the way you went about getting it, but," Jamie's eyes searched mine. "I appreciate ya. No one has ever done anything like that for me."

I shook my head at him, really not trying to get emotional that night. "It was no big deal, Jamie. I did it for my son."

Jamie nodded. "You did it for me, too, shawty. I never got the chance to tell you how sorry I am for the way I treated you for almost two years. You didn't deserve that. I blamed you for losing that girl when I was the one to blame. You and me, we've been cool all my life. You know I never meant to hurt you, Charlene."

I nodded, fixing the collar of his shirt, trying to distract myself from crying. "I know, boo. You don't have to apologize, okay? It's obvious that I forgive you, or we wouldn't be standing here talking to each other tonight."

"So, you comin' home with me tonight, shawty?" Jamie held my waist, pulling my body closer to his.

I sighed, thinking about Ashton and the number of times he'd texted me that night. I had lied to him, telling him that I was staying over my cousin's crib because

I had a photo shoot in the morning. I knew from the moment I slid into that dress that I was going to Jamie's place just so he could take it off.

"I don't know, Jamie." That bit of information Misty gave me had me feeling some type of way. "I should go back home. Ashton has been calling and texting me. He got off at seven. I forgot we were supposed to be going to dinner and a movie tonight. He actually wants to spend time with me. Meanwhile"—I looked Jamie up and down as he laughed—"your smooth-talkin' ass just wants to take me home and remove some clothing. You don't love anyone but yourself, Jamie. Ashton loves me regardless of what everyone else thinks about me. Maybe I should give this boy a chance."

"Maybe you should." Jamie's brown eyes searched my body. "But not tonight."

I looked into Jamie's face. "Why you always wanna take my clothes off, Jamie?"

Jamie grinned lookin' back into my face. "Shit, we can do it with the dress on if you want to. C'mon, let's get out of here. I haven't seen you in two months. I'm sure the nigga can spare you for one night. Just for an hour. You don't live that far from me. I'll get you home by one o'clock, I promise."

Boy, did he lie. From the moment we stepped inside of his mansion, panties were coming off. He just couldn't wait. He fucked me up against the wall, in the corridor. The first words out of Jamie's mouth after he came were, "Spend the night with me." I hadn't heard him ask me that since we spent the night on that beach. I don't know if it was the loneliness that was talking, but whatever it was, I wish he'd felt that way before Ashton got a hold of me. Damn. Fuck. Shit.

***

"Charlie, get your ass up!" I awoke to someone shaking the hell out of my arm.

"Lilia, bitch, you're fired," I muttered, burying my head under the pillow.

"No, dummy, it's not Lilia. This is Jamie's house, fool." It finally registered in my brain that the sound of the woman's voice was my damn sister's.

"Heather?" I sat straight up in the bed, hair covering my face. "What the fuck? What are you doing here?" I pushed my hair from my face, covering up with the blanket.

Heather shook her head at me, standing there in her purple and black workout shorts and a tank top. Her dirty-blond hair was pulled up into my messy ponytail. "Girl, it's ten o'clock. I told your ass when I picked August up yesterday that I would be droppin' him off over here at ten today. What the fuck are you doing here?"

I looked over to my left, where Jamie had been sleeping the night before. I looked up at Heather. I didn't have to ask how she got to Jamie's place; I already knew whose broomstick she'd rode in on. "Where is Jamie?" I was reluctant to ask.

"Downstairs with mama." She nodded, watching me hop my naked ass out of the bed, rushing over to the chair in the corner of the room where my clothes were laid. She shook her head at me. "I thought you were seeing Ashton. How the fuck did you end up over here last night?"

"Girl, why don't you just concentrate on how to eat your girl's pussy and stay the fuck out of my business? Damn, you're just like mama, always in my shit when your shit doesn't smell any better than mine." I slid into my panties and threw on my dress.

Heather laughed a little. "Me and my girl are engaged. At least I have only been with one girl in my entire life.

How many dicks been up in you? You got Ashton's nose wide the fuck open, and you're still chasing after Jamie's ass? This dude will never love you like he loves Ne'Vaeh, so you might as well stop fooling yourself."

I picked up my shoes, pushing past her. "Bitch, move. I don't have time for your shit today." I hurried out of Jamie's room and down the steps to see my mother standing there, already with her finger in Jamie's face, little August on her hip.

Mother looked up at me, watching me walk down the steps, bra and heels in my hand. She handed August to Jamie as I reached the bottom of the steps. She looked at Jamie and then back at me, shaking her head. "Charlie here has been dating Ashton for the past two months. Has she told you that?" Mama looked back at Jamie.

I sighed. "Mama, me and Ashton are just friends."

Mother rolled her eyes from Jamie over to me. "Does he know that? He may be just your 'friend,' but you're definitely not just his. That boy has worshipped the ground you walk on since you were like two years old, Charlene! He is too fragile for this shit! You're really still seeing Jamie knowing how that boy feels about you?"

"Mama, please, stay the fuck out of my business this time. I don't need you to do any more damage than you already have. Let me handle things my way this time, okay?" I slipped into my heels.

Mother shook her head at me. "Ya know, I was supposed to keep this a secret, but I thought you should know. I went with Ashton two weeks ago to help him pick out an engagement ring."

I gasped, looking at Jamie.

Jamie grinned, shaking his head to himself, "I told you so" written all over his face.

"He was going to propose to you last night over dinner." Mother shook her head at me, her blue eyes shimmering.

"Baby, that boy loves you. Despite all that you are and all the bullshit that you do, he loves you! But instead of love, your ass seems to want to feel pain. You want some more pain?" Mother dug through her purse to pull out a beige envelope wrapped in a purple bow. She shoved it at me. "Here! Feel this!"

I looked at her, holding the envelope in my hands. "What is this?"

"An invitation to Ne'Vaeh and Aaron's wedding reception. It's next week, you know, at the same place where your wedding reception was supposed to be." Mother smirked a little before kissing her grandson on the forehead. "Bye, baby. Come on, Heather. Let's leave the foolish couple alone."

Watching Ne'Vaeh and Aaron shoving cake into one another's face at their extended wedding was heartbreaking, I must admit. You should have seen him kissing and licking the cake off her face, while she giggled and cried at the same time. She wore the most beautiful tight, backless pearl-colored dress, covered in tiny pearls from her tiny little waist, to the end of her eight-foot train. I sat at a table in the far corner of the room with Ashton, his brother Trenton, his cousin Korel, Kelissa, Danita, Dana, Lailah, and Tyra. I didn't want to sit with those bitches, but I had to sit far enough away from everyone so no one would see me crying. I couldn't get the thought out of my head of what Misty had told me the night before. All I kept thinking was maybe little August wasn't Jamie's baby after all.

I couldn't bear to watch them dancing together to Ne'Vaeh's favorite R & B song entitled "Ah Yeah." From the moment she heard that song, she told everyone that she was going to dance with her husband to that song.

And there she was, face pressed against Aaron's chest, dancing in his arms. They looked so cute together, they had damn near everyone, even Aaron's mother, in tears. I couldn't watch. I had to sneak away to the ladies' room.

I sat on a bench in the bathroom, blowing my nose when Kelissa, Danita, Dana, Tyra, and Lailah made their way into the bathroom.

I rolled my eyes, drying my face. "Really? How the fuck is damn near our whole table gonna get up and walk the fuck out in the middle of a dance?"

"Girl, shut up." Tyra went over to the mirror to blot her face. "Girl, that song had me in my feelings. I had to walk the fuck out before I grabbed some random dude and started kissin' on him. Did you see those men in Aaron's family? Every last one of them muthafuckas—white, black, Senegalese, Arabian—were fine as fuck!"

"For real!" Danita high-fived my cousin, standing alongside her at the mirror.

I had to clear my head. I had to ask them about Misty's party. "Ummm," I ran my fingers through my hair. "Y'all remember Misty's party back in 2014, right?"

Lailah giggled. "Shit, barely! All I know is when I woke up, I was at the airport with you chicas, ready to board our flight to Miami."

"What about the rest of y'all?" I looked at Kelissa, then Dana and Danita.

Kelissa rolled her eyes. "Well, I was the fuckin' designated driver, so I didn't drink shit. I spent most of my night making sure none of y'all ended up fuckin' some random nigga at Misty's crib."

"And what about me?" I hesitated to ask.

Dana and Danita just looked at one another, and then at me.

Tyra looked at their reflection in the mirror, then turned around and looked at them. "What was that look for?"

"You don't remember anything about the night before our trip to Miami? You really don't remember going home with Ashton?" Dana looked at me.

Kelissa damn near tripped over her heels, falling down on the stool next to mine. "Say what?" She looked at me.

Tyra's eyes were big as hell. "What are they talking about?"

I shrugged. "I don't know."

"Then why are you asking about Misty's party? And Dana, what the fuck do you mean she went home with Ashton?" Kelissa exclaimed.

Danita sighed. "When it was getting late, we were trying to round up all the girls that we knew had to be on the plane the next morning, headed to Miami. Like Lailah said, just about half of the squad was drunk as fuck. Alisha rounded up all the girls we could find, and we helped her put them in Kelissa's Tahoe, and Alisha rode with her to take them back to the hotel. When we asked around if anyone had seen you, they said you had left with Ashton. Girl, me and Danita did a high-speed chase down that highway to make it to you before Alisha did! Good thing Aaron was out of town with his cousins. You were high as fuck, knowing good and damn well you can't drink anything Misty's brothers put together! They're always trying to get them young bitches drunk at their parties so they can do whatever to them. You know Ashton's square ass didn't know there was anything put in that punch. Anyway, we got to Ashton's crib, used Alisha's key and went inside. We found you and Ashton naked on the bathroom floor!"

Tyra looked at the clueless expression on my face.

"It took me, Dana, and that chick Tisha who used to dance with us to get you up off of Ashton, dressed, and back to Dana's apartment." Danita shook her head at me.

"And the reason y'all never mentioned this shit to Charlene is because?" Kelissa took the words right out of my mouth.

Dana looked at me, her hazel eyes searching my face. "Alisha was already on Charlie's ass enough as it was. She had suspected something happened between y'all years before, ya know? Why would we wanna cause more drama than was necessary?"

I just sat there in shock, letting Kelissa and my cousin Tyra do the arguing for me.

"The fuck you mean? Bitch, look at the damage that has been done!" Kelissa exclaimed. "Have you seen little August? I'm not saying he looks like Ashton, 'cause he looks like Charlie, but come on now, there's not much a resemblance to Jamie, and now I see why!"

All five women in the bathroom looked at me, watching my chest heave in and out. I hadn't had a DNA test done when I had the baby because I just knew that Jamie was his father. Aaron and I weren't having sex during that time, and I found out that I was pregnant a few weeks after returning home from Miami. It wasn't until the day Ashton kissed me that the memories started to come back. And if I hadn't mentioned anything to Dana or Danita, they would have never mentioned it to me.

"Y'all could have told me this shit." I shook my head at the both of them.

"What difference does it all make now? The damage has already been done." Dana shook her head back at me. "You made this bed for yourself, Charlie, now you gotta be a woman and lay in that bitch."

I stood from the bench, stepping up to her, getting in her face so she could hear me loud and clear. "Y'all bitches just like drama, that's all this is! You knew I was too high and faded to know what the fuck I was doing, let alone remember it! Y'all had plenty of time to tell me what I had done!"

Dana shoved me, pushing me out of her personal space. "Are you serious? We didn't even go on that Miami trip with you girls. How the fuck were we supposed to know that you'd end up sleeping with Jamie? As soon as we found out that you slept with Jamie during that retreat, we stayed out of your business."

"Do you know what I've done? Ne'Vaeh was in love with Jamie!" I exclaimed.

Danita laughed a little. "Did you not just see that girl crying while Aaron recited his wedding vows to her? She couldn't even say hers back to him, she was crying so much! Did she look like she was even thinking about Jamie to you?"

"Li'l Ne'Vaeh was like 'Jamie, who?'" Lailah laughed.

"Exactly." Danita shook her head at me.

I was so irritated with everyone's thinking. "Are y'all serious? Y'all must not remember my baby shower, when that girl hit me in the face with that key, splitting my face the fuck in half! Y'all don't remember that bullshit? Well, I do, because I had to pay thousands to get rid of that scar! I can barely chew on that side of my mouth! I pushed her to Aaron because I fucked up what she had with Jamie! And Jamie loves my son! And my son hasn't woken up once not asking for Jamie!"

They all started to see my point then.

"Oh my goodness, what have I done?" I moaned.

"Charlie, you have to get a DNA test!" Tyra shook her head at me, her light eyes glistening. "If you don't wanna tell Jamie, you can at least talk with Ashton. Or did you sleep with some more niggas that I don't know about during that time?"

I looked at her. "Tyra, you're my cousin, but don't get fucked up. This shit isn't funny."

Tyra shook her head at me. "Who's laughing?"

Kelissa looked at me. "Word on the street is you actually started dating Ashton."

Danita gasped. "But I heard you were still fuckin' with Jamie!"

Tyra was disgusted with me. "See, that's the shit I'm talkin' about! Charlie, I told you not to fuck with Ashton, so what are you doing?"

"I—I don't know," I whispered.

Kelissa threw her hands up, not sure what else she could say that would make a difference in my situation. "Girl, I don't even know what to say to you that will help your situation. All I know is that boy Ashton has been in love with you since we were kids. And drunk, high, gone, faded or not, I'm sure that nigga has some sort of memory of what happened that night. You need to go ahead and get a DNA test. And if the baby is Ashton's, you need to tell him. And if he's not the man you wanna be with, you need to tell him that, too. The whole while Jamie was on the road, doing his acting thing, I'm sure you were fuckin' Ashton. Now am I wrong?"

They all looked at me.

I sat back down on the bench, not answering the question.

Kelissa exhaled deeply, really not in the mood to lecture me or to start another fight like the one we had less than two years ago. "Yes, you hurt that girl when she found out the baby was Jamie's. And yes, you'll hurt Jamie if he finds out this baby is not his. You're playing with Ashton's heart when you know he loves you. You are his crutch now that Alisha is gone. If you don't wanna be with him, you need to let him know and stop fuckin' with his head. Dana's right, the damage has already been done. From this point on, people are gonna get hurt. There's no way around that, so stop lookin' for it, shit. Just get the damn DNA test done, Charlie."

Just then, Renée strolled into the bathroom, in a beautiful purple chiffon dress. Her hair was in a curly updo. She looked just like Marilyn Monroe. "The hell y'all doing in here?" She made a face at us as she strolled over to the mirror to check her makeup. "Y'all missing everything. She's about to throw the bouquet."

Everyone, including myself, rolled their eyes at Renée.

"Girl, ain't nobody trying to catch that shit." Danita smacked her lips. "But I am hungry. I'm about to go get me some of that shrimp cocktail, yessir!"

"Oh!" Renée turned around facing us, just as we were about to make our way out of the bathroom. And there she was again with another got-damn invitation. She handed the canary yellow envelope to me.

I sighed, taking the envelope in my hands, looking her in her face. "Let me guess, an invitation to home girl's baby shower?"

"Yes, hunti!" Renée squealed. "Since she's here for another few days, I figured I'd throw my boo a baby shower. And I expect each and every last one of you bitches to be there, a'ight? Ain't gonna be no shit like there was at Charlie's baby shower, I'm gonna let y'all hoes know that shit right now. Now, c'mon, let's go reach for that bouquet."

Just as we left the bathroom, I ran smack into Jamie. He was dressed in Gorgio Armani from head to toe, looking delectable as ever. Tyra nudged me in the back as she made her way back into the reception area with the rest of the girls.

Jamie grinned down at me, looking my body over. I'll admit, I did look sexy in my teal backless dress and gold Giuseppe stilettos.

I knew we needed to talk, but it wasn't the time. "Wow," I looked him over, too. "You actually showed up. You're making progress."

Jamie laughed a little, knowing I was mocking him. "Slowly but surely, shawty."

"C'mon, chica, let's go get this bouquet!" Lailah grabbed my arm, pulling me along with her.

You should have seen everyone fighting for that bouquet. I was just standing there like, *What the hell am I doing here?* The men stood back on one side of the room; you know Jamie's ass was as far from the festivities as possible. I couldn't believe Ashton had the nerve to join in. Ne'Vaeh was so happy, preparing herself to toss that expensive bouquet of flowers in her hand. She tossed it in the air, and all those bitches pushed each other out of the way to get to it. But despite of all of their efforts, the bouquet fell right at my feet. I watched them fight for the bouquet, and guess who got a hold of it? Renée's ass. And guess who caught the garter belt? One of Aaron's nineteen-year-old cousins, this cute little white boy named Richie. You should have seen Renée's ass squirming in that chair as that cute-ass boy slid that garter belt up her leg. I'm pretty sure her panties were soaked. That young boy was gonna have her ass sprung. Yeah, it's about time that bitch got some dick in her life, dick that she didn't have to share with another woman that is.

Jamie never once walked up to Ne'Vaeh to say his congratulations, but she knew that he was there. I saw them catch each other's eye for a second or two. Her eyes lit up when she saw him, and he winked at her. She grinned a little before winking back. And that was that. They didn't need words to say they still loved each other. Aaron couldn't compare to Jamie, and Jamie couldn't compare to Aaron. I don't think Ne'Vaeh was looking to replace Jamie when she married Aaron. I think she was just trying to stop her heart from feeling the pain of losing both him and their baby. Jamie watched as

Aaron held her hands in his, holding her close, letting everyone know that he was never letting her go. I'm sure that Jamie had to be thinking that the moment Ne'Vaeh was sharing with Aaron was meant for him, but Jamie kept his thoughts to himself. Jamie saw that Ne'Vaeh was taken care of, and I think that was assurance enough to him that she'd be okay.

Chapter 12: The Test

Charlene

"Miss Ella did her thing planning that wedding." Ashton removed his tie that evening in my bedroom.

I tried to smile, but I couldn't. I kicked off my shoes and tossed my clutch on my bed. "Yeah, it was beautiful."

Ashton watched my lips tremble as I fought back the tears as hard as I could. "Charlene, what's wrong?"

I shook my head, unzipping my dress.

Ashton held my hand, pulling me to him, looking down into my face. "Baby, talk to me."

I looked up at him. "I talked to Misty two weeks ago. She said that she had a party the night before the Morgan Girls went to Miami for our retreat. She remembers me leaving her party with you. And that I was pretty faded."

Ashton let go of my hand, just looking down into my face.

"When I asked around at the wedding reception who remembered anything about that party, they also said that they found me and you naked in your bathroom, me on top of you, passed the fuck out." I shook my head to myself.

At that moment, little August comes racing into the bathroom, running straight into my legs, face first. I looked down at my son with tears in my eyes, struggling to smile. I picked my little boy up, who was excited to see me. He looked at Ashton, grinning from ear to ear. "Ashy!" he called out to Ashton.

Ashton's eyes glistened. He looked at August, then back at me.

I nodded. "Ashton, we need to get a DNA test."

The very next morning, me, Ashton, and little August went to have the DNA test done. I cried as the doctor swiped the cotton swab across my gums. I couldn't believe that I had caused so much chaos in my life as well as everyone else's. Alisha told me that I would hang myself. I couldn't even blame Dana and Danita for not telling me what I had done. I should have known my partying would catch up to me sooner or later.

I sat in the front passenger's seat of Ashton's ride that morning, in a daze, staring out of the window. Little August was knocked out in the back seat. Ashton didn't say much to me that entire morning. I'm pretty sure he was hurting just as much as, if not more than I was.

Ashton grabbed my hand.

I looked at him, heart in total shock.

Ashton looked at me, light eyes glistening, "All we can do is wait a few days for the results, baby; that's pretty much all we can do."

"I–I know." I stuttered. "It's just what if Jamie isn't . . . What if you're . . ." I burst out crying.

Ashton leaned forward and gently kissed my lips, holding my face in his hands. "Baby, we just have to wait and see."

"He–he wanted Ne'Vaeh so bad, and I ruined it for him," I whispered, drying my face. "I didn't mean to cause him any pain. I didn't mean to hurt you or anyone else."

"I know. What's done is done. If little man is mine, you know I'm here for you. If he's not, well, you know I'm here for you regardless," Ashton assured me.

"Ashton, I'm so sorry." I continued to cry until I couldn't cry anymore.

***

After Ashton went to work and I dropped my son over at my mother's house,

I paid Jamie a visit at Flex, a gym that mostly celebrities and sports stars frequented in DC. I didn't have a membership, but I used to go to school with the couple who owned the gym, so they'd let me in for free just as long as I got a few people to sign up for a membership.

"Hey, Selena." I sighed, running my hands through my curls at the front desk.

"Hey, supermodel! What's up?" Selena smiled, pearly whites gleaming. Selena was about five foot one, long dark hair, perfect beach tan, and the perfect body. She opened the gym with her rich husband about three years ago. Selena was twenty, and Russell was twenty-three. Russell's parents were both Circuit Court judges. Russell was already the head of the department that Ashton worked in at the University of Maryland Medical Center.

"Have you seen Jamie around?" I asked, pulling my hair back into a ponytail. I was dressed in a black crop top, hot pink boy shorts, and pink Reeboks. I knew good and well I wasn't going to work out, but I knew I had to look the part if I wanted to not look too suspicious. Russell and Ashton were pretty good friends, and if Russell saw me talking to Jamie, I knew word would get back to Ashton. Though Ashton knew of my feelings for Jamie, that didn't mean he wanted me anywhere near him, especially once Ashton and I had started sleeping together. I was getting tired of sneaking off to be with Jamie. We'd been sleeping together just about every day since he'd gotten back from Atlanta.

"Last I saw Jamie was down in the private weight room. Room B123. Here." She tossed me a set of keys. "You need a key to get in."

I looked at her. "Is there anyone with him?"

"I haven't seen Jamie with any girls down there in since he's been back in town, sweetie," Selena replied, watching the relieved expression on my face.

"Thanks, Selena." I hurried off to find Jamie.

The private weight room was on the basement level of the gym. As seductive as the theme of that floor was, I knew the only workout going on down there was fuckin'. As I unlocked the door to the room Jamie was in, I was hit in the face by a Zesty mist. Each weight room had its own shower and sauna. I walked into the room, closing the door behind me. Jamie's gym bag was on the floor, and the clothes that he had taken off were lying next to it. I removed my socks and shoes, then made my way into the shower room.

"Jamie?" I called out, eying him standing directly underneath the shower head. Suds ran from his head down his back, sliding through the crack of his ass. Why, oh why, did he have to be so damn sexy?

Jamie turned toward me, wiping the excess water from his face. "What's good wit'cha, shawty?" He rinsed off.

I had almost forgotten what I had to say. His body had me speechless. He looked edible, like a fuckin' piece of hot fudge, all wet and slippery. I inched my way near him, grabbing his towel along the way. I just watched as he rinsed off. I didn't regain my ability to speak until he turned off the water and reached for the towel that I was bringing him.

"Hey." I finally spoke.

Jamie grinned, drying himself off. "What'cha doing here?"

"I–I just had a lot on my mind." I watched him running the towel over his chocolaty skin.

"Has he proposed yet?" Jamie wrapped the towel around his waist.

"No, but I know he will. That wedding has everyone feeling some type of way." I rolled my eyes. "It's probably got you in your feelings, too, huh?"

Jamie just looked at me.

My eyes widened. "Not you, too! What did you do? Go and hunt Ne'Vaeh down at the hotel where she's staying? No, wait, you must have gave her the engagement ring that you wanted to give her when she left Maryland last year. I bet after I left the reception, your ass gave that shit to her right in front of Aaron, didn't you?"

Jamie laughed at all of my ideas, though he knew he had thought about each and every one of them. "Naw. I just been thinkin' about life, that's all."

I sighed. I had to talk to him about the DNA test, but first I had to talk to him about ending whatever it was that we had going on. "Jamie, we have to stop doing this. Whatever this is, we can't do it anymore. Ashton isn't my boyfriend, but he means a lot to me. So we need to stop."

Jamie looked down into my face, pulling me closer to him by the elastic in my shorts. I wasn't wearing any panties underneath, by the way. "Well, what if I don't wanna stop? What if I wanna keep doing this?"

I let out a long sigh, as Jamie ran his hands up my thighs, cupping each ass cheek in his hands. I looked up into his face. "Jamie, I can't be your favorite anymore. I don't wanna be someone's favorite, I wanna be someone's only. I'm just your *daily*, but I'm Ashton's *only*."

"Let's try this." Jamie's eyes searched my face.

I pushed him in his chest, pushing him off of me. "Jamie, please, stop playing. I don't have time for this. I came here to talk to you about something serious, and you're playing with my emotions again!"

"Naw, shawty," Jamie grabbed my hand in his, pulling me up against him. "There's no drama with us. There's no secrets with us. There's no pretending to be something that we're not. I can talk to you about anything, and you always set it to me straight. We have a son together. Maybe this is meant to be. I wanna try this; just you and me, nobody else."

My heart nearly stopped in my chest. My mind kept screaming, "What about Ashton? You're just gonna hurt Ashton! That boy is in love with you! He waited all of his life for you! What if this baby is Ashton's?"

But my heart was in complete control: "Jamie wants you, Charlene, you better jump at this chance. He doesn't have to know about the DNA test, or the results, which-ever way they turn out. You have been waiting your whole life for this boy to want you, so what are you waiting for?"

"What about Ashton?" I whispered, looking up into Jamie's face as he backed me up into the shower, drop-ping his towel. "What do I tell Ashton?"

"Shawty, I want you. I have a son with you. We owe it to ourselves to give this a try. You've been in my bed every night for the past two weeks. Don't it feel good to be together?" He reached for the faucet handle, turning the water back on, steam instantly filling the room again.

I gasped as he swooped my shirt up and over my head, tossing it on the tile floor. "Yes, Jamie, you know it feels so good to me, but—"

Jamie slid my shorts down, down my thighs and past my calves.

I stepped out of them, and he tossed them on the floor, too.

He backed me up against the wall of the shower. "Don't you wanna be with me?" He gently kissed my lips. "Huh? Don'tcha?"

I kissed him back, holding his face in my hands. Our hearts were finally on the same beat, and it felt so damn good. "Jamie, you know I do, but—"

"Then fuck him." Jamie lift my body up, wrapping my legs around his waist,

"And fuck with me."

I knew what I was doing was wrong. I knew I didn't deserve to be with either Ashton or Jamie. With the DNA test pending, I had no business letting Jamie finally decide it was the right time to try and dedicate his heart to someone again. I should have told him the truth right then, but I didn't. I let that boy make love to me in that shower, knowing in the back of my mind that the son he thought we shared might not be his.

I didn't go home that night. I went out with Jamie and a few of his friends to Whip, a club in downtown Baltimore. Turns out, Anastasia Jones was in town and was throwing Jamie an album release party. You should have seen the look on her face when she saw me strolling into the club, hand in hand with Jamie. I knew she had a problem with me, and I couldn't have cared less.

I'd never seen Jamie sing in person, though I had heard a few of his songs on iTunes. I was blown away by the strength and power in his voice when he performed one of his songs that night in V.I.P. The name of his song was "51515" or in other words, May 15, 2015, the day little August was born. I couldn't even make it halfway through watching him sing that song when I had to make an exit from VIP. I couldn't take it. I could feel the chunks start to rise in my throat as I rushed into the bathroom. The thought of August not being Jamie's baby was literally making me sick. I made it into the bathroom stall just as the chunks spewed from my mouth into the toilet.

I sat there, face buried in the toilet, on my knees, crying and gagging at the same time. I was so ashamed of myself. My mother was right; my lifestyle was catching up with me in the worst way possible. Why did I have to drink that got-damn punch at Misty's party? Shit, why was I even at the bitch's party? Why did I have to put myself in the position to even question the paternity of my baby? Why did Jamie have to tell me that he was ready for me? And why was Ashton in love with me when I was in love with Jamie?

The door to the bathroom opened, and I heard the sound of heels prancing across the linoleum floor, stopping abruptly, probably to primp in the mirror.

"Are you okay in there?" I heard Anastasia's voice.

"Yeah." I wiped my lips, peeling myself off of the floor. I slowly opened the door to the stall, seeing Anastasia standing back against the sink, facing my stall with her arms folding. Guess she wasn't primping after all.

I made a face at her, then walked over to the sink to rinse my mouth out with water. I cupped my hands, holding it under the running faucet.

She turned to me, arms still folded, glare tracing my profile. "The fuck are you doing here with him?" She watched me drink water from my hand, then spit it out into the sink. She moved aside as I grabbed a paper towel from the dispenser.

I lifted my eyebrow at her as I dried my face, the tears from my cheeks, and the water from my mouth. "Excuse me?"

"You heard what I said, Charlene," Anastasia rolled her neck at me. The bitch was richer than Bank of America, and yet she had the audacity to give two cents about my mediocre life. "What are you doing with him besides fuckin' him?"

I just looked at her like she'd lost her mind. "You need to be worrying about making sure he gets everything you promised him in that contract and stay out of his personal business, Mrs. Jones. I don't give a fuck how you thought you could talk to Ne'Vaeh, but I'm not the one to fuck with."

Anastasia laughed a little. "You know, that girl talked about you and Jamie all the time. It really hurt her that you never came to see her while she lived in Atlanta. I told her to not even sweat it, because you weren't shit but someone trying to steal her life and her man. That boy was everything to that girl, and you took him from her."

I rolled my eyes at her, turning back to the mirror to fix my face before I stepped back out into the crowd. "I heard about that grimy shit that went down in Atlanta, so don't try to throw salt at me, Anastasia. If you cared so much about her, why did you damn near work her to death? It was my idea for Jamie to try out for the play, but I had no idea that shit would escalate so far as to you sending Aaron to jail."

"The only reason why Ne'Vaeh even came to Atlanta was to get away from you and Jamie. It shouldn't even surprise me that you'd come here with him. I couldn't make it to Ne'Vaeh's reception because I had a concert in New York, but Jamie called me afterward. Said that Ne'Vaeh sang what was supposed to be her first single off of her second album, called 'White Gold,' to Aaron. He said Aaron's mother was crying watching her son getting married to Ne'Vaeh. Watching Ne'Vaeh hugging Aaron's mother had Jamie in tears, he said. Ne'Vaeh lost her brother, lost her sister, never had the mother she wanted, never knew her father. Jamie said the day she married Aaron, she got all that back. Watching Ne'Vaeh find true happiness made that boy realize he needed to find that, too. That he wasn't complete until he had a family of his own." Anastasia's stare nearly burned a hole in the side of my face.

I looked at her.

"I wish he would have gotten his shit together with my cousin, because I sure as hell didn't wanna see him with your thottish ass." Anastasia looked me up and down.

I couldn't help but laugh. "Don't you have better *thangs* to do with your time than to worry about what I do with mine? If your two cents isn't going toward any of my bills, I could give a fuck about anything that you say to me."

"Well, there's no shame in your game, I can at least say that much about you. Just remember that sooner or later, you'll run out of cards to play." Anastasia grinned.

I rolled my eyes. I should have listened to her, but I didn't, the same way I brushed off everything that everyone else said to me.

"You're gonna hurt him," Anastasia shook her head at me. "I just know it." And she left the bathroom, leaving me standing there to face my reflection in the mirror alone.

I sat there at the bar in VIP that night, sipping on a melon cocktail and watching Jamie mingle with a few people. Just when I asked the bartender to fix me another drink, she looked at me and then pointed to the VIP entrance. I turned around to see Ashton standing in the entrance, eyes scanning the room. I stared at him long enough for our eyes to meet. Once he saw me, he made his way through the crowd of people over to the bar. I looked over at Jamie as Ashton approached me. Jamie wasn't paying Ashton any attention until one of his associates directed his attention at Ashton walking over to me.

Ashton stood before me, looking around the room at the group of people that I was associating with. He already knew they were Jamie's people. I guess he wanted to read the expressions on their faces to see if their faces revealed anything to him that let him know that I was there with Jamie and not there alone.

Ashton looked at me, temples twitching. "Charlene, you forgot we had plans tonight?"

I looked up at him, heart pounding in my chest. He was taking me out to eat at my favorite Italian restaurant in Silver Springs. I remembered, I just knew he was planning on proposing to me, and I couldn't break his heart. I should have known that he'd find out where I was. Like I told you, Russell must have looked at the log-in book at the gym, saw that Selena had given me the keys to the weight room that Jamie was using, and told Ashton that I had gone to the gym to meet Jamie.

"I forgot, boo. Ummm, I was invited to Jamie's album release party." I watched the vein in Ashton's temples throbbing. He was pissed.

"Hi, sweetie." Anastasia made her way over to us, holding out her hand to shake Ashton's. "We never formally met at Alisha's funeral, but I'm sure you know my name."

Ashton looked at her, then back at me.

Anastasia lowered her hand when she realized Ashton had no intentions of shaking it. "You should stay a while, Ashton, there's plenty to drink, and it looks to me like you're gonna need one." She patted me on the back, then walked away from us.

"The fuck you doing here with this muthafucka, Charlene?" Ashton's eyes searched my face. He looked over at the leather couch where Jamie was sitting, dressed in black and white.

Jamie grinned, grill gleaming, with that "you should have known better than to let your girl come around me" face.

Ashton looked back at me, "C'mon, Charlene, let's go."

I looked up at him, shaking my head, "What? No, I just got here!"

Ashton grabbed my arm, pulling me to him, about to take me out of that club if he had to drag me out. "I said, let's go, Charlene!"

Jamie rose from the couch. "Aye, nigga, she said she didn't wanna leave. If you wanna leave, why don't you take your ass the fuck up out of here?" He walked up to us.

Ashton was still gripping my arm tight in his hands, standing there looking at Jamie like he wanted to slam Jamie's head into the bar. "Muthafucka, was I talkin' to you? I was talkin' to my girl, so back the fuck up."

Jamie grinned. "Your 'girl?' Did your 'girl' come in this muthafucka with you? Did you put a ring on this finger yet? If not, she ain't your muthafuckin' girl. So you need to back the fuck up and get the fuck out this muthafucka before I put you out this muthafucka."

Just then, one of Jamie's teammates walked by us, instigating, singing, "It's not my fault she wanna know me. She told me you was just a homie!"

Muthafuckas were already starting to clown.

I sighed.

Jamie chuckled to himself, grill gleaming under the club lights. "Oh, you thought she was your girl? I'm sorry, dude, my bad."

Ashton let go of my arm, about to get in Jamie's shit, when I pulled Ashton away from him. "No, Ashton, no, we're not gonna go here tonight!"

Ashton yanked his arm from my hands. "Tell this nigga to back the fuck up then, Charlie. You're the one who got this nigga thinkin' he's runnin' shit! He keeps running his mouth, I'ma put my fist in that bitch!"

Before Jamie came back with something real ignorant, I put my hands up to stop him, not realizing that Ashton's eyes were fixated on the diamond bracelet that Jamie had given me that night. "Jamie, please, just let me talk to him." I looked up into Jamie's face.

Jamie looked down at me and then back at Ashton. Jamie didn't budge; he stood right there, ready if Ashton was ready. Jamie was ready to fight for me, something no one had done for me. You know my heart was racing, because I knew my life was about to change, only I wasn't sure which direction it would go in.

I looked up at Ashton, whose eyes were still on the bracelet.

Ashton laughed to himself. "You're still fuckin' this nigga, Charlie?" He looked back into my face.

My heart was racing, and my entire body was shaking.

"Just tell me the truth." Ashton snatched the wrist that had Jamie's bracelet wrapped around it. "A muthafucka ain't giving you shit like this unless you're giving him something in return that's worth just as much."

I pulled from him. "Ashton, I told you two months ago that we weren't exclusive!"

Ashton couldn't help but laugh. "Not muthafuckin' exclusive? When the only people we're fuckin' is each other, Charlene? What the fuck would anyone take from that? So, you're telling me that I was just keeping the pussy warm while Jamie was out of town, is that it?"

People were cracking the fuck up around us, like what Ashton was saying was an act in a comedy show.

"Ashton, you know how I feel about you." I looked up into his face.

"Naw," Ashton looked at Jamie, "I know how you feel about *him*." Ashton looked back at me. "After everything I've done for you, after everything that we've been through, even after everything that happened this fuckin' morning, you still wanna chose this muthafucka over me? Did you even tell him about this morning?"

My lips trembled. I shook my head at Ashton, "Please, don't do this." I begged him. I couldn't tell Jamie about the DNA test. Little August was everything to Jamie. And Jamie was everything to him. I wasn't sure who fathered my son at that moment. The thought of August being Ashton's son scared the hell out of me. I knew what I was doing was hurting Ashton, but I just couldn't tell Jamie the truth just yet. "Don't do this here; I'm begging you."

"Tell me you don't love me, and I'll walk away. You won't see or hear from me anymore." Ashton's eyes searched mine.

I looked over at Anastasia, who was shaking her head at me and my situation. I looked at Jamie who had "I told you not to play with this dude's head" written all over his face. I looked back at Ashton. My heart was confused, but it knew who I desired the most. So I just said the first thing that came to my mind. "I love Jamie," I whispered.

Ashton shook his head at me. "Charlene, you know I need you. You wanna throw what we had away for some nigga who doesn't know how to show his love for you other than to buy you shit and take you out to fancy clubs? Then do what you do, shorty. I'm not gonna stop you." His eyes glistened. "I'm not gonna pretend that I'm not hurt. You know I wanted you since we were kids. To hold you, kiss you, touch you, everything to you felt good as a muthafucka—I'm not gonna stand here and say that it didn't. If this man makes you feel the way that you make me feel, then I can't come between that. I love you more than life itself, and if I can't have you, well, there really is no point in saying anything else, is there?" Ashton looked around the room at all the muthafuckas who were snickering. Then he looked back at me. "What am I even here for?"

I couldn't fight the tears back any longer. "Ashton, sweetie, I'm so sorry."

"Naw, don't be sorry, you made your choice. I hope he takes care of you the way I did. It's just sad that you'd chose him over me. Him, a muthafucka who chooses when to and when not to fuck with you." Ashton looked at Jamie, "You hurt her, they'll be hell to pay, muthafucka." He looked at me one last time, then walked away from us, making his way through the nosy bystanders.

I watched Ashton walk out of that club. It took everything in me not to scream out his name, for him not to leave me, for him to come back. Maybe my heart knew that night would be the very last time that I talked to Ashton.

Chapter 13: Gone

Charlene

I avoided Jamie for the entire weekend. He must have called fifty times. I felt so bad about what I had done, especially when I got home the night of our 'break up,' only to see that Ashton had left a tiny velvet box from Tiffany's on my pillow. I was bawling, tears and snot were running everywhere as I popped open the box to find the most beautiful ring I'd ever seen. There, mounted in platinum, sat a diamond that had to weigh at least 3.8 carats. Tiny, brilliant round diamonds created a halo around it. And I was pretty sure the amount that he invested into that ring could have bought him a four-bedroom, two-story house with a complete basement in Maryland, paid for in full.

That following Monday, I received the results to the DNA test by way of FedEx. Terrified to open it alone, I slid the envelope in my purse. I tried calling Ashton, but he never answered. I had been calling him from the night he left me at the club until the day of Ne'Vach's baby shower. I didn't want to open the envelope without him. I decided that after the baby shower, I would stop by his apartment and pay him a visit.

Renée threw Ne'Vaeh a baby shower at her new condominium in Columbia that Monday afternoon. Ne'Vaeh was so cute, sitting there in her canary yellow strapless dress. Her hair was up in a perfect bun. Her long bangs were swooped to the side. Her Estee Lauder dual finish makeup was flawless. She sat there in the center of us, sniffling as she opened all of our gifts. We weren't best friends anymore, and it sure as hell didn't feel like we were sisters. You should have seen the eye rolls that I'd gotten from Ne'Vaeh's family members, not to mention from a few of the girls on my dance team from the moment that I entered the door. I knew that more than anything, the gifts that always meant the most to her were the ones that came from the heart. So that's what I decided to give to her that day.

"Oh, here's mine!" I grinned, picking my gifts off of Renée's glass dining room table. I walked over to Ne'Vaeh, handing her the first gift.

Ne'Vaeh tried not to grin as she took the gift from my hands, placing it in her lap. She tore open the box.

"Oh, that's pretty," Danita commented as Ne'Vaeh held the gift in her hands.

The first gift was this red-headed porcelain doll, dressed in a raincoat and rain boots that Ne'Vaeh always loved that sat on my nightstand, in my old bedroom at my mother's house. Ne'Vaeh would play with it and sleep with it when we were in kindergarten. She loved that doll and always wanted it, though she never said it.

Ne'Vaeh looked at me, holding the doll in her hands.

"Open this one, too." I handed her another box.

Ne'Vaeh was reluctant to take the next box from my hands. She tore the paper from the box, immediately covering her mouth to fight back the tears. It was the box of Ninja Turtles that my mother bought for her little brother the night before he was killed.

Ne'Vaeh looked up at me, lips trembling.

"Since my sister seems to be speechless," I winked my eye at her, "the first gift is the doll that used to sit on my dresser. She always loved that doll and would sleep with it when she spent the night at my house when we were kids. The second gift is a set of Kevin's favorite toys, the Teenage Mutant Ninja Turtles. My mother bought it for him, but he never got the chance to play with him because . . ." I watched the tears begin to roll down Ne'Vaeh's cheeks. ". . . because he was killed the next morning. Ne'Vaeh, sweetie, I don't know if you're having a girl or a boy, so I gave you toys for both."

"Thank you, Charlie," she whispered.

I sighed, looking at everyone around me, who all looked shocked that I'd brought her such thoughtful gifts. "I know I haven't been much of a friend or a sister to Ne'Vaeh these past few years. I've done and said some things that a sister, let alone a friend, should have never done." I looked at Ne'Vaeh, "You deserve to be happy, Ne'Vaeh, more than anyone that I know. And I'm glad that you finally have someone who will make sure to keep a smile on your face. Aaron would give you the moon, stars, Heaven, and Earth if he could. It's good to know that your heart is finally in good hands." I wiped the tears that escaped from my eyes. "I love you, Ne'Vaeh Washington-Whitehaven. I know I don't say it enough, but I love you, and I really miss you."

Ne'Vaeh reached for a hug, and I gave it to her. I hadn't hugged my girl in so long, and it felt so good. I believed I cried more than she did in her arms. I tried to ignore the Morgan Girls shaking their heads at me. I'm pretty sure Dana and Danita's big-mouthed asses told them about my foggy night with Ashton. I'm pretty sure they wanted to bust me out, but they knew that Ne'Vaeh didn't deserve to go through the pain that my lifestyle caused. I wasn't the only one that was paying for my mistakes. It seemed like the rope that I'd used to hang myself was slowly making a victim out of the people closest to me.

Though Ne'Vaeh was grateful for the gifts, she still wasn't so sure how to deal with me. I'd neglected her when she needed me the most. I played on her guilt of sleeping with Jamie when I knew I was wrong for tricking Aaron into marrying me, knowing I was pregnant with a baby that he had no idea wasn't even his. Though Ne'Vaeh had found her happy ending with Aaron, she'd never forgive me for messing up what she had with Jamie. The love she had for Aaron was no comparison to that do-anything-for-you love she felt for Jamie. It hurt her to be with Aaron when all she ever wanted was Jamie. When we were kids, she told me that she would follow Jamie to the moon and back. That she'd be with him forever. That only God could keep her from him. And I believed it. I finally had Jamie to myself, and all I could think about was the fact that I didn't deserve him.

It had to be about 9:30 at night when the baby shower had come to a close. Aaron arrived at Renée's condo to pick up Ne'Vaeh and the gifts around 9:15. The girls left around 9:45 after helping Renée straighten up her place a little. I was in the kitchen, washing Renée's dishes when she noticed that I hadn't left with the others. She closed the door behind Kelissa, looking over at me.

"Sweetie, you can leave, too. My new boo thang is coming over in about thirty minutes, and I need to go shower." Renée walked into her newly modeled kitchen. "I plan on gettin' fucked tonight by that sexy ass white boy, so you need to bounce. Deuces."

"Girl," I rolled my eyes, drying my hands on her dish towel, "I'm not trying to fuck up your groove; I just wanted to help you clean up your apartment."

Renée grinned. "That was nice what you did for your 'sister,' Charlie, really nice. Who would have ever guessed a girl as grimy as you actually had a heart in there?"

I looked at her, "Not tonight, okay, Renée? I'm feeling like shit enough as it is."

"I don't see why. I heard from one of your girls that you started seeing Jamie again." Renée shook her head at me. "You should be happy. You've always wanted your 'sister's' man, and now you have him."

Renée always had a way of making me feel worse than I was already feeling. Just when you thought you couldn't feel any lower, there Renée's ass was, stomping you more into the ground with her Manolo's.

I shook my head back at her. "You know, Jamie always wanted that girl. He wanted her more than any-thing. Do you know how many times he's called me 'Ne'Vaeh' while having sex without even realizing it?" I cringed at the thought that I had even imagined that I was her while having sex with him, so I could feel how it felt to have Jamie's heart all to myself. "Do you know he has that girl's name tattooed over his heart? Do you know that he wears that engagement ring that he tried to give to her last year dangling from a chain on his neck? The nigga just got the tattoo of baby Sara's name tattooed right underneath Ne'Vaeh's name! He will never love me the way that he loves her! I should have left well enough alone and just let them be together! I should have had the abortion before anyone found out so that they two could live happily ever after, then I wouldn't be in this mess!"

Renée just looked at me, not really sure what to say.

I exhaled deeply, looking at her, bracing myself, because what I was about to say was going to blow her mind. "I started dating Ashton about two and a half months ago."

Renée's eyes grew big. "What? Why would you do that boy like that when he just lost Alisha? You know you don't love him! Why would you play with his heart like that?"

I shook my head to myself. "I know, Renée. I know I was wrong, but it felt so good to be with him. He always cherished me, you know that. Jamie didn't want me, and Ashton was the next best thing."

Renée was shocked that even I could be that cruel. "So, let me guess, when Jamie came back from his tour with Anastasia, y'all started seeing each other? And you broke things off with Ashton?"

I hesitated. "Well, no, I was still seeing Ashton. I couldn't just cut him off like that because . . ." I reached over to my purse, which sat on her countertop, and took out the envelope that contained the results to the DNA test. And I handed the envelope to her.

Renée looked down at the envelope, reading the return address. "'Quest Diagnostic'?" She looked back up at me. "Charlie, you went and got a DNA test for August? Why—why do you need a DNA test?"

"Because I found out that Ashton and I slept together back in 2014." I watched Renée stumbled over her own two feet.

"Hold up, wait a muthafuckin' minute!" She exclaimed. "What the fuck do you mean you 'found out?' You fucked so many different niggas that you can't remember whose dick is whose?"

I looked at her. Even when she was angry she was a fuckin' smart-ass. "I went to one of Misty's parties, and her brother's spiked the drink with all types of shit. Apparently, a lot of us girls drank that shit. I guess Ashton got to me before anyone could find me and take me home."

"And when did this happen?" Renée's light eyes searched my face.

"The night before we went to Miami." I watched Renée toss the envelope back onto the counter before walking out of the kitchen to go sit down at her dining room table.

Renée sat there, at the table, covering her face with her hands, leg shaking in frustration. She was speechless for about five minutes. I am sure she was thinking the same things that I was thinking. "Throw that shit away." Renée removed her hands from her face, her light face turning red. Well, I wasn't thinking that.

"What?" I laughed a little, not meaning to laugh out loud. "Throw what away?"

"The results to that fuckin' test. Throw it out! The results don't matter now, and I swear"—Renée stood back up from the table—"I won't let you hurt my cousin again!"

"Renée, are you serious? I need to tell Jamie about this!" I exclaimed.

"If this would have been a year ago, yeah, I would have told you to tell my cousin about this bullshit. But you saw my cousin, she is so happy with Aaron. I can't let you steal that from her like you did last year! She was pregnant with Jamie's baby, and she left him, only to lose that baby, too! Leave my cousin alone! Let this shit go, Charlie!" Renée was outraged.

I opened my mouth to speak, but Renée just kept on talking.

"You got who you want, and my cousin has who she needs! No need to go starting any more shit than you've already started! You started a chain of events that just keeps on keepin' the fuck on! My cousin deserves to be happy, isn't that what you told her a few hours ago? She's having Aaron's baby! Do you know what confusion this will cause her if she finds out that the reason she left Jamie didn't even exist? You will fuck everyone's world up, including Jamie's! He loves that little boy!"

"Well, what about Ashton? What if this baby is his? What is he supposed to do?" My head was spinning with all sorts of questions and what-if scenarios.

"Just don't tell him. You're good at keeping secrets, aren't you?" Renée fired more shots at me.

"Fuck this shit!" I shook my head, picking up the envelope off of the countertop, about to just rip it open.

"Ne'Vaeh said every moment with Aaron is so sweet." Renée walked back into the kitchen, laughing to herself. "She makes her life with this boy sound like a Nineties R&B video, for real! She says she wakes up every morning to the smell of bacon, eggs, and French toast. He gives her the choice of fresh-squeezed orange juice or lemonade. She says every night, they have dinner by candlelight on their back porch. She says this dude has a package delivered to their house every muthafuckin' Friday! And do you know what is in that box?" She stood before me, looking down at me, standing five feet eleven inches from the ground.

I looked up at her, still gripping the envelope in my hands. "No. What's in it?"

"The dress that he wants her to wear that night for their date! The muthafucka takes her out on a date every Friday night like they just met!" Renée exclaimed. "He is making up for the time that he missed with her in high school while he was wasting his time fuckin' around with you!"

It was hard fighting back the tears. The truth hurt like a muthafucka.

"You know I never really liked that boy, especially when I found out that he was trying to get at my cousin when he was dating you. But I had a change of heart last year when he came to rescue my baby, Ne'Vaeh. You should've seen her last year." Tears lined Renée's false lashes. "She was a mess when she lost that beautiful baby. The doctors had to pry that baby out of her arms. She went weeks without being able to sleep, the same way she couldn't sleep when she lost Kevin. She was afraid to go to sleep, because every time she closed her eyes, she saw little Sara's face. She went almost a month without eating. Doctors had to sedate her to put an IV in just to get her to at least take in some fluids. I used up all of my sick and vacation leave to stay with her in Atlanta. That girl would rip the IV out as soon as they put that shit in! I watched the doctors pump her stomach after she over-dosed on prescription meds! She needed both you and Jamie, and neither one of you muthafuckas were there!" She shoved me into the counter, knocking the envelope out of my hands.

I looked at her, unable to fight back my tears any longer.

"Aaron went halfway around the world to get away from this bullshit with y'all; he didn't have to come back to check on Ne'Vaeh, but he did! It took me a while to see it, but he really loves her. He loved her so much that he gave her up, let her find out on her own what Jamie was all about. When Ne'Vaeh needed a friend, Aaron was there, and I will always respect him for that. My cousin loses everything that she loves. Please, don't do this to her. Just leave them alone. Let them be happy." Renée dried her face with her fingertips.

"I never meant for any of this shit to happen. I don't wanna hurt her, but what am I supposed to do? You know I love Jamie, but I don't deserve him. Not like this." I looked up into Renée's face.

Renée went over to her front door and opened it, showing me the way out. "I really wished you would've kept this shit to yourself. I don't wanna have this shit floating around in my head, Charlene!"

I picked up the envelope, putting it in my purse. "I'm sorry, Renée." I threw my Hermes Himalayan Croc Birkin bag over my shoulder. "I didn't know who else to tell."

"You could have told anyone but me! You did this shit on purpose, because you know it's hard for me to keep a secret from this girl! Get the fuck out, Charlene," Renée hissed as I walked toward her. Renée grabbed my arm as I walked passed her.

I looked up into her face.

"I'm telling you, Charlene, rip that shit up now," Renée warned me.

"Why have you been avoiding my calls, Charlie?" Jamie asked as he strolled through the front doors of my mansion the following day, around lunch time. He looked at me as my butler closed the door behind him.

I stood on the last step, holding little August in my arms. As soon as he saw Jamie, he damn near jumped out of my arms to get to Jamie.

Jamie approached me as August ran into his arms. Jamie smiled at his son, "Hey, little man. You been givin' your mama a hard time today?"

Little August giggled, hugging his father tightly around his neck. I loved the way they loved each other. I tried to listen to Renée's advice, but I couldn't throw the envelope away. And it took everything in me not to look at it. I'd been calling Ashton non-stop since the day he left the club, but I'd received no answer. And when his mother and cousin called me looking for Ashton, too, I started to worry.

Jamie looked at me. My hair was a mess, and I was still dressed in the clothes that I wore to Ne'Vaeh's baby shower the day before. I was standing there, holding the tiny velvet box that Ashton had left on my pillow. Jamie looked down at the box in my hand. He reached for my hand, taking the box from it. He flipped the box open. The light from the diamonds danced across his face.

Jamie looked at me, closing the box, handing the box back to me. "Shawty, didn't I tell you? I told you he had a ring for you, you thought I was playin'!" Jamie shook his head, watching the tears slide down my cheeks. He put August down on the floor.

August clung to Jamie's legs, looking up at the two of us in wonder. "Mommy cry," he whispered, looking up at me.

"Mommy will be okay, August. She's just sad," Jamie whispered back.

I looked at Jamie as he reached for my face, drying my tears. He held my face with one hand and dried my tears with the other. I looked up into his face, holding the hand that held my face. "I've been trying to call him for four days. I know he said that he didn't wanna talk to me anymore, but he's never avoided my phone calls! Not to mention his family has been calling me looking for him. I'm worried, Jamie. He's my best friend!" I cried out loud. "Look at this ring that he gave me! I don't deserve shit like this! He could have bought himself a new house! Jamie, Ashton practically bought me a house!"

Jamie grabbed me in his arms, squeezing me tight. "Charlene, everything will be alright. Just give him some time to adjust. You probably need some time to adjust, too."

I looked up into his face. I did need time to adjust to life with Jamie. He was trying to do the right thing for a change. He was giving me a chance to be with him. He wanted to be my boyfriend, possibly even more. I wanted to tell him about the DNA test, but the way he held me felt oh-so-good, and I wasn't ready to lose that. "Jamie, I didn't wanna hurt him like that. I love you. I wanna be with you forever if I can, but not like this. I could have picked a better way to tell him that it was over between us, that it never should have started. I've always wanted you, and he's always wanted me. I should have left things the way that they were."

Jamie looked down into my face. "With who? Him or me?"

I hesitated. "I don't know." The only reason why I didn't know was that my heart wouldn't allow me to open the results to the DNA test.

"Agosto, niño!" Lilia called as she came down the hallway. "It's time to eat, little boy!"

Lilia was in a cheerful mood until she saw Jamie standing there talking to me. She rolled her eyes, walking up to Jamie, picking August up, holding him in her arms. She started to walk away from us when I felt the urge to say something to her about her funky-ass attitude.

"Look, Lilia. Your attitude is starting to get on my last got-damn nerve!" I called out to her as Jamie let go of me.

Lilia sighed, turning around to face me, her lips pursed together.

I walked off the last step, walking over to meet her.

Lilia looked me up and down, shaking her head at me. "Eres patéticio," she sucked her teeth at me.

I rolled my eyes. "Look bitch, I'm going through too much shit. I don't have my Spanish translator turned on in my head right now, so if you're gonna talk shit, you're gonna have to speak in English, or at least Ebonics."

"You're pathetic!" she exclaimed, her Spanish accent almost non-existent. "Ashton really loves you! The night that you went out to the club with this," Lilia rolled her eyes over to Jamie and then back to me, "asshole, Ashton was over here lighting candles and sprinkling rose petals for you! He had a trail that led from the front door all the way to your bedroom! It was the most romantic thing that either of us maids had ever seen."

I dried my face, feeling as pathetic as she was making me sound.

"He helped your cook make the most spectacular seafood platter. Ashton sat at that dining room table for hours. When you didn't show up, he called your mother, who already knew that Ashton planned on proposing to you. It just so happened that Ashton stayed over long enough to hear Selena from that celebrity gym leave a message on your answering ma—" Lilia's voice was drowned out for a few seconds from the loud ringing of my house phone. "She left a message saying that she found your gold ankle bracelet in the shower in the weight room that Jamie had reserved for that day. If you're gonna fuck around on someone, why'd it have to be a man like that? If you didn't want him, you should have stayed the fuck away from him! You have men calling here for you all day! That police officer that was here a few months ago has been calling you all morning! That's probably him calling right now!"

Jamie and I both looked at her.

"Jayson? Jayson Taylor?" I felt an awful burning sensation in the pit of my stomach.

Lilia looked at me, her hazel eyes searching my face. By the look on my face, she could tell that he wasn't calling about sex, but about something that may have had to do with my Ashton hadn't been returning any of my calls. "Sí. He called about five times already. I just—"

I put my hands up to stop her from talking. "Why didn't you come get me out of bed? Why hadn't anyone told me that he called?"

Carlita walked slowly into the corridor, with the cordless phone pressed against her chest. "Señorita, it's the police."

I rushed to her, slowly taking the phone from her hands. I heard Jayson's voice through the receiver before I even placed it to my ear. "Charlene? Charlene, can you hear me?"

I stuttered, pressing the phone to my ear. "Y–yes, I can hear you. Jayson?"

"Charlene, you need to come to Ashton's house right away." Jayson's voice shook.

"Why?" My lips quivered.

"Just come, Charlene, please." Jayson hung up the phone.

All types of thoughts were running through my head as Jamie flew down the highway, doing about ninety trying to get to Ashton's place. Ashton lived right outside of Baltimore City, and we were way on the other side of the state, outside of D.C. It took about an hour to work our way through traffic to get to Ashton's condo. Jamie barely put the car in park when I jumped out of the passenger's seat and stepped right onto what looked like a crime scene straight out of *Law and Order*. Yellow police tape was stretched out around the entrance to Ashton's building.

I covered my mouth in shock as I walked up the sidewalk to meet Jayson, standing alongside other police officers. Jayson was dressed in his civilian clothes and looked like he'd just gotten out of bed. Jayson eyed Jamie and me approaching him. Jayson looked at Jamie and then looked at me.

"Jayson, what happened?" I looked passed him and at paramedics as they made their way into the building. "What's going on?"

Jayson hesitated, "I've been trying to call you all morning." His eyes glistened.

"About what?" I looked at him, heart slamming against my ribcage.

"How well do you know Ashton Brookes?" The police officer who was standing next to Jayson, turned toward me, notepad in his hand.

I looked at the blond-haired police officer, and then back at Jayson. "What the fuck is this?"

Jayson sighed. "Charlene, just answer him."

I looked at the police's badge, then back into his face. "Officer Norman, the fuck you mean how well do I know Ashton? He's my best friend; we grew up together. Why?"

"When the maintenance man got word of water leaking from the ceiling from the bathroom in the condominium below Ashton's, he knocked on Ashton's front door. This was taped to the front door." Officer Norman handed me a card-sized envelope that had been opened.

"Why are y'all opening Ashton's mail?" I snatched it from him, seeing my name was written on the back of the envelope. "What is this?"

"A–a suicide note." Jayson watched as I dropped the envelope from my hands.

I would have dropped to my knees hadn't Jamie caught me in his arms. I couldn't make a sound, I couldn't move, my mind wasn't functioning for an unknown amount of time. Everything went black before I came to my senses. Or should I say came out screaming?

"Charlie, shawty, breathe!" Jamie exclaimed, watching me screaming out and hyperventilating at the same time. I was hysterical, so much that the paramedics rushed over to where we stood with a stretcher. I pushed everyone, including Jamie, off of me.

"No, where is Ashton? Where is he? Why hasn't he been answering my calls?" I screamed out, beating Jayson in his chest.

Jayson caught my arms. "He's gone, Charlie! He's been gone for about four days! The maintenance man found him in the bathroom . . . hanging from the shower curtain rod by a rope."

I screamed out, "No!" I squealed, falling against Jayson's chest. "Where is he? Where is Ashton?" I sobbed, feeling awful pains in my chest and head. I must have passed out twice in Jayson's arms, because the next thing I knew I was in the back of the ambulance, laid out on a stretcher.

I came to, screaming and fighting again. The paramedics practically had to fight me to get me to stay in the ambulance. It took a few minutes for the male paramedic to calm me down a little. I started to hyperventilate. The paramedic placed a mask over my face. The air supply calmed me down a little—that was until I saw paramedics wheeling a body enclosed in a body bag out of the apartment building on a stretcher. I fought to get out of the ambulance. The paramedics attempted to hold me back. I pushed them off of me, and I jumped out of the ambulance on my way over to the paramedics who were carrying Ashton's body.

Jamie, who was talking to the police officers about what had happened, rushed over to me when he saw me damn near pushing the paramedics out of the way to see my best friend.

"Take him out of this bag! He can't breathe! Take that off of him!" I screeched.

Jamie grabbed me, pulling me away from the stretcher. "Shawty, I know this hurts, but you need to calm down and let them do their job!"

"But they're suffocating him! He can't breathe! Why is he is that bag?" My heart and mind were in denial. I couldn't admit to myself that he was gone, even though I was faced with the evidence.

"Baby, he's gone!" Jamie shook me a little, tears in his eyes.

I looked up into his face, shaking my head frantically. "No!" I screamed.

Jamie nodded, tears sliding down his face. "He's gone, Charlie."

Just then, a few of Ashton's family members pulled up in their cars, showing up to the scene. His mother got out of the car, already screaming for her son. The police stopped her in her tracks, holding her back, questioning her the same way that they tried to do me.

I looked at the body bag that contained Ashton's body. The screams and wails from his mother were drowned out by my own thoughts. "I wanna see him," I cried, looking at the paramedics. "Please."

They hesitated before unzipping the bag just a little. They didn't even unzip the bag three inches before I was screaming out in agony. As soon as I saw his pale blue forehead, I collapsed to the ground.

Chapter 14: The Final Good-bye

Charlene

I sat on the edge of my bed the day of Ashton's funeral. I hadn't had anything to eat or drink, let alone get a wink of sleep, in four days. I was a wreck. I had been sitting in the same spot since Jamie brought me back home the day they found Ashton's body hanging from the shower curtain pole. Images of the pictures the police showed me of Ashton hanging from the rope were embedded in my mind. I wouldn't take anyone's calls, not even my mother's—especially not my mother's. My manager and his wife had been calling me non-stop. News reporters stayed parked outside of my house for days trying to get a story from anyone who walked out of my house. I was a fashion model, but I was nowhere near as famous as Jamie was. He had only been in the spot light for almost two years and had only been singing for a few months, yet by the amount of paparazzi outside of my home those few days, you would have thought he was one of the damn Kardashians. He stayed by my side the entire time and only left my house that morning to go pick up my dress for me.

My house was buzzing with people. I stayed in my room the entire morning, staring at the envelope that sat on my nightstand. I'd placed the unopened DNA test results in a card-sized envelope and sealed it shut. I couldn't bring myself to open it. Since Ashton was dead, did the results really matter? There was no way that I was going to tell Jamie the truth and lose him. Even though it was hard to look at him and not think about Ashton, I still desperately needed Jamie. Jamie was trying to do right by me for a change. We were a family, and I planned on keeping it that way.

There was a knock at my room. "Señorita," Lilia's voice called through the door. "You have a visitor."

"Go away!" I screamed out, drying the tears from my face.

"Charlene," I heard Ne'Vaeh's voice through the door, "sweetie, it's Ne'Vaeh."

My heart jumped in my chest, as the door to my bedroom crept open. I turned around to see Ne'Vaeh coming into my room, dressed in a tight white silk blouse and tight pinstriped pants. Her jet-black hair had been cut into the cutest layered bob. She looked amazing and healthy, glowing in her first trimester. She watched the tears strolling down my cheeks as she stepped into my room, closing the door behind her.

I looked up at her, body quivering as she came over and sat beside me on the bed. The last person I expected to see was Ne'Vaeh. She had no idea that I was harboring a secret about the paternity of my son. I had created so much chaos in her life. I pushed her life into a direction I'm sure she had never thought it would go. She was happy, but still, Aaron wasn't Jamie. She'd left Maryland with Jamie's baby because of what I did. Had she never found out about me being pregnant with what was supposed to be Jamie's son, she wouldn't have had to go through that pain alone if at all. Who knows, maybe the stress of what was going on between Jamie and me caused her to lose that baby. Regardless, I was nowhere in sight when her baby died. I didn't call her for almost a year and a half. When she needed me, I wasn't there for her. Yet when she knew I needed her, she was right there.

Ne'Vaeh took my hand in hers, and I broke down.

"He's gone, Ne'Vaeh! My boo is gone!" I cried on her shoulder.

Ne'Vaeh cried too, surrounding me in her arms. "Ssshhh." She tried consoling me, "I'm so sorry, Charlie."

"He killed himself because of me, Ne'Vaeh!" I screamed out. "My best friend is gone because I chose Jamie!"

She looked at me, not sure what to say. She had read the tabloids. Shit, everyone had. The day after Ashton caught Jamie and me at the club, our picture was in the got-damn paper. "Supermodel Trades Doctor for Football Player" was the headline. She knew I was fuckin' around with Ashton for two months, only to turn around and diss him for Jamie. She knew, like everyone else did, that Ashton was fragile, that he needed me, and that he couldn't live without me. She knew that I should have never slept with Ashton. She knew that I should not have played with his head the way that I did. Everyone told me to stop playing around, but I wouldn't listen. I never listened. I shut everyone out, and now my best friend is gone.

Ne'Vaeh could have gloated in my face, but she didn't. Instead, she unwrapped her arms from around me, and just intertwined her finger with mine. She looked into my face. "We all make mistakes, Charlie. Ashton knew you loved Jamie, yet he involved his heart with yours anyway. You were a risk that he was willing to take."

I looked into her face. "What does Aaron think? I know your husband had something to say about the way that I did his friend."

Ne'Vaeh sighed. "I really don't need to tell you what he said, 'cause you already know how he feels when it comes to Ashton. They were homies. Ashton was the first friend that Aaron made when he moved here. They moved in together. They were on the same basketball team. Do you think that Aaron didn't know Ashton felt some type of way about you while y'all were dating? That boy was in love with you, but for whatever reason, you didn't love him. Aaron warned you about screwing with his head, Charlie, but you wouldn't listen. You never listen."

"So," I dried my face, "you think it's my fault that he's dead, too?"

Ne'Vaeh stated bluntly, "I think it's your fault that he's not alive, take it how you wish."

The tears started rolling again, and my heart pumped overtime in my chest. "I can't help who I love," I whispered.

"Neither could he." Ne'Vaeh's eyes searched mine. "There's a lot of people waiting for you downstairs. Some you may wanna see, others you may not. You know Ashton's family is down there, too."

I exhaled deeply. It was going to be hard facing Ashton's family that day. I had already gotten a few threats from his female cousins in the days prior to Ashton's funeral, so I was prepared for that. What I wasn't prepared for was facing his mother.

"How long are you staying?" I pushed my hair from my face.

"Just until they bury Ashton. Aaron is really hurt, so we're just gonna stay until they lower his body, and then we gotta go catch our flight." Ne'Vaeh pushed my hair over my shoulders. "He didn't even wanna come at first. I had to convince him to come. When he heard it was a closed casket funeral, he was furious. Ashton's mother showed him the pictures from the bathroom. Aaron threw up when he saw them, Charlie."

I looked at her. "You didn't have to come up here. I know Aaron didn't want you talking to me."

Ne'Vaeh shook her head, "Girl, you know Aaron ain't even like that. Just because he doesn't have any words for you doesn't mean I don't. You're my sister. And even though we don't talk as much as we used to, I knew you needed me, and that's why I'm here. You don't deserve for me to be, but that's another story." She grinned at me a little.

But I just cried.

"Charlene, I got your dr—" Jamie entered my room, dressed in a crisp white t-shirt, dark denim jean shorts that touched the middle of his calves, a clean white baseball cap, and fresh white Nikes. He was carrying a dress box in his arms. He stopped in his tracks when he saw Ne'Vaeh sitting beside me on the bed.

Ne'Vaeh stood from the bed, watching him standing there looking at her.

My hairstylist and makeup artist flew in the room behind Jamie, rushing over to me.

"Charlene, Golden has been calling your ass for days!" Holly immediately took a brush to my hair. "Do you know how many people are downstairs waiting on you? The press is even here!" She took me by the arm and led me over to my vanity mirror, sitting me down on the stool. "Oh my goodness, look at your hair! And good grief—when is the last time you showered, girl?"

The bitch yapped at me for a good fifteen minutes straight, but I wasn't paying her any attention. Once Ne'Vaeh caught Jamie's gaze, that's all I was concentrating on. You should have seen the way that they were looking at one another; looking each other over like they were making sure everything was still there, that nothing about one another had changed. They didn't really need words to say anything to one another. Jamie knew Ne'Vaeh was disappointed, that he should have known better than to get involved with me, baby or not.

"Charlie, I gotta get back downstairs." Ne'Vaeh cleared her throat, trying to hurry past Jamie and out of my room.

As she passed him, Jamie grabbed her hand, pulling her back to him.

The way she looked up at him helplessly was priceless. If I had had a camera, I would have taken a picture. There was no competing with the love they still had for one another, wedding ring, baby mama, or not.

"You came, shawty," he whispered to her, but I heard him loud and clear.

Ne'Vaeh slipped her hand from his, looking back at me looking at her. She looked back at him. "She's my sister," she whispered back. "Take care of her the way you should have taken care of me."

Jamie looked at me as she left.

I sighed, watching him sit the dress box on my dresser. He sat in the chair that sat in the corner of my room. He slouched back in the chair, hands over his face, probably asking himself what he'd gotten himself into. I knew how he felt, because I was thinking the exact same thing.

That morning I sat in the bathtub for damn near an hour, thinking about my life and the pain that I had caused. I couldn't believe what had happened in such a short amount of time. My life had caught up with me, no matter how much I had tried to avoid it. Just when I felt like giving up and ending it all, Lilia entered the bathroom, carrying little August in her arms. He was wrapped in a white towel and smiling from ear to ear. His brown curly hair was all over the place.

I looked up at the both of them, tears sliding down my cheeks.

Lilia sighed. "Señorita, you're going to ruin your makeup. You have to get to the church in an hour. Your family is waiting downstairs for you."

I didn't say anything; I just reached for my son.

She walked over to me, handing him to me. She reached for the faucet, turning on the hot water to heat the lukewarm water. She watched as I cried, holding August against my chest. "Charlie, no matter what people feel about you right now, just know that God will forgive you," she whispered.

I looked up at her, lips trembling. "My mother hasn't even came up here to talk to me! Even the Morgan Girls tried, though I turned them all away. I'll never forgive myself for this, Lilia."

Lilia's hazel eyes sparkled. "It takes time. A lot of time. But your heart will heal, chica. You have to remember that everything and everyone around you doesn't belong to you. Everything you have belongs to God. So when He decides to take it all back, you have to be ready to give it to Him."

It wasn't easy facing Ashton's family that morning. Not only was Ashton's mother there to confront me, but Alisha's mother was standing right there by her side. It took about five people to stop either of the two from slapping me dead across my face. My mother stood there, watching as these two women attempted to jump me. She didn't step in until she saw Kelissa jumping to my defense. I so didn't deserve for anyone to defend me. I definitely wasn't Kelissa's favorite person; she and Alisha had both warned me about my reckless life. I deserved for Kelissa to toast to my pain, the same way she'd done at my wedding rehearsal a few years earlier. Instead, she jumped to my defense, reminding Ashton's and Alisha's mothers the reason why we were all gathered together that day.

When I attempted to get into the hearse that carried my best friend's body, his mother stopped me in my tracks, telling me that I didn't deserve to go anywhere near Ashton, dead or alive. I couldn't even argue back with that woman, because she was right. My mother finally decided it was time to step in to aid me. She grabbed my arm, pulling me to her car. Reluctantly, I got into the front passenger's side of my mother's Porsche.

"I understand how bad it hurts when the man you love is in love with someone else," my mother finally decided to say to me after not speaking to me since the day she caught me over at Jamie's house.

I looked at her, then rolled my eyes, staring back out the window. "Are you really talking to me? The world's biggest slut?"

My mother sighed. "Charlie, I never called you a slut."

"You might as well have!" I exclaimed. "You made me feel like shit for dating different guys because the man who I loved was in love with my best friend! No, my sister! You made it seem like I wasn't good enough for Aaron or for Jamie! Every time you look at me, you see a slut!"

"No, I see myself," my mother interjected before I could see anything else.

I looked at her.

My mother shook her head to herself. "Kristopher never loved me. No matter what I did, he always loved Juanita. He tried to love me, but he couldn't. We only got married because my parents refused to let their daughter walk across that stage to get her diploma, pregnant, without a ring on my finger. His father was a senator. His mother was a judge. Their son wanted to be a record executive, which is how he got involved with Juanita. I wasn't his first choice. I was skinny, I was a nerd, and I wouldn't put out. Juanita did it all, and your father fell in love. When I look at you, it just reminds me of how much he loved her. I took Ne'Vaeh in to hurt

Juanita. Not because I loved Ne'Vaeh any more than I loved you, but because I wanted to take something away from Juanita that I knew that she loved. Juanita wasn't a bad person. She had been through hell, and that was all she knew."

I dried my tears. "Why are you telling me this now, Mama? What does all of this have to do with me?"

"You need to leave Jamie alone. He's never gonna love you, no matter what you do. It's nothing personal against you, honey. He can't help who he loves. Your best friend killed himself to hurt you. He's gone because you left him for Jamie. You're gonna have to live with that pain. Every time you look at Jamie, you're gonna think about that boy." My mother looked at me as she stopped at a stop light. "Jamie's gonna leave you, whether it's physically or mentally. Your father did it to me, so I'm telling you from experience. My marriage was for show. I commend Jamie for doing the right thing. But I promise you, he's only with you to prove something to her. And there is absolutely nothing that you can do to undo what that girl has done to that boy's heart. Let him go, now."

I shook my head at my mother. Leave it to her to make me feel even guiltier than I was already feeling. I just sat there in that seat, clutching the envelope that contained the DNA test inside of it.

I looked across the room at Ashton's family. They all sat in the pews, wailing and screaming as the preacher gave his sermon at Ashton's home going. I watched as Aaron cried for his friend, leaned over, head between his knees. Ne'Vaeh rubbed his back, trying to soothe him. The intensity of the screams was too much for Aaron. He got up from the pew, grabbing Ne'Vaeh's hand

and taking her outside with him. I thought it would be easier for everyone to attend the funeral because it was a closed-casket funeral, but that fact alone made the event more horrifying.

The worst part of the funeral was at his burial. It reminded me of the day I held Ashton's hand, watching them throw dirt over Alisha's casket. His mother had his body buried right next to Alisha's. I had buried both friends within a few months' time. When everyone else was placing a rose on Ashton's casket, I was placing the envelope that carried the DNA test. I looked up to see Renée staring right back at me, shaking her head in disgust. She wasn't stupid, she knew what I'd hidden in that card-sized envelope.

I stayed there until the final pile of dirt was thrown on Ashton's casket, just to make sure that the results of the test were buried with his body. I didn't want to know the results of the test, because at that point, they really didn't matter. I had lost Ashton because of my decision to choose Jamie. What difference did it make who the biological father of my son was at that point? I know I was dead wrong. Alisha was probably cursing me out, asking God to give me a one-way ticket to Hell.

That evening, my mother had a gathering at her house. Of course, Ashton's family wasn't there. Of course, Alisha's family wasn't there. All of my classmates and family members came to my mother's house, including those I went to college with. A few of the Morgan Girls were there. Though Ne'Vaeh and Aaron left right after the funeral, Renée decided to stay at my house that evening. Jamie sat in the living room, holding August close. It was bad enough that the press was hanging outside my house before and during the funeral, but they had the nerve to camp themselves and their fuckin' camera equipment outside of my mother's door that night.

I didn't mingle with anyone that night. I stayed hidden out in the kitchen, drinking Tequila straight from the bottle. I was an emotional wreck. Liquor was the only way to compose myself that night. Just when I started to pop a few oxycodone pills along with that alcohol, Kelissa, Dana, Danita, Tyra and muthafuckin' Renée come strolling their pretty asses into the kitchen. I rolled my eyes, sitting the bottle of pills and Tequila down on the island countertop.

"The fuck y'all want?" I wiped the tears from my face with my fingertips. "What, y'all came in here to gloat? Or better yet curse me out, blaming me for what happened to my best friend? Go ahead! Curse me out! Call me a high-yellow, dick-suckin', bust-it-wide-open-for-everybody, triflin' ass bitch!" I watched as they all stood around me with their arms folded.

Tyra snatched the pills and bottle of liquor for me. "These aren't gonna make you forget about what happened, Charlene!" She tossed my shit in the trash. "I told you a long time ago that Ashton was in dangerously in love with your ass! You just had to play with his head. Yeah, I'm gonna rub in all in your pretty face! I'm not cutting your ass any slack! You don't deserve any slack!"

I got up off of the stool about to leave the kitchen, when Tyra grabbed my arm, slinging my ass back down. "I don't have to sit here and hear this shit, Tyra! Don't you think I feel bad enough?" I screamed.

"No," Kelissa interjected, "you don't!"

I looked at her. Tears saturated her cheeks. Losing Ashton probably hurt her just as much as losing Alisha did. Both Kelissa and I had grown up with Ashton. We both knew him before he'd even started dating Alisha. Ashton was like a brother to Kelissa. The kind of brother who you could go to about anything. If he had it, it was hers.

"I'm not gonna lie to you." Kelissa dried her face, "I'm pissed than a muthafucka at you! I grew up with Ashton! He was my muthafuckin' homie for life! You had no business getting involved with this boy if you knew you weren't gonna give your all to him! You should have kept your muthafuckin' hands, lips, pussy, ass, everything off of him!"

"Okay, sweetie, calm down!" Dana pulled Kelissa's arm, pulling her back.

Kelissa was two steps from yanking me by my hair from the stool that I was sitting on. She pulled from Dana. "Dana, you and your sister, Danita, are always pulling somebody back! One day, one of y'all are gonna catch some of those punches that you keep trying to block!"

"What I wanna know is," Renée stepped in to add more fuel to the fire as usual, "did you open up the results of the test before you tried to bury the shit with Ashton?"

Everyone looked at me.

I didn't respond to her. I just ran my fingers through my hair anxiously.

Tyra laughed a little. "So, in your twisted little world, you think that burying the test results will hide the fact that August might not be Jamie's son?"

"Wait a minute, you mean to tell me that you had a DNA test done and didn't tell Ashton nor Jamie the results?" Kelissa exclaimed. She looked at Renée, "And how did you know about this shit?"

"She came to me with that fuckin' envelope the day that I gave Ne'Vaeh that baby shower," Renée hated to admit.

Tyra was confused. "So, you agree with her keeping this shit from both Jamie and from Ne'Vaeh? The whole muthafuckin' reason why Ne'Vaeh left this muthafucka in the first place is because of that baby! The whole fuckin' reason why she's with Aaron is because of that baby!"

"My cousin is finally happy, y'all! The results of this test aren't gonna bring Ashton back! As a matter of fact, I am sure that boy probably already knew the results to this test, and that was probably what made him kill himself!" Renée shouted.

We all looked at her. None of us had really thought about that.

They all looked at me. If looks could kill, I would have had ten bullet holes shot straight through my head.

"You know that boy knew, y'all. He worked at the got-damn hospital!" Renée shook her head at me in disgust. "You know they called that boy as soon as the results were in. He knew every nurse practitioner, nurse, phlebotomist, physician, and medical technician in Baltimore!"

"This shit is crazy!" Kelissa started to cry again. "Ashton is gone, all because you wanna be with a nigga who only paid your ass any attention when it was convenient for him! He ignored your ass until he saw Ne'Vaeh stroll up in Alisha's funeral with Aaron, and you know that shit! You want a nigga who ignores your ass until it's convenient for him? You killed my friend over a man who will always love another woman! You don't deserve to be happy while my friend is out there, six-feet fuckin' deep!"

Danita looked at me, her dark eyes glaring at me. "We told you years ago that your shit was gonna come back to haunt not just you, but everyone else. What if this baby isn't Jamie's? What will Ne'Vaeh think? What will Jamie think? You're gonna fuck this girl's entire world up, and Jamie's, too!"

Renée shook her head, "I'm telling y'all, just let the shit go!"

"Y'all muthafuckas is trippin'!" Kelissa was so irritated with Renée. "Charlie thinks it's cool to just try and bury the evidence with the man who she claims was her best friend, and Renée's over here talkin' about keepin' the shit sealed is the best thing to do! Renée, you're always the one talkin' about doing the right thing! You were always tryin' to play Ne'Vaeh's mama! And now you wanna keep this shit from her?"

Renée looked at Kelissa, "And just like a mama, I wanna protect my baby."

Before the two could continue back and forth, Heather came through the kitchen door. "Charlie, Officer Taylor is in the living room."

I looked at her. *What could he possibly want?* I thought to myself.

We all made out way into the living room where the rest of my guests were sitting. Mother was standing at the door with Office Taylor. Jamie was standing by the chair where he once sat, little August clinging to his leg.

Jayson looked at me, walking into the living room. He stood there dressed in his crisp, clean police uniform, holding an envelope in his hands. "Good evening, Miss Campbell. I'm not here to disturb you all. I just came to give my condolences for loss. I went to school with Ashton as well. I've known him since we were in the third grade. He was probably the most talented, genuine, and honest person that I've ever met. He will be missed." He started to hand me the envelope that he held in his hand.

My heart was pounding like a snare drum in my chest. "What is this?"

Jayson hesitated. "The envelope we found on Ashton's door the day that his body was found. You never read it."

I backed up a little. It was Ashton's suicide note. I shook my head frantically. "No, I can't read it."

My mother snatched the envelope from him, opening it.

I shut my eyes as tight as I could as she took what I thought was a letter out of the envelope.

"It's—it's a picture," my mother stuttered.

I opened my eyes, looking up at Jayson, who was shaking his head at me. I looked at my mother as she eyed the picture. "Picture of what?" I hesitated to ask, as Jamie walked over to my mother, taking the picture from my mother's hands.

Jamie looked at me. "A picture of me and August."

My heart continued to slam against my chest.

"It says something on the back," Jayson cleared his throat as Jamie turned the picture over.

Jamie's eyebrows knitted themselves together for a few seconds before his eyes coated over in tears. He looked up at me, about to say something, when little August ran back up to him, grabbing his leg. He looked down at August and then back up at me.

"What's the picture say?" people around the room began to question.

My mother took back the picture from Jamie, reading the words to herself instead of reading them out loud. Her eyes squinted looking at the words. Not because she couldn't see the words, but as if she was trying to make sure she had interpreted correctly whatever was written on the back of the picture. She gasped, looking up at me, and then looking at Jamie as he picked up August.

Jamie hugged August as tight as he could before the tears started racing down Jamie's face. "I'll see you later, little man. Take care of your mother for me, a'ight?" He spoke softly before trying to let August down.

"No!" Little August squealed, clinging to Jamie with both his arms and his legs.

"C'mon, August, Jamie has to go bye-bye, okay?" My mother started to cry too, taking August from Jamie's arms.

Jamie looked at me, shaking his head before leaving the living room.

"What's wrong with Jamie?" Heather asked, watching Jamie walk out of the living room, into the corridor. "Ma."

She looked back at my mother. "Where is he going? And what does the picture say?"

My mother looked at me, nostrils flaring. "It says . . . 'When you left me, you left me no choice. I couldn't live without you. Now you can raise my son with him.'"

I nearly fell to the floor. My heart had literally stopped beating. And my brain forgot how to allow my lungs to breathe. I nearly lost control of all bodily functions at that moment. All I could hear over and over in my head were the words that had just come from my mother's mouth. The silence in the room was deafening. Everyone was staring at me, not even sure what to say to me. My mother, who has an opinion about everything, was without words.

Once I regained my senses, the first thing my mind forced me to do was run and catch Jamie before he walked out of my life for good. I raced out of the living room and through the corridor, making it outside just before Jamie made it to his black and burgundy brand new Bugatti which was parked in the driveway, right out front. The camera crew was outside, snapping pictures at me as I ran to catch up with Jamie.

"Jamie!" I screamed out to him, pushing past the camera crew.

But he wouldn't turn around. When he got to his car, he opened the door about to get in, cameras flashing in his face, camera men blocking him from driving off if he wanted to. Jamie was such in a hurry to get away from me, he probably would have run everyone over if I hadn't stopped him.

And I said the only thing that I could think of to make him stop. "Jamie, please don't leave August!"

You should have seen the expressions on the faces of the camera crew. They just knew they had themselves a story. You could hear my mother's voice in the corridor, asking Jayson to tell them to leave before they were all arrested for trespassing.

Jamie stopped in his tracks. Even though he wasn't facing me, I could tell by his body language that Jamie was crying. He wiped his face before turning around to see me running up to him.

Jamie's temples twitched. He looked over my shoulder to see my mother and Renée standing at my front floor.

Officer Jayson came down the front steps, telling the camera crew they had to leave, but they weren't going to budge until they got their story.

Jamie looked back at me, clearing his throat. "You knew that boy wasn't mine, Charlie?" He tried to be as calm as he could.

I shook my head. "No, Jamie, I didn't, I swear!"

"So tell me how the fuck Ashton knew then, huh?" Jamie leaned back against his car. He was trying his best not to blow up in front of the camera, giving them the show that they wanted. Jamie's attitude was reckless, and it always seemed like they were ready to capture that about him on camera. It appeared that he was always causing trouble. Little did they know, I was always the catalyst.

I sighed, bracing myself for Jamie's response. "Apparently I slept with Ashton the night before my team and I flew out to Miami. I was high, I was drugged, and I was drunk. Neither of us remembered what happened that night. It wasn't until a few weeks ago that I found out about it and had a DNA test done. I didn't even open the envelope."

Jamie had to laugh to keep from smacking me. "You had a DNA test done, shawty, and you didn't tell a muthafucka? Apparently, you told him! I guess he found out the results before you did! The crazy muthafucka wrote that shit on the back of that got-damn picture!" Jamie's anger could no longer be suppressed.

I reached for his hand, "Jamie, please, I'm sorry!"

Jamie pushed me away from him. Cameras flashed. "Don't fuckin' touch me! Ashton is dead because of your decision to be with me after he already knew that August was his son! He left you because you left him! He left his son behind to pay you back, to pay me back for taking you from him when I knew that he needed you! Look what we've done!" Jamie screamed out, his voice echoing in my chest.

I cried out loud.

"Ne'Vaeh left Maryland because of this little boy! I lost her because of him! And losing him hurts just as bad as losing her did! I love that little boy with everything in me! I spend more time with him than you do, shawty! He is my fuckin' life, and you took him from me!" Jamie cried out. "I just killed that little boy's father? What the fuck am I supposed to tell that little boy?"

I shook my head, not even sure what to say to him. All I could say was, "Jamie, I need you. Please, August needs you."

Jamie shook his head at me, drying his tears. "Again, all you can think of is yourself. You aren't thinking about that little boy in there who's gonna have to grow up without a father!"

"You're all he knows! You're his father, Jamie!" I pushed him. "I had no idea about that night, Jamie, I swear I didn't! Dana and Danita found me naked on top of Ashton that night! They're the ones—"

"This is your fault, Charlene, no one else's!" Jamie exclaimed. "You were about that living-on-the-edge shit since we were kids, yo. I should have known better than to trust you when you told me that you were pregnant with my son. I never thought you'd be the one to hurt me like this, shawty. I watched the girl I loved get married right in front of my face! And the only reason why she ended up with that muthafucka is because of you!"

"Daddy!" Little August ran outside the front door, past my mother before she could catch him.

Renée ran after my baby, catching him at the bottom of my front porch steps. She swooped him up in her arms.

Jamie looked at August, and then back at me. "Take care of little man. He's all you have left of Ashton. Hold on to him, shawty. He's gonna need you." Jamie's temples twitched. "Tell my son—I'm sorry, your son—I said good-bye."

I shook my head, trying to grab Jamie's arm before he got into the car. "No, you need to tell him!"

Jamie pushed me off of him. "Naw, shawty. I'm not gonna be the one to break his heart. You're good at that shit. I'll let you do it."

"Look at him, Jamie!" I screamed, pushing Jamie in his chest. "Don't leave him! He doesn't deserve this shit! He didn't do anything wrong! It was my mistake, not his!"

Tears slid down Jamie's face. He shook his head at me before looking up at August, who was screaming at the top of his lungs, reaching out for Jamie. Jamie looked back at me. "Ne'Vaeh hates me because I never reached out to her while she was in Georgia. When she left me, I was hurt so I did whatever I could not to think about her. I was fuckin' all types of bitches left and right, trying to get over that girl. Meanwhile, she's in the hospital, giving birth to my dead baby. Our baby died while I was here taking care of you and yours! Do you know what I'm feeling inside right now, Charlie?" Jamie exclaimed.

"Jamie, I'm so sorry." I cried out.

"What do we tell August? You gonna lie to him all of his life about who his father is? Are you gonna tell him what kind of woman that you are, and how you got caught up in a fuckin' situation that made his father kill himself?" Jamie dried his face.

I had no idea what to say to Jamie. Everything he was saying was right about me.

"You're right, Charlene, August doesn't deserve this shit. He's got my last name! Not yours, not Ashton's! I'll be in his life, Charlene, but I want no part of yours." Jamie looked down into my face. "Tell little man the truth. You lied to everyone else. Don't lie to him." Jamie got into his car, closing the door behind him. And in seconds, I was watching his Bugatti racing out of my driveway.

I looked back at Renée and my mother. They both stood there, not really sure what to say. Renée let little August down. He ran straight into me, burying his face in my legs, crying his eyes out because his "daddy" had left without him. I picked up my son, wrapping my arms around him. He clung to me, arms wrapped around my neck. I cried with him.

"You already know where that boy is headed." Mother shook her head at me, watching me walking up the steps to my front porch, holding my son in my arms.

"And the drama continues." Renée sighed. "This shit ain't never gonna end."